Hurricane Reese

Forces of Nature Book One

R.L. Merrill

Celie Bay Publications LLC

Published By: Celie Bay Publications LLC
Edited By: Liz Fitzgerald
Cover Design: KaNaXa

 Created with Vellum

HURRICANE REESE

Forces of Nature Book One
   By R.L. Merrill

The life of Tony-winning musician Reese Matheson resembles a natural disaster, and caregiver Jude De La Torre is caught in the eye of the storm. But can the love of two opposites survive caring for an ornery octogenarian with wayward balls and a meddling family insistent upon tradition?

Fresh off the successful London run of his musical, the last thing Reese expects when he comes home is a house surrounded by paparazzi and his girlfriend throwing his stuff into the pool. All he wants to do is spend time with his beloved grandfather and musical mentor who suffers from Alzheimer's. Reese knows he doesn't have much time left before the elder Matheson forgets who he is. In classic "Hurricane Reese" form, he moves into the cottage by the sea and displaces Jude, the intriguing caregiver he hired two years before. When Grandpa proves too much for Reese to handle on his own, Jude comes to his rescue, taming Grandpa... and the Hurricane as well. Soon all Reese can think about is how to get Jude out of his scrubs and into his bed—permanently. Will Hurricane Reese destroy everything in his path, or will this odd couple learn to harmonize together?

To Jojo Imana, my confidante and co-conspirator.
Thank you for applying your hair-guru skills to keep me beautiful for the
past fifteen years. Our conversations helped to breathe life into this story,
and I'll be forever grateful for your friendship and trust.

ONE

"JADA, HONEY, can we please just—"

SPLASH!

Reese Matheson had been arguing with his girl and banging on the front door of his condo for twenty minutes, and it seemed she'd finally gone ahead with her threats.

"Shit."

Reese flew down the steps and around their unit to the pool in time to see his photo album plummet over the railing of their balcony and into the deep end to join his surfboard.

Reese focused on his family pictures, quickly sinking to the bottom. He climbed over the iron fence that surrounded the pool, dove in fully clothed, and swam frantically to collect his precious photos. As he surfaced he could practically see the fire in Jada's eyes as she hurled a stack of his songbooks over the rail.

"You love those books more than anything! Now you can swim with them."

On and on it went. She continued to clear the bookshelves of his irreplaceable music collection. He halfheartedly begged her to stop. She tossed them over into the pool. He rescued them. A crowd formed.

Paparazzi snapped pictures.... Suddenly Reese knew exactly why this was happening.

The London photos.

"Jada, please. Can we—"

"We most certainly can*not*! We're through! You can pick up your shit and get out! You want to go traipsing around the world, having fun without me, hanging all over people? I'm too young to be sitting here cooped up!"

Reese snorted. The drama was too much. "Oh, please. You're older than me."

That did it. She squealed and disappeared from his sight only long enough to run back in and grab the pièce de résistance—his Tony.

"No, Jada. Please!"

The hunk of matter of which he was the most proud sailed effortlessly through the air. It landed in the water a foot out of Reese's long reach. He dove after the heavy statue and surfaced in time to see his ex-girlfriend's sorrow-filled gaze. She slammed the sliding door shut so hard that he was shocked the sound of breaking glass didn't echo through the complex.

"Señor Matheson. Oh, I'll help you."

The little old man who tended the grounds took the statue from Reese and held out a hand to help him out of the water. A pile of soggy books lay at his feet—books that chronicled his brief but unbelievably successful music career. He'd gone from jam-band singer, to songwriter for a pop princess, to her tour mate, to singing a pair of smash-hit singles, to landing a movie soundtrack, and finally, co-writing a Broadway musical with his longtime friend and collaborator, Toby Griffiths. It was that last endeavor that earned them the coveted award.

Reese should be celebrating the end of their London run, not rescuing his memories from a saltwater pool. But if he stopped to really think about it, all the warning signs of impending disaster were there— no cute selfie texts recently and complete radio silence over the past week. Apparently she'd been building up to a blowout for seven whole days, during which every television, tabloid, and internet service had plastered his face and that of the lead in his show, Ethan Bradley, all over the planet. He couldn't totally blame her. She was concerned with appearances, and appearing to be someone's beard didn't appeal to her, even if *she* knew it wasn't true.

Reese slowly gathered up his belongings and, with the help of Enrique, loaded them all into his Tesla Model X. He tried to give the man soggy money from his wallet to say thank you, but the sweet guy refused it.

So now what? The condo was leased in his name, and he'd been paying all of their bills for the last two years, but he didn't have it in him to fight anymore. He'd rushed home to drop off his stuff as soon as his flight landed and then planned to go directly to see his beloved grandfather, with or without Jada. Now he needed a new plan, one that involved dry clothes. He turned on the car and pointed it in the direction of the cottage he'd bought for Grandpa on the beach in the gorgeous Southern California town of Malibu. The little two-bedroom house had beach access and was perfect for Reese's passion for surfing. The thought of working off his frustrations by riding some choice waves appealed to him. The whole setup appealed to him.

That was it. Since Jada had made the decision for him, he would move in with Grandpa. He'd already taken an indefinite hiatus to spend time with the old man. Now he'd be right across the hall.

The catch was that the place had only two bedrooms, and the other room was currently occupied by the caregiver Reese had hired for Grandpa, Jude De La Torre. The old man had suffered a series of minor strokes and then was diagnosed with Alzheimer's just over two years prior. He was sure Jude would understand. Reese was determined to have quality time with his grandfather before he'd have to make some difficult decisions. No time like the present. His heart felt considerably lighter as he drove toward his next adventure.

Two

"REESE, MY boy, I wash my own balls. Don't think because you're taking over I need that kinda help. You got that? And I need you to get me them underwear from JCPenney, not this designer crap you brought me. They hold your balls in better, and my boys need all the support they can get."

Reese had been sole caregiver of his grandfather, Thomas Matheson, for exactly two hours, and the old man hadn't stopped peppering him with gems of geriatric wisdom.

"You know, I can deal with diapers, but old man balls is not exactly the topic of conversation I thought we'd be having right about now."

"Well you better be ready for it. You reach my age, and your balls move into a new zip code. Right now it's time for *Jeopardy*. I'm not missing my shows tonight."

"Old man, *Jeopardy* doesn't start until seven. It's only five thirty. How about we go to Mulberry and have some pizza?"

"But I'll miss my show. Jude never let me miss my shows."

Jude. The name alone sent Reese into a whirlwind of guilt, irritation, and, well, feelings he wasn't ready to admit. Reese showed up that afternoon after the debacle at the condo and sprang the news that he was moving in. Jude had remained infuriatingly quiet.

"Jude you've been wonderful, but I need this time with him. I'll pay you for the next month, but I'm moving back in today. You understand, don't you? Thank you for everything."

Reese had hoped for some sort of reaction—anything other than silence. He never knew where he stood with his grandfather's caregiver, nor could he figure out why it mattered to him.

Jude crossed his arms, stuck out a hip, and raised a perfectly formed eyebrow at him. "Very well. I'll pack my things." Jude moved swiftly from the room. He had his things together in thirty minutes and took another fifteen to carefully type up Grandpa's medication and schedule.

Grandpa had been confused and downright ornery. The old man liked his caregiver, but Reese was family. They were it for each other.

"I'm your grandson and I love you. I thought we could have some time together, just you and me. I'm off tour indefinitely, and I want to focus on you. We've got your music to catalog, and I want us to work on my next show."

But Reese had a sinking feeling that he might be too late. Jude had warned him over the past year that his grandfather's Alzheimer's was advancing at a rapid rate.

Before he left, though, Jude let Reese have it, albeit in his calm voice.

"What do you know about caring for an old man? You only know about taking care of yourself, Reese Matheson. What're you going to do when he wanders? Have you thought about that?"

Ridiculous. How much trouble could his grandfather be? Reese was absolutely competent enough to take care of his beloved eighty-seven-year-old grandfather on his own. He'd been footing the bills for his care anyway. Moving in hadn't been part of his plan, but it was a great idea.

That brought him back to thoughts of Jude. The guy had a big family. He knew from Grandpa that Jude had aunts and uncles and cousins in the area. Reese was sure he'd have a place to stay. It wasn't like he was making him homeless or anything.

But no aspect of the transition was meant to go smoothly.

A Week Later

. . .

JUDE DE La Torre drove his ancient Nissan Pathfinder along the sunny Southern California coast toward yet another interview—his third in the week since he was abruptly let go from his last job as a live-in caregiver. The sounds of Neon Trees filled the vehicle, and Jude tried to let go of his stress. It wouldn't do to go in all wound up and with a frown on his face.

Tita Germaine had set up the interview for him through her contacts as a labor-and-delivery nurse. Germaine knew everyone in the Santa Monica nursing community. If she didn't know them, Tita Gemma had sold them a house or knew them from her volunteer work with the Filipino community. Everyone knew everyone, and that was why he needed to be discreet with his current living situation.

He'd gotten quite adept at grooming using the tiny mirror on the Pathfinder's visor. He'd showered at Tito Rommel's house early that morning, before his uncle got home from his night job, to avoid looking like he'd been sleeping in his car—which he had—and thanked the Lord once again that he still had a set of clean scrubs to wear for his interview. He'd have to hit the laundromat that night.

Jude needed a break. Ever since that entitled, clueless, spoiled brat Reese came waltzing in and told him he was no longer required to care for Mr. Matheson at the job he'd cherished for the past two years, he'd been in damage-control mode. Jude wet his hair with a spray bottle, used some product to even out the bedhead, and applied the last of his deodorant. He'd have to buy some toiletries. His meager savings didn't allow for many purchases, but looking his best and being put together was the only way he was *keeping* it together.

His phone rang somewhere under a pile of papers on the passenger seat, and he dug frantically for it.

Reese Matheson.

Huh.

He'd called Jude several times over the past week with questions about Mr. Matheson's medications and where his doctor's office was located. The man had a college degree and a successful music career, but he couldn't manage to look up a phone number, much less follow the directions Jude had written out.

He'd warned Reese that he wasn't capable of taking care of his grandfather, who was suffering from Alzheimer's and needed full-time care. But Reese was adamant. He said he wanted time with him and could handle it. Jude admired his determination, but Reese was foolish to think he could do it on his own. But try as he might, Jude couldn't just walk away from their situation, nor could he refuse Reese.

Despite how much he hated himself for it, he'd been terribly attracted to Reese since the day he interviewed for the home health care position. Reese's wavy blond hair had hung down past his shoulders and covered one eye until he pulled it back in a ridiculously self-absorbed man bun and smiled with those stupid-white teeth and eyes so deep blue they were ludicrous. Jude had stumbled over his words, but somehow managed to land the job. He'd spent two long years watching Reese pop in and out of the house to visit his grandfather.

"What do you want, *Mister* Matheson?" Jude didn't even try to keep the sneer out of his voice. The man, more like man-*child*, had taken away his job and left him homeless with his determination to do things *his* way. He wasn't about—

"I need you."

Reese's voice was devoid of the swagger Jude had experienced from him in the past. It turned his blood cold.

"I don't work for you or your grandfather anymore, Mister Matheson. You'll need to call—"

"Jude, he's gone. I woke up this morning, and the front door was standing wide open. I drove all over and called the police, but there's no sign of him."

Jude could hear Reese breathing heavy on the other end of the phone, as though he were power walking.

"I...." He paused. What did Reese expect from him?

"You know him. You know his routines, where he likes to go, what he likes to do. I've been gone for so long, I don't even know where to start looking." His voice broke on that last sentence.

Jude looked at his watch. He had ten minutes until his interview. They might reschedule. They might tell him to take a hike. He still had two more assisted living facilities he could contact, but he was running out of options. No one in his family had the room or the resources to take him in or feed one more. He'd been sleeping in the back of his SUV and parking outside the homes of various family members to be near help if he needed it. He always claimed to be at someone else's house so no one would suspect his ruse.

Nope. Jude was going to find a job and a room to rent. He'd been on his own for years. He could handle his own business.

But Jude couldn't walk away from Mr. Matheson. He'd become like Jude's own grandfather. When he was having moments of clarity, they walked along the beach, and he sang to Jude and told him stories. He'd given Jude life advice that he found priceless. His own parents had been summoned back to the Philippines to care for his paternal grandparents, and they'd left him on his own at twenty.

Thankfully he'd finished a two-year Nursing Assistant program so he could support himself. Living with Mr. Matheson meant he could continue to take online courses toward his nursing degree and help financially with his younger siblings. It hadn't meant saving money.

"I'll help you on one condition," he said to Reese.

"Anything."

It was a bit evil to make Reese promise him anything while he was frantically looking for his grandfather, but it was nonnegotiable.

"When we get him back, we do things *my* way."

Jude heard cursing on the other end of the line and what sounded like Reese fumbling with the phone.

"Fine. Meet me at the house. Please, Jude. I'm so worried."

That melted his heart a little.

"On my way."

THREE

REESE PACED frantically in front of the cottage. The past week had been exhausting and his sleep deprivation was a serious hindrance. Grandpa was much worse off than he'd originally thought. Jude had left lists of medications and routines that could have easily been for an entire hospital. Reese was never very good at keeping schedules. Even on the road, he had to be constantly reminded by the tour manager where he was supposed to be and when. Grandpa was up during the night several times, trying to get out the door. Once he even got as far as the back gate to the property, which led down to the beach. Reese had called an alarm company, but they couldn't come out for another several weeks. Turned out that was too late.

It would be hell admitting to Jude that he'd bitten off more than he could chew. Something about the young man put him off his game. He was so damned *intense* all the time. Reese had visited many times over the past two years, and always admired the quiet way Jude entered the room, gave Grandpa his medicine, and breezed right out without even disturbing anything. By contrast Reese moved like a hurricane, wreaked havoc with his crazy energy and enthusiasm, and then left the place a disaster in his wake. It was probably one of the many reasons his relationship with Jada hadn't worked out.

When Reese asked him how Grandpa was doing during these visits, Jude always started with the positives and then said, "His disease will worsen, so it's important he stay on a routine. It will be easier for him that way." His gentle voice sounded older than a twenty-two-year old's should. It made Reese wonder why a young man would take on a job that basically required round-the-clock care. When Reese was his age, he'd been living the fraternity life at UC Santa Bonita, surfing, and making music with his friends.

A beat-up Pathfinder parked at the curb, and Reese felt his stomach clench. He hated the way he'd left things with Jude. He hadn't meant to waltz in and disrupt everything, but he really thought he should finally step up and take care of his beloved grandfather. He'd been trying to figure out how best to apologize when Jude climbed out of the cab of his truck and rendered Reese speechless for a moment. He almost forgot the purpose for the younger man's visit. Jude moved with a purpose, every step graceful and efficient. Reese watched as Jude lifted his chin and sucked in a breath as he walked toward him.

"Did you check the pool hall?" Jude called out. "The senior center? Have you called Lefty and Harry?"

Jude passed right by him and into the house, his sturdy frame covered in worn scrubs. Reese had only ever seen him dressed that way. It made him wonder what Jude did with the rest of his life. And if he were in scrubs, perhaps he'd already found another job, which could be a good thing for Reese's guilt, a bad thing if he wasn't able to help.

"I called Lefty. He said he hadn't seen Grandpa since Tuesday when we met him for coffee. Harry didn't answer his phone. And did you say pool hall? I don't know any—"

"The one downtown. I doubt he could have walked it. Did you check your phone to see if he called a cab? He tried that once with me when I wouldn't take him out at night. The guys have a room in the back at Lucky's where they play cards every Thursday. Perhaps he was confused and went down there. What time did you say you woke up?"

Shit. "About ten I think? I don't know. He's been getting up at night. I was up with him last night around three, and then I couldn't sleep so I was working on music, and—"

"And you didn't hear him leave," Jude finished, irritated. "Let me go down to the pool hall."

"I'll grab a coat and come with you," Reese said as Jude headed for the door. He hurried into his room, which had clothes strewn all over. He tossed piles around until he found a hoodie. Then he dashed into the short hallway as he pulled it over his head and crashed into something. Or someone.

"Oh, Jesus. Jude, I'm sorry."

Jude stood holding a hand to his head with his eyes closed as though he were taking cleansing breaths for patience.

"It's fine, Mr. Matheson. I was going to say—"

"Please. Call me Reese. Look, Jude, I'm sorry. I really thought—"

"Let's go. He'll be hungry soon, and if no one is there to bring him food, he'll wander."

Jude turned on his heel and left the cottage. Reese cursed his clumsiness as he watched Jude walk away. He'd run right over the poor guy so many times. How could he ever get into his good graces?

FOUR

J UDE WAS trying really hard not to lose his cool, but the infuriating man would not get out of his way. Reese insisted on driving, which meant he was practically touching Jude in the front seat of his sporty electric car. His long arm stretched past the steering wheel, and his other one rested on the back of Jude's seat as he was driving. He kept leaning close to Jude to look out the passenger window. Jude leaned back in his seat and tried to breathe.

"I've never even heard him talk about this place."

Lucky's was a short drive from the cottage, just over the border into Santa Monica. Jude had been taking Mr. Matheson there weekly to meet his friends for two hours every Thursday for the past year. He'd included that in the instructions he left for Reese, of course. Apparently he hadn't paid attention. And why did he have to smell so good? Reese leaned across him once more to look around, and Jude sucked in a breath. He said a silent prayer for his sanity.

"The card game moved here from Lefty's bar when he sold it. Mostly they eat the popcorn and peanuts, hassle the young waitresses, and play cards in the back room. Your grandfather tends to bet too much money and then forget how much he bet, and then there's a big fuss. Hopefully things aren't out of control."

Just then a police car pulled up, thankfully with no lights or sirens. Reese and Jude watched in horror as two officers walked into Lucky's. Through the window they could see the bartender pointing toward the back.

"Oh, shit," Jude whispered as he let himself out of the car. Jude felt Reese hulking behind him as they entered the room. The bartender, a thirtysomething blonde named Darla, shook her head and offered a sad smile. Jude greeted her with a kiss to her cheek.

"So glad to see you, Jude. I'm sorry I had to call the cops, but things got out of hand today."

"I'm sorry. We'll take care of it," Jude said to the woman he'd befriended in his many trips there. She'd always helped keep an eye on Mr. Matheson, especially if Jude had to leave him for a bit to pick up medications or whatnot.

Darla glanced at Reese curiously as she continued to clean up. Jude thanked her and walked through the pool tables toward a doorway covered in drapes. Shouting could be heard from inside.

"Mr. Matheson, if you don't calm down, I'm going to be forced to handcuff you and put you in the back of my squad car. Now, can we please settle this?"

"Settle this?"

Jude flinched as his former charge shouted, pointed his finger at his best friend, and shook it vigorously. "This bastard ain't gonna call me no cheat and get away with it. I'll show you how we used to settle things back in Jersey."

"Mr. Matheson," Jude said softly. Though his voice was considerably lower than all the shouting, Mr. Matheson stopped arguing.

"Jude," Mr. Matheson said, and most of the fight bled out of him. He looked hurt and confused more than anything. "Tell these sons of bitches that I don't welsh. Tell them."

Jude hurried to his side, put a hand on his arm, and gently coaxed him to take a seat. Mr. Matheson still wore his slippers and pajama pants with a sweater, a blazer, and a fedora. He brought a shaky hand up to steady his hat and glared at the cops.

"I'm sorry, officers. I'm Reese Matheson. Thomas is my grandfather." Reese sidestepped Jude and approached the officers with his hand extended. The officers' faces lit up as they shook the celebrity's hand. Reese pulled them off to the side and left Jude to deal with his confused grandfather.

"Mr. Matheson, you left home without waking Reese. He's been very worried about you."

"That boy sleeps all day. I can't wait around for him. I called a cab. You should be the one taking me to my places. Why weren't you there this morning?"

Jude had already explained to Mr. Matheson that his grandson would be caring for him. He'd understood at the time.

"I just want to go home. I can't believe they think I stiffed them. I always pay my debts."

Lefty, the former gangster, now "retired businessman," came over and placed a hand on Mr. Matheson's shoulder.

"Now, Tommy, you can't be coming in here betting these high amounts without no money on ya. It ain't right, and these guys ain't gonna take too kindly to being stiffed."

Jude swallowed hard. "How much does he owe, Mr. Mancuso?"

Lefty glanced between Jude and Mr. Matheson and sighed. He knew exactly why Mr. Matheson was confused and had been incredibly patient. But it seemed his patience had run out. "I'll take care of it, but you see to it that he ain't here without his stake, you got me?"

"Yes, sir."

Reese wandered over, and the police left, autographs in hand, no doubt. Jude wanted to ream him for letting the situation get out of hand. Reese had no idea that his grandfather played some serious cards with those old guys, and most of them had all of their faculties. They knew exactly how much Mr. Matheson was in for.

"Hey, Grandpa. You scared me this morning."

Mr. Matheson gave him a blank look and turned to Jude. "I think I'm ready to go home now."

Jude helped him to his feet and supported his weight when he suddenly seemed very weak. He likely hadn't eaten since the night before, and it was going on two o'clock in the afternoon.

"Grandpa, how about we—"

Jude shot Reese a look over his shoulder that shut him up. He almost felt sympathetic when Reese's handsome face fell like a kid being told he was grounded. The man-child had no comprehension of the severity of the situation.

The drive back to the cottage by the sea was quiet. Mr. Matheson hummed an old Sinatra tune to himself. Jude had become versed in the classics from the Rat Pack era while he lived with him. Thomas Matheson had been friends with those men after he left the Navy and moved to Las Vegas from New Jersey in the 1960s. He'd played with big bands in the casinos and became the go-to guy for the crooners when they needed a fantastic pianist. Thomas could sing and play anything, and he'd done it for hours with Jude as his biggest fan.

Reese had learned at his knee and made a career for himself as a singer-songwriter. He sold out shows all across the country, had been nominated for a Grammy, and had even won a Tony for work he'd done co-writing an original Broadway musical. Jude knew all about the younger Matheson's career, as his grandfather bragged endlessly about him. The two were close, and very much alike—exactly why Jude knew the arrangement for Mr. Matheson's care would never work. Reese was a wonderfully generous man and extremely charismatic, but he didn't have the discipline it took to care for a man with his grandfather's needs.

Reese pulled up in front of the cottage, and Jude immediately hopped out of the back seat to assist Mr. Matheson. Reese started to come around, but Jude waved him toward the door.

"If you can let us in, please," he said in his calmest voice. "I think Mr. Matheson could use some supper and then take a nice nap."

"That sounds fantastic, Jude my boy. How about them noodles you make for me? I miss them noodles."

"Of course, Mr. Matheson. You come inside and have a seat in your recliner. I'll have the soup ready in no time."

REESE WATCHED helplessly. He sat across from Grandpa and tried to ask him what happened, but Grandpa dozed in his chair. Reese covered him with a blanket—the fall afternoon was chilly on the Southern California coast. It was the most beautiful time of the year. The sun showed off grandly after hiding behind the stubborn fog the past few weeks, and

Reese wished he could pull on his wetsuit, paddle out into the waves, and let all of his stress from the past week flow away. At least he could breathe easier with Jude there taking care of things.

Jude. *Lord*, how that young man handled everything like a pro. His grandfather had fought him at every turn, but Grandpa did everything Jude asked with a smile and a nod. He had a magic touch. Reese wondered what it was about him that tamed his larger-than-life grandfather. He wanted to know him, wanted to understand where that magic came from.

The delicious smell coming from the kitchen reminded Reese that he too had gone without food. He turned the corner and watched Jude cut up vegetables and fry some shrimp in a skillet that crackled and popped next to a pot with boiling water.

"Your grandfather loves ramen. What can I say? I add veggies and meat to it to ensure he gets all of his nutritional needs met. He loves it."

Reese was mesmerized by Jude's graceful hands as he expertly chopped the carrots, green onions, and mushrooms. He scooped them into his hands and brushed them off into the pot with the boiling water. He moved through the kitchen as though he'd done it a million times. Which he had. God, what had he done, letting him go like that? What if he didn't want to come back? Reese was at his wit's end. He couldn't do it alone any longer.

"I can't thank you enough," Reese murmured. He stood next to Jude by the sink.

Jude's lips turned up slightly in a closed-mouth grin.

"I did this for Mr. Matheson. He's been wonderful to me. I hate to see him...."

"You can say it," Reese said with a sad smile. "I fucked up. I never should have taken this on by myself. I'm sorry."

Jude shrugged. "You've always wanted the best for your grandfather. I know you thought what you were doing was right."

Reese laughed at the backhanded compliment. "I just wanted to have the time with him. Things are finally settled enough that I can stay with him and—"

"And you found yourself needing a place to live. Look, Mr. Matheson—"

Reese couldn't help himself. He reached out and placed a hand on Jude's shoulder.

"Do you hate me that much that you won't call me Reese?"

Jude's dark eyes were wide as he turned to look up at him. He glanced at the hand still on his shoulder and then back into Reese's face.

"I don't. No. I don't hate you. I just want to see Mr. Matheson cared for. I worry about him."

Reese realized the second time Jude looked down at his hand that he hadn't moved it yet. Jude's shoulder was hard and firm beneath Reese's hand. Muscular. His hand slid down involuntarily over an equally firm bicep. Jude cleared his throat.

"Will you stay?" Reese asked, his voice cracking. He stepped back and took a deep breath. *What am I doing?* "I need help." *Obviously. I just fondled his biceps. Really nice biceps.* Reese shook his head. "I'd like to work out an arrangement with you."

Jude turned back to the skillet, took the shrimp out with a spoon, and added them to the boiling water. He added the noodles and set the timer and then turned back around and faced Reese with determination on his face.

"I told you if I came back, we'd do this my way. Mr. Matheson needs round-the-clock care, and that's too much for one person. Even I had assistance from a day nurse three days a week and my *tita* Germaine came over in the evenings so I could go to class. You do need help, Mr. Matheson. Reese. I'm happy to take the early shift, since that seems to be problematic for you. We can work out a schedule that you'll promise to keep this time."

Reese couldn't help but notice that eyebrow again. Jude's arms were crossed over his chest like they'd been when Reese let him go before, the same hip cocked out to the side. But this time Reese saw more than a man in scrubs. Jude may have been younger than him, but he had a commanding presence when it mattered. And he expected Reese to listen to him.

"And you must follow the routines I prescribe for Mr. Matheson so we don't have a repeat of today. You can't let him get off schedule. He becomes confused. We were lucky today. Next time might be worse."

Reese needed to sit down. The idea that he could have lost his grandfather out there somewhere made him nauseated. He dropped his head into his hands and exhaled. Exhaustion weighed his body down, and he was near tears. A gentle hand squeezed his shoulder. Reese looked up, surprised to find Jude standing over him with a sympathetic expression that Reese probably didn't deserve.

"I'll do whatever you say," Reese whispered. "Just help me, please? He means everything to me. I know he's getting worse. I need a little more time with him."

"He's very special," Jude said and, he smiled. Reese's heart instantly felt lighter at the sight. Jude started to pull his hand away, and Reese caught it in his own.

"I can't thank you enough for being here."

Jude looked down at their hands together and paused. The timer beeped loudly, announcing the soup was ready, and made them both jump. Jude pulled his hand back and held it almost as though he'd been burned.

"I'll get this ready for him. Will you please rouse him from sleep and help get his tray set up? Oh, and it's almost four. He likes to watch *Ellen* while he has his supper."

Now why didn't I know that? Reese scolded himself that he hadn't paid more attention to the notes Jude left for him. He stood with some effort, trudged into the living room, and patted Grandpa's shoulder.

"Hey, old man. Time to eat."

Grandpa sat up and blinked a few times. "Help me to the can, son." Reese helped Grandpa out of the chair and down the short hallway to the bathroom. The two bedrooms were off to either side of the bathroom, and he cursed when he realized how messy he'd let things get since Jude left.

He waited in the hall until Grandpa was finished, sort of swaying on his feet and wishing he could fall into bed. Jude stepped into the living room with the bowl of soup for Grandpa.

"Is that noodles I smell, Jude my boy? Hot damn. I love that stuff. You got any of that hot sauce? I like it hot. Yes, indeed. Son, you gotta try this sauce Jude here puts in my soup. It'll burn the hair off your balls," he said and cackled as he sat slowly back down in his chair.

Jude shot Reese an amused look and then frowned at him. He

hurried to Grandpa's chair and made sure he was comfortable. Then he held the bowl for Grandpa and waited for him to get situated. Grandpa tucked a cloth napkin into his collar, held his spoon up in his hand, and licked his lips as Jude set the bowl on the tray in his lap.

"Here you go, Mr. Matheson. I'll go grab the sriracha for you."

Reese watched Jude do that thing where he practically floated through the room, his feet not even making a sound on the floor—unlike his own heavy stomping that used to drive his grandmother crazy when he visited them as a kid. Damn, he missed that lady.

FIVE

REESE WAS still standing in the same spot by the bathroom looking as though he were ready to drop at any moment. Once Mr. Matheson was settled and the TV was turned to *Ellen*, Jude made his way to Reese's side in the narrow hallway. Reese seemed to take up all the space and probably all of the oxygen in the room.

"Why don't you get some rest, Mr. Matheson? I'll stay and care for your grandfather until I need to leave for my class at seven o'clock. I can have my aunt come and sit with him then, if you like."

"No, that's all right. I just need a couple of hours. I can't thank you enough, Jude. He's so much better when you're here."

Jude looked down at his feet. "It's my pleasure. He's a wonderful man."

Reese stretched out his massively long arms and groaned as he arched his back and yawned. "I feel like I could sleep for a week. Thank you. And I'll, ah, clean up when I wake."

Jude raised an eyebrow when he got a glimpse inside Mr. Matheson's room for the first time since he'd moved out. He gasped at the piles of clothes everywhere.

"*Ohjesuslord*," he said quietly. He glanced out at his charge and then glared at Reese. "He'll trip over those clothes. You can't leave things on the floor. Sometimes he doesn't look where he's going and...." He brought a hand up to his forehead as he realized just how far gone the well-kept world he'd created really was.

"I know. It's a lot to keep up, and I get distracted," Reese said.

Jude shook his head. He started to pick up clothes and place them in the hamper. But he felt Reese's presence behind him and became flustered. *Does he even know how he affects people?*

Oh, right. *Sure he does.* Women threw themselves at him. Men too. Jude wondered how many of the stories he'd heard were true. He knew Reese had lived with a woman for a couple of years before he came back to the home he bought for his grandfather. But Jude had also heard from some of his theater friends that Reese didn't discriminate when it came to who he shared his affections with. He was discreet, but there'd been talk. Some even thought the girlfriend was for show, for his career, but he'd seen them during a few dinners with his grandfather and watched how attentive Reese was with her. She was standoffish with Jude, but Reese catered to her every whim. Mr. Matheson didn't speak fondly of her, though. Jude chuckled to himself as he remembered one very spirited diatribe Mr. Matheson had spouted after a Thanksgiving meal.

"That diva wouldn't know a hit song if it slapped her upside the head. Can you believe her sitting up here in my house telling me that tribute show in Vegas was the best live performance she'd ever seen? Has she never seen my grandson? That boy can sing circles around all of those performers out there. And the quality of his music? Fuhgedaboutit. He learned at my knee, and I wouldn't have pushed him so hard if I didn't think he had star quality. That little brat is using him."

Jude let him carry on, only because he knew that, after one of his rants, he'd usually take out his frustrations on the piano, and Jude was his biggest fan. He'd play for hours and tell Jude stories about all of the songs and what was happening in his life when he'd played them.

"What's so funny over there?"

Jude turned around and dropped the clothes he'd just picked up. Reese was standing in the doorway, shirtless, holding a towel in one hand and leaning against the doorjamb.

"Oh, just um... nothing. Did you need something?"

Reese smiled broadly, as though he'd caught Jude stealing cookies from the cookie jar. "I've never heard you laugh before."

Well, if that didn't just make things awkward?

The men stood staring at each other. Reese's smile grew wider, and Jude's discomfort increased rapidly.

"I'm just going to shower, and then, if you really don't mind, I'm going to nap. I appreciate this, Jude. I'll be up in time for you to make it to class. Are you working on your degree?"

Jude nodded as he bent to pick up the clothes he'd dropped. "Trying to finish up my RN. I take at least one class each term, whatever my schedule and finances will allow."

Reese frowned and shifted his weight, which caused his iliac furrow to flex under his tanned skin.

Could he please hide that broad chest? And that V-line? Or just do the world's hormones a favor and go shower? Get out of my sight? Jude struggled to maintain his carefully crafted composure.

"Won't it take you forever doing it that way?"

"I'll make it. I need to work."

Reese didn't know how much that was true. Jude's younger siblings stayed with their aunt, uncle, and grandmother, and Jude pitched in to pay for their private Catholic school. He had no living expenses while he lived with Mr. Matheson, so he'd been able to swing their tuition, no problem. It would break his heart if he couldn't pay and they got stuck returning to the public high school. They'd have to give up their passion —color guard—which would devastate them.

Jude looked at his watch and hoped it would kick-start Mr. Shirtless Wonder into his planned shower and nap. Anything would be better than being trapped in the room by those shoulders. And his hands... they were so *big*.

Reese hovered a moment longer and then moved back.

"I'll just go—"

"Yes. Fine. Thank you." *Ugh. Keep. It. Together.*

Reese chuckled as he closed the bathroom door... and began to sing.

. . .

REESE STOOD under the hot spray and wished it could wash away not just the muck of his situation, but also his guilt, shame, and frustration. But then a new feeling cropped up. *Lust.*

Damn. Watching Jude move about the house with his graceful way was intoxicating. If he didn't know better, he'd swear Jude was a dancer, he was that elegant. He wasn't very tall, maybe five six or five seven, but he had a build that reminded Reese of the men in his show. That got Reese thinking about Jude in tighter clothes, which led to fantasizing what he'd look like naked, which led to an almost-painful erection. Was he really contemplating jacking off in his grandfather's shower thinking about Jude? Yeah, that's exactly what he was about to do.

Reese had been celibate for at least six months. His tour schedule kept him away from opportunities probably even more than the repercussions of a private tryst going public. He and Jada had an arrangement while he was on tour—just don't get caught. They loved each other in their own way and had pretty phenomenal sexual chemistry, but their relationship was more for show. He liked having a built-in "plus one." She liked being built-in and liked sharing his spotlight. An aspiring actress, she wanted what he had to offer—connections and money.

Unfortunately, while attending a benefit in London, he'd been photographed with one of the actors in his musical. They weren't even in a compromising position, but it had been enough to fuel rumors about their relationship. He had no problem allowing Jada to save face by throwing him out. The paparazzi had eaten up the show and given Jada the exposure she wanted so desperately. She even received a call from producers of *The Marrying Kind*. Reality TV. That thought made Reese cringe, but whatever made her happy was fine by him.

No. What would really make Reese happy would be to get through the controlled exterior of the enticing young man occupying space in his home. Reese couldn't care less that their ten-year age difference might cause a stir. He wanted Jude. He wanted to watch him come apart, preferably under Reese's own greedy hands. He began to stroke *his* own tender flesh, which was made even more sensitive from months without the touch of another. He cupped himself, groaned at the feel, and imagined Jude's skin likely felt as smooth as his own. He rested one arm on the shower wall and allowed his tension to build and build.

Pictures of Jude bending over to help his grandfather, cutting vegetables, rolling his shoulders after carrying in the laundry, all flowed through his mind and acted like an aphrodisiac. Reese wanted to massage those shoulders and feel what he'd only briefly touched earlier in the kitchen.

"*Oh God*," Reese moaned as he imagined what he could have done if they'd been alone and not in the middle of a crisis. He'd have loved to slide Jude's scrubs down and run his hands over his strong body—a body that had been teasing him for the longest time. The way he moved was almost erotic. Sensual.

Reese began to shudder as he felt his orgasm forming at the base of his spine, his fantasy now moving way out of any realm of appropriateness. He pictured spinning Jude to face him and falling to his knees before him, finally discovering what he could do to make the stern young man lose his mind. As he saw himself leaning forward and taking Jude into his mouth....

"*Fuuuuuck*," he roared as he came and came into the spray of water. Whimpering moans came from his throat as the waves of pleasure rolled through him. He'd apparently had a lot built up. Either that or he wanted Jude even more than he'd previously thought. If he wasn't careful, his curiosity and lust were going to turn into obsession with a man he barely knew anything about. Which could go wrong. Very wrong. But would feel so goddamn—

"Reese? Are you all right?"

Reese slipped in the shower at his surprise and caught himself by the ledge of the window, but not before he knocked the shampoo bottles over and the handheld nozzle loose. The heavy metal showerhead crashed down on the bridge of his nose and sliced the thin skin. Blood poured down his face, and he groaned from the pain. As he sank to his knees in the shower, Jude burst into the bathroom.

"JESUS, MARY, and Joseph. What have you done to yourself?" Jude's voice was barely above a whispered, so horrified by the sight in front of him that he could hardly move. The blond Adonis knelt awkwardly in the shower stall, covered in blood like a scene right out of *Psycho*.

"Can you just hand me a towel? Preferably not the cream one?" Reese spoke from behind cupped hands covered in blood.

Jude rushed into action like the professional he was and forced himself to forget that his crush was naked in front of him like some perfect Greek statue. He grabbed a navy blue towel from the rack with one hand as he pulled open the glass door with the other.

"Thank goodness you didn't come crashing through this," he murmured as he knelt to assess the damage. "Move your hands, Reese. Sit back against the wall."

Reese did as he was told and allowed Jude to see his wound. Jude hissed at the sight of Reese's perfect face marred with a good-sized gash across his nose. He was certainly not a registered nurse yet, but he knew enough to ascertain that the cut could probably be closed with Steri-Strips. "Press this firmly to stop the bleeding."

He turned from Reese and attempted to ignore his semi-erect penis lying exposed. Jude focused on the task at hand, rather than his own physiological reaction to being so close to all that naked flesh. He stepped into the hallway and dug around in the linen closet until he found what he needed—an extra towel to cover his distraction, an instant ice pack, and bandages. He returned to the shower and casually dropped the towel in Reese's lap.

Jude knelt beside him once more, sat back on his haunches, and ignored the water seeping through his scrubs. He pulled the towel away and used some gauze to clean the area.

"I can bandage this well enough, but if the bleeding doesn't stop, I'll have to take you to the ER."

Reese cursed under his breath. "What a fucking disaster. I'm sorry, Jude. I'll be all right." He laughed at himself. "I really did a bang-up job, didn't I?" His chuckles grew into belly laughs.

Jude shook his head, unable to hide his smile.

"Let me just try to close this up," he said as he leaned over Reese's body to apply the strips to the wound. He pushed up on one knee, and the knee holding his weight slipped. Jude lurched forward and sprawled across Reese's broad chest.

"Whoa," Reese said with a laugh as his arms came up to catch Jude's weight. Reese's smile faded into a lust-filled gaze. He tightened his hands on Jude's arms, and pulled him closer. Their faces were inches apart and Jude could feel himself trembling.

"Does this really work for you, Mr. Matheson? Making people fall for you?" Jude's sarcastic tone belied a nervous reaction. Reese must have picked right up on it as his voice was husky when he spoke.

"Why are you shaking, then, Mister De La Torre?"

Jude scrambled to his feet and backed out of the shower just as the elder Mr. Matheson hollered from the living room.

"Jude, my boy. I need the remote. *Ellen*'s over, and it's time for the news."

The senior Matheson's voice acted as ice-cold water on them both. Reese's eyes widened, and he covered himself with the towel as he stood. Jude frowned as he noticed blood seeping from the bandages.

"That's not going to work. They're gonna need to glue it," he said quietly and reached up to dab at the blood with some tissue. Reese caught his hand with an awkward smile and took the tissue from him.

"I'll take care of it." He turned to look in the mirror. Whatever the hell that moment had been, it was long gone, like the steam from the shower.

Jude hurried into the living room to see to Mr. Matheson. As he approached him in the chair he cursed.

"Where'd all that blood come from? Who's hurt?"

"Reese had an accident in the shower," Jude said as he handed Mr. Matheson the remote and carried away his tray and soup bowl. "I think he may have to go to the hospital and have his nose looked at."

"Damn it all to hell, Reese. What the hell kind of clumsy stunt did you pull this time?"

Reese came down the hallway in a pair of loose sweatpants that exposed the waistband of his Diesel briefs.

"Hey old man, you've got more scars than me. Admit it."

"Sure I do, but that's because I boxed in the Navy. Not because I pranced my pansy ass all over a stage in those tight pants that crush your balls."

Reese barked out a laugh that sounded like a cross between embarrassed and annoyed. "Yes, well, not all of us have led such a colorful life—Jersey street fights, the Navy, boxing, working for the mob, pounding the keys for Frank. How can anyone possibly keep up?"

He shook his head and then took an elastic band from around his wrist and began to pile his hair into some complicated twist that ended with that ridiculous-looking man bun once again. Jude wanted to hate it —hate him. Too bad he was so stunning, that his chest had been such a tempting place to fall, and that his charm was going to land Jude in some serious trouble.

The last thing Jude needed to do was screw up his reinstated job working for a wonderful, if not a little intolerant, man and get his heart broken in the process. Jude didn't do casual. He didn't invest himself in anything or anyone halfway—which was precisely why he remained single at twenty-two. He'd been content to care for Mr. Matheson, work with his brother and sister, and attend school. Luckily his family had always been supportive of him, and he never wanted to bring any sort of embarrassment upon them. His father and uncle were very involved in their church and community, and they didn't need a gay son/nephew. Discretion was Jude's first rule of thumb when it came to getting involved, and Reese didn't have an ounce of discretion to speak of. Just look at the debacle of his last breakup.

And he'd been staring the whole time. *Jesuslordgodinheaven.*

"I should take you to the emergency room."

Reese was still holding the towel against his face.

"Come here, son," Mr. Matheson gestured for Reese to come closer for his inspection. Reese pulled the towel away and showed his grandfather that the blood was not stopping.

"Well, hell. It's just a scratch. I've had worse. That should close up with just a bandage, or does my grandson need a cute little nurse to kiss it and make it all better?"

Reese and Jude both coughed simultaneously.

Thankfully Mr. Matheson was ignorant of the tension in the room. "Let me just call Tita Germaine to come sit with you."

"Oh yeah. Speaking of hot little nurses, Reese, you oughta get a load of that Germaine. I might need me a sponge bath tonight."

"Very funny. Germaine will take care of your necessities. A sponge bath is not necessary. I'm leaving strict orders for her to make you take a walk in the backyard and then get to bed at a decent time. Perhaps I'll have her give you a shave, since it looks like you've lost your razor."

Jude shot Reese a pointed look with that comment. Then he looked down at himself and frowned. "I'll be back in just a moment, and then we'll get you to the hospital."

"I can drive myself. I don't want you to miss class," Reese offered, his expression full of guilt.

"You can't drive safely while keeping pressure on that wound. And what if you pass out? Squeamish people often have a delayed reaction—"

"*Squeamish?* I'll have you know—"

"Will you old biddies get on with it? I can't hear the news."

Reese and Jude studied each other.

"I'll just change clothes," Jude said quietly and hurried out the front door.

Six

REESE GLANCED at his grandfather once more to be sure he was engrossed in the nightly news, only to find him frowning and talking back to the TV. He went to his room and tried to put on a shirt, but he didn't want to pull anything over his head and get blood on it. He opted for a flannel button-down he could slip on, but then got stuck between keeping the blood from dripping everywhere and....

"Let me do that," Jude said in a huff. Reese couldn't help but grin at the flustered way Jude was moving now that he'd unsettled him. Jude set down a fresh set of scrubs on Reese's unmade bed and turned to face him. He took the shirt from Reese and moved behind him to slide the sleeves on from each side. When Jude returned to his front, Reese couldn't help himself. He rested his hand on Jude's narrow waist. Jude flinched as though he were startled and then started at the bottom, methodically pushing the buttons through the holes.

"Can we talk about what just happened?" Reese said, a smile forming.

Jude glanced up with that eyebrow raised again and batted at Reese's hand like he would at a pestering child.

"What happened? You mean your careless shower activities?" He bit his lip as he reached the top of Reese's abdomen. Reese mentally groaned as Jude's hands worked so close to his skin. He could almost feel the heat coming off of them if he fantasized hard enough.

"Maybe I should tell you what really happened," Reese said, his bravado startling even himself. *Should I?*

"I can only imagine, Fabio, that you got conditioner in your eye? Or maybe you dropped the soap?"

Reese's hand tightened, and the tips of his fingers dug into Jude's hipbones. Jude gasped softly.

"Are you going to pretend you don't feel the same as me right now?" *God, please let him be feeling what I feel.* He needed to know that Jude was just as affected. Otherwise he'd cut his losses and avoid any further embarrassment for either of them.

Jude continued to button, painstakingly slowly. "Doesn't matter how I feel. There's nothing even remotely appropriate about this situation."

Reese knew he was right, but he couldn't help himself. He stepped closer, forcing Jude's hands against his chest.

"It's just the two of us here, Jude. You can be honest with me. Am I imagining things? Tell me the truth."

"But it's *not* just the two of us here. We should both keep that in mind."

Reese desperately wanted to pull Jude flush against his body and discover physically whether or not Jude was feeling him too. But he didn't dare. The poor man definitely wouldn't appreciate being groped like that.

It took all kinds of self-control for Reese to step back and away from temptation.

"I'm sorry. I got carried away. Look. I'll call a friend to come take me to the hospital. I don't want you to miss class."

And he really needed to put some distance between them before he had Jude on his back on his bed. Where the hell did his libido come from all of a sudden? Did sleep deprivation remove sexual inhibitions? He'd missed that part of psychology, apparently, and he needed to extricate himself before he made Jude any more uncomfortable.

"I.... Are you sure? It's no trouble. My class meets not too far."

He was just being nice. Reese felt as though he were the one being let down easily. It was a role he'd never experienced before. But everything about Jude was different—his devotion to detail, his quiet manner, the honorable way he cared for Grandpa, and his patience dealing with Reese's fuck-ups, which were growing in number every minute he stood there.

"No, it's fine. I'll call a friend. You go ahead and change. I'm sorry I got blood on you. I'm sorry... for a lot of things."

"Please," Jude said, his voice barely above a whisper. "Don't."

He turned hurriedly and grabbed for his scrubs, then blew out the door as gracefully as a plastic bag in the wind.

Reese was in trouble.

He pulled out his cell and dialed Toby, but cursed when he remembered that Toby was vacationing in some exotic location. Fiji? Bali? Some place. *Shit.*

So he called the only other person he could think of.

"Jada? I need a favor."

WHAT A mess. He had to have his skin glued together at the hospital. The doctor really had to work to get it back together, and he told Reese his scar was definitely going to be noticeable with such a jagged cut. Jada laughed at him and said she was surprised he hadn't messed up his pretty face sooner with his crazy lifestyle. Surfing, skateboarding, snowboarding—any of his favorite activities could have messed him up before then, but no. He'd managed to keep his natural good looks intact. It drove her nuts.

Once he was patched up and they left the hospital, she spent the drive back to the cottage talking about *The Marrying Kind*, for which producers had offered her the lead. She apparently had "star potential" after tabloids picked up on their public breakup. Audiences would sympathize with her. Reese's mind wandered after a bit. He was preoccupied with Jude, irritated by how he'd left things, and he missed what Jada said.

"Are you even paying attention, Reese Matheson? For Christ's sake.

I drive all the way out here to take you to the hospital, and you can't even do one thing for me?"

Reese wanted to remind her that he was still paying the lease on their apartment for the next three months and that he'd made her last two car payments for her.

"I'm sorry, darling. It's this darn bandage on my nose. It must be interfering with my capacity to listen to your constant nitpicking."

He wasn't even mad at her for their breakup, which surprised him. Sure, he was pissed about his photo albums and songbooks, but they'd been mostly salvageable. He never stayed mad for long. It wasn't in his constitution.

He gave her his most charming smile, which made her laugh.

"You know you miss it." She paused for a moment and sighed. "Did you really sleep with Ethan? Please just tell me the truth. Of anyone you could have fucked around with, why him?"

It was Reese's turn to sigh heavily. "I've told you a million times already, I did not have sex with Ethan. We went to the gala in London together. That's it. I have no interest in him other than his acting ability, which earned my show a Tony or two. I don't even remember what we were talking about when that picture was taken."

The picture that reached across the ocean and disturbed his domestic bliss was of Reese and the star of his musical, Ethan Bradley, laughing heartily. Reese, being the touchy-feely guy that he was, had a hand on Ethan's shoulder. That was it. Suddenly they're fucking? If that's all it took, he might have spent the night with Jude.

"But obviously he's attracted to you. Who's to say you wouldn't have slept with him eventually?"

"And that's exactly why you and I agreed that when I was on tour, it was fair game. I know you had *your* fun, and I never cared."

"Yeah. And why didn't you care? I cared, Reese. I never said anything, but I cared."

They pulled up to the cottage, and Reese was too shocked to move. "Why didn't you ever say anything? Honestly, Jada, I hardly ever touched anyone. It wasn't that important to me. You said you didn't want to be alone for so long, so I went along with it."

Jada turned off the engine, fell back against the seat, and put her hand to her forehead. "Maybe it bothered me because they were men."

Reese turned his body to look at her. *The hits just keep on coming.* "What does that mean? You knew who I was when we got together. I made it very clear I'm pansexual. I like who I like. I loved you. I still love you, but I don't think love means the same thing to you." His voice turned soft, and he took her hand in his, lacing their fingers together.

Jada sniffled and smiled sadly. "I just thought that... I don't know. You know I'm a vain woman, Reese. I figured, once you had all this," she said, gesturing to herself, "you'd never go back. Stupid, huh?"

Reese brought her hand up and kissed it. "Not stupid, no. Naïve, maybe? Presumptuous?"

Jada elbowed him, but she laughed softly. "I love you, too, Reese. But I'm not meant to be alone so much. I need someone who needs only me in their life and is completely enamored of me. I guess I always knew you didn't need me like I needed you."

"Jada," Reese said as he moved closer to her. "How could you think I wasn't enamored of you? I spent a fortune on you. I gave you everything you could desire." He was so confused. He'd done everything for her.

"I desired *you*. Here with me," she sobbed, and tears ran down her lovely face. "I thought eventually, if you loved me enough, you'd stay here and stop touring."

Reese groaned and brought his hands up to rub his face in exasperation, forgetting his bandage.

"Owwwwww," they both said simultaneously. Jada reached for him, but Reese intercepted her touch.

"I'm fine. Look. You hoped to change me, and that wasn't going to happen. Babe, I'm a musician. I tour. I go where my music goes, wherever it takes me. This is my passion. I thought you understood that."

"I guess not enough to accept it. I'm sorry, Reese, about the way I acted. I didn't mean to embarrass you or anything, but I'm not sorry I broke up with you. I want more than you can give me, and that's the bottom line. I hope we can stay friends, and I hope you'll consider what I asked you."

Reese frowned and then winced. Damn, that was inconvenient.

"What did you ask me? I can't quite remember what we were talking about before all of this."

Jada rolled her eyes. "I asked you if you'd come on the show. The producer wants to do a segment where we talk about things, either a setup, or we, like, casually run into each other and have a conversation."

"More public performances, huh? Jada, I'm tired. Can we talk about this later? I haven't slept much this past week. I'm trying to take care of Grandpa. I had to ask Jude to come back because I can't handle him on my own."

"*Jude?* You asked him back? Huh," she said. Then she climbed out of the car and headed for the door of the cottage. Reese opened his door.

"What? What does that mean?"

Jada turned dramatically. "You think I don't know?"

Reese slammed his door, angry that she was continuing this nonsense and a little concerned about Jude's aunt and his grandfather hearing whatever came out of her next.

"Just what do you think you know? And please, I know you love the attention, but can we use our library voices? I'd rather my grandfather not be disturbed."

She crossed her arms and frowned at him. She was nearly his height, her ebony skin a contrast to his. She was slender like her model counterparts, fierce in attitude, and she was gearing up for another big scene.

"What I know, Reese Matheson, is that you are attracted to that funny little man. I've seen the way you look at him. You just better watch yourself. I doubt he's the kind of person that will put up with your crap either." She took two steps up the porch. "I'm going in to say good night to your grandfather, and then I'm leaving. The producers will be contacting you this week to set up a time to meet. I hope you don't ruin this chance for me. I gave you two years. The least you can do is give me this."

Reese watched her strut through the front door and turn on the charm as she greeted his grandfather. Little did she know that Grandpa had her all figured out already. Old man Matheson had been glad to see her go. He'd even offered to have some of his old "contacts" take care of her. But Reese would let her continue to think she'd be missed. He was anxious for her to be gone... for several reasons.

SEVEN

J UDE WAS exhausted after class and didn't relish the idea of sleeping in the rear of his truck another night, but he had no choice. And he had no more clean clothes. He'd promised Reese he'd return in the morning so he could take the early shift. He turned the Pathfinder in the direction of the cottage, pulled up to the curb, and sighed heavily.

He should be able to go inside, strip out of his funky clothes, and take a quick shower while Tita Germaine sat on the sofa reading a romance novel. She'd stay and talk for a bit, give him a hug and a kiss on the cheek, then go home to her toddler and husband in their one-bedroom apartment. She was only eight years older than him, so they'd been more like friends than aunt and nephew. He probably would have confessed everything he was feeling after that afternoon since he could tell her anything. But just as Jude was preparing to get out of the truck, Reese's Tesla pulled up into the driveway.

Jude watched in shock as Jada stepped out of the driver's seat and sashayed up the steps to the front door with Reese behind her. *She* was the friend he called to take him to the hospital?

With the windows rolled up, he couldn't hear them talking, but it appeared they were having a heated discussion, if Reese's expression was to be believed. Then he heard her laugh. Hadn't he seen TMZ footage of her throwing all of Reese's belongings out the window and into the pool? How could she have gone from scorned lover to laughing companion just like that?

Mr. Matheson had said she wanted to be an actress, and with her Naomi Campbell physique, she certainly could be. Too bad she had the nasty attitude to go with it. Or at least according to Mr. Matheson, she did. Perhaps she really was the sweet and caring woman Reese made her out to be. He'd overheard Reese arguing with his grandfather not too long after the last Thanksgiving they spent together.

"Old man, you just think every woman other than Grandma is bad news. Jada and I are fine together. She deals with my crazy, and I buy her expensive shit. It works for now."

Reese wasn't crazy. He was a lot to take, but he was a kind and generous, if somewhat oblivious, man. Did he really have to ask what Jude felt after their impromptu embrace in the shower?

Jude's heart had pounded out of control. The sight of Reese's blood was the only thing that kept him from closing the distance between them, desperate to know Reese intimately, starting with his lips. He wished the two of them could have been anyplace else and able to see just how compatible they might be with fewer clothes on.

Jude dropped his head against the steering wheel with a groan. Leave it to him to have a crush on the beyond-unattainable Reese Matheson.

A knock at the window startled him and he hit his elbow on the horn.

"What are you so damn jumpy about?" Germaine asked him, laughing.

He really needed to get centered.

"Carjack much? You scared me out of my skin. I just got home from class. What do you think I'm doing?"

"Stalking the Matheson residence?" she asked with a giggle. Then she grew serious. "He seemed really tired tonight. Grandpa, that is. What's been going on?"

"Reese got in over his head. He called me today because Mr. Matheson went missing. I told him I'd help him out. I can't just let him flounder. I care too much about Mr. Matheson."

Germaine seemed to know he was bullshitting her. "Uh-huh. I'm sure that's the only reason you're back here. I'm not stupid. I know just what effect that *man* can have. Hey, I thought you told me he broke up with his girlfriend? Why's she here?"

"Reese apparently called her to take him to the hospital. He cut his nose falling down in the shower. He, umm... didn't want me to miss class."

Her eyes flared at him. She shook her head. "Oh, Jude. Your poor heart."

Another sigh. "You're telling me." He'd confided before to Germaine that he found Reese frustratingly attractive. She'd listened sympathetically, understanding that it was an impossible situation.

"You talk to Brianna or Bailey?"

Jude's younger brother and sister, a junior and senior respectively, were what had kept him going the past week. He needed to get his life together before their next tuition payment was due.

"I haven't. I canceled practice last week, since I needed to look for a job."

Germaine tilted her head to the side. "They miss your mom and dad. Things aren't going so well at Rommel's."

Jude knew they hated the strict rules and really hated sharing a room with their cousin. It wasn't right for siblings their age to be rooming together, much less with a four-year-old.

"I know. If I can just get a job lined up, I'll be able to get an apartment finally, and they can live with me. Mom and Dad said they may come back next summer, that Tito Francisco would take over care of Lola and Lolo. I don't think they can wait that long, though."

Germaine looked down at her feet. "I really wish we had room for you guys. I'm sorry things have been so tough. Who knew my sister would have to be gone so long? I promise, if Paolo's boss gets him that raise, we can—"

"We'll be fine. You have the baby to take care of." He knew she wanted to help, but he needed to do it on his own. She'd already helped him out so he could take over coaching the kids' color guard team at school.

They spoke for a few more minutes, and then he told her he needed to get inside—but he was lying through his teeth to his favorite tita. When she drove off in her late-model Volkswagen Jetta, Jude started up the Pathfinder and decided to go to the all-night laundromat so he would have clean clothes. He really wanted a shower. He wanted a bed. He wanted peace and order back in his life. Instead he powered up his laptop and tried to concentrate on the week's classwork while he watched his clothes tumble around in the dryer. All the same color, spinning round and round, getting nowhere.

When his laundry was finished and folded neatly, he stored it in the back seat. Then he drove across town to park outside his *tito*'s house so he could catch a couple hours of sleep. He couldn't exactly blame Reese for falling asleep on the job if he did the same.

Jude knew how tough his tito Rommel was on his brother and sister. He was even stricter than their father, and his father had made Jude's high school years tough. Academics, color guard, and church were his life then. There was no time to socialize. Perhaps it had prepared him well for his current life.

He curled up in the cargo area of his truck and tried to calm his mind. Just a few hours of sleep and he'd return to the Mathesons'. He had to keep it together. He absolutely could not dwell on the image of Reese wet and naked in the shower.

EIGHT

REESE WOKE with a start the next morning, petrified that he'd overslept again and hadn't heard Grandpa wake up. He sat up too quickly, and the pain in his face reminded him of his embarrassment the night before.

"Fuck," he groaned as he sat on the side of the bed. Where had Jude gone? He almost hoped he'd come back last night, but they hadn't discussed it. And that conversation with Jada still unsettled him. Reese found himself wondering why she had it in her mind that he was attracted to Jude. Had he said something?

There was that one night they were over for Grandpa's birthday, and he sang with the old man. Reese had a lot to drink and he remembered Grandpa egging him on to sing the old songs. Reese asked Jude to make a request, and it had kind of turned into a serenade. He'd been messing around, got down on one knee in front of Jude. *Oh, yeah*. That might have given off an impression.

And so what? Jada was not the right partner for him. He wanted more than just arm candy hell-bent on stardom. He wanted... family.

He was thirty-two years old and had been an orphan for the past eight years. Perhaps all of his relentless touring had truly been an escape from his loneliness. His parents had been dead for a long time, a fact he thought he'd come to terms with, but being back with his grandfather really drove the point home. He was soon to be the sole surviving Matheson. He didn't even have any cousins. He was it.

And watching how well Jude took care of his grandfather made him realize he'd been missing that in his life as well.

Reese wandered into the kitchen and found a pot of glorious coffee. The smell energized him, and his mind started to spin with all the things he could accomplish now that Jude was there to help out. He could get out Grandpa's trunk of sheet music—music he'd written during the years he worked for Frank Sinatra and the boys. Reese had a story idea, and he was ready to work on it.

A crash from the living room sent Reese running. He heard his grandfather shout as he rounded the corner. Jude was bent over picking up broken dishes.

"Everyone okay?" Reese asked. Jude looked up at him, and Reese blanched. He looked exhausted. Where once his brown skin was the picture of health, his face looked pale. There were dark circles under his eyes, and his usually full dark lips were cracked and lacked color.

"I must have slipped as I was lifting the tray off your grandfather. I'm so sorry," he said softly.

"I'm just glad that coffee had cooled. You coulda boiled my balls."

"Jesus, old man. Enough with the ball cracks."

"Well, I'm serious. At least I don't need to use the boys for anything anymore, but they hang down so low in my chair, they woulda been scalded for sure."

Reese groaned as he stepped around Jude and tried to help.

"I've got it," Jude grumbled. Reese fought the laugh that almost slipped out. The unshakable Jude De La Torre was in a foul mood. Reese was entertained, but he was also worried.

"No, I've got it. Why don't you just sit down, Jude? You look like you're about to drop. Are you not feeling well?"

Jude stood slowly and brought his hand to his lower back. He moved to the couch and plopped down in an uncharacteristically awkward way. Reese continued to clean up the mess, but he could see Grandpa trying to get up.

"Just wait, old man. I'll get you cleaned up. Just let me get these shards picked up. I don't want you to cut yourself."

The old man grumbled, and Jude stared off into the distance. Reese stood, piled the broken dishes on the tray, took them to the garbage, and dumped them. Then he hurried back to his grandfather, helped him down the hall to the bathroom, and chanced a glance back at Jude. Jude's eyes met his and his heart clenched at the sight. Jude was seriously a wreck. Seemed Reese needed to care for *him* today.

"Let's get you into the shower." Reese helped him get undressed and left Grandpa to get his own drawers off.

"I wash my own balls, son. Remember that."

"Lord. Enough with the balls."

Grandpa chuckled his way through his shower and only paused a couple of times to hold on to the handrails. Reese should have remembered to grab them when he slipped last night. Reese stood next to the open stall door, at the ready in case Grandpa lost his balance. He needed to get a chair to put in there.

When Grandpa finished, Reese handed him a towel and grabbed his bathrobe. Reese helped him into it and then stood beside him as he combed his hair and put on his aftershave. Grandpa shuffled into his room next, and Reese glanced down the hall to see Jude had moved from the couch. He frowned but continued into the bedroom with Grandpa... and stopped cold.

Jude had cleaned his grandfather's room—top to bottom. There wasn't a speck of dust on anything. All of the clothes were put away. There was nothing on the floor, and the bed had been freshly made. No wonder the guy was exhausted. That would have taken Reese a week, not a couple of hours. What the hell time had he shown up that morning?

Grandpa hummed to himself as he went about his dressing routine, and Reese beamed. He loved it when Grandpa sang. The times were few and far between these days, but he relished them.

"Hey, Grandpa? How about I take you out back. I'll play for you, and you can sing. What do you say? I want to pull out some of your sheet music."

"My grandson wants to write a play about me, did ya know that?"

Reese frowned, but Grandpa continued.

"My grandson is a great musician. Taught him just about everything he knows. Well, the guitar he picked up on his own. I love that boy. He should be back soon from his tour. Did you want to meet him?"

He looked at Reese expectantly, but he didn't even recognize the man he'd just been heaping praise on.

"Yeah," Reese said, choking back tears. "I'd like to meet him."

"Mr. Matheson, *Judge Judy* is on. Would you like to come back to your chair? I've cleaned it up for you."

Reese turned to find Jude had composed himself. Jude stepped forward and took Grandpa by the elbow and led him out the door. He raised an eyebrow at Reese, but the look wasn't one of reproach. He genuinely looked sorry for him.

Reese couldn't get his feet moving. There'd been a couple of times when his grandfather briefly hadn't recognized him, but he snapped out of it. Today he'd carried on as though Reese weren't there in front of him.

Were they really out of time? The thought broke his heart. He knew once he placed him in a care facility, their time would be up. He'd read that many of the places discouraged visits from family members as it just disturbed and agitated the Alzheimer's patients. Reese's chest felt heavy just thinking about it. He sank to his knees—a fitting metaphor for his situation. He was all alone.

His parents had been traveling in South America when the car they rented went over the side of a cliff in rainy weather. Reese had just graduated from college and was touring across the US with his band when he got the call. It hurt, sure. But they'd been traveling since he was a kid, sometimes for six or eight months at a time because his father's film-production company worked all over the planet. Reese spent so much time with his grandparents that their house felt more like home than any house he'd lived in with his parents. Losing his grandmother four years ago was more difficult—for him and for Grandpa. Reese wished that tough woman were still here to guide him.

A gentle hand on his shoulder stirred him from the painful memories. Reese looked up into Jude's comforting gaze. His dark eyes held compassion—something Reese hadn't felt from anyone in a long time.

"He's resting in his chair. He sleeps more during the day now."

Reese couldn't fight the tears any longer. He rubbed at his eyes and bumped his nose.

"Fuck, that hurts." He wiped gingerly with the hem of his shirt just as Jude held a tissue out to him.

"Thanks," Reese said. He hadn't cried when his parents died, evidence enough that his present situation hurt on a much deeper level.

"You have a little more time, Reese, if that's what you're thinking."

Reese blew out a breath and tried to get his breathing under control, but his chin wouldn't stop quivering as he spoke.

"He talked about me. *To* me. As if *I* weren't *me* standing there. Jude, he didn't recognize me at all."

JUDE KNELT before Reese and wrapped his arms around him to offer solace. Reese seemed so lost. Jude didn't know how to help him come to grips with the fact that he could very well lose his grandfather sooner rather than later. How could he? Jude didn't know what that meant. Even without his parents and grandparents, he had a large extended family. Reese had his grandfather. Period.

Reese clung to him as he let his feelings out quietly. Jude felt the shudders going through Reese's much larger frame. When it seemed like he was getting himself under control, Jude tried to lean back, but Reese held on.

"We'll care for him together," Jude said softly against Reese's hair. They held each other a few moments longer until it was obvious that things were moving from the realm of comfort toward something more like a caress. Their eyes held as they separated, and neither was able to look away.

"Thank you," Reese finally said, his bright smile returning although he looked a little ridiculous with the bandage on his nose. His eyes hadn't blackened, but they still might.

"You're very welcome," Jude said, his cheeks flushed. The full force of Reese's charisma hit him like a tractor beam and threatened to pull him back in. He didn't want to fight that pull any longer.

"It's nice to know we're in this together." Reese's smile was intoxicating.

"You called Jada last night," Jude blurted out, unable to stand the tension between them. Reese's eyes widened in surprise, and he barked out a laugh.

"I did. My songwriting partner is out of town. She was the only other person I could think of who had nothing better to do." He chuckled at his own statement, but Jude needed the wake-up call. He had absolutely no business on his knees in front of Reese Matheson, especially in his grandfather's room. He scrambled rather ungracefully to his feet and backed up to the door.

"Well, I'm certain she was glad to help. Excuse me."

He turned to run, or at least flee to the kitchen, the porch, the closet —anything to be away from Reese at that moment. A knock on the door almost saved him. He turned back meaning to say "That must be the nurse," only to find Reese standing inches away.

"She told me she knew I was attracted to you," Reese said, blushing.

Jude was dumbfounded. "Why would she say that?" he asked rather lamely.

Reese reached up a large hand and ran his thumb over Jude's lip. "Because it's true," he whispered. He sucked in a breath and blew it out as he pushed past Jude's unmoving and confused form and walked toward the living room, probably to open the door for whoever was knocking so insistently. Jude caught himself against the doorjamb.

"Sleep deprivation," he mumbled and shook his head. "That has to be the explanation. Why else would I be feeling light-headed?"

Lack of food could have been the culprit as well, but Jude had been going without sleep for a week. Since the nurse was there, he could leave for a while, maybe go catch a shower at Tita Germaine's. She'd be home with the baby, but she wouldn't mind. He'd just explain that he wanted to freshen up before he headed over to the kids' school for color guard practice.

Not only was Jude trying to finish up his degree, one course at a time, he'd taken on the color guard choreographer position to ensure that his brother and sister were able to experience a championship season. He'd missed the dancing anyway, and it was a great outlet for his frustration. Now that he'd determined the best course of action to get him away from Reese and all the temptation he personified, Jude had the gumption to put one foot in front of the other and join them in the living room.

"Well, hello Jude. It's so nice to see you back."

He kissed cheeks with Kyla, a friend of his from high school. She'd been a year ahead of him and had completed her nursing degree in the past year. She'd taken a job with the home-care service Mr. Matheson's insurance contracted with and came three to four times a week to check his vitals and follow up on his medications. She'd been upset when Reese let Jude go, but being the professional she was, she didn't outright yell at him. She just snuck in little digs while Jude was still around that made it clear who she sided with.

"You too, girl. Hey, I might need to ask you for a reference, if you don't mind. I'm looking into—"

"Of course," she said as she gave Reese a scolding look. "You're probably looking for work, huh. I'd be happy to write you a letter. Where should I send it? Are you staying at your uncle's?"

Jude's eyes darted between Reese's very attentive ones and Kyla's expectant ones.

"Uh, no. I'm staying with my, umm, cousin. Adrian. He lives not too far from here. It's quicker than going to Tito's. Would you excuse me? I need to get ready for class."

Feeling incredibly nervous, agitated, hungry, and exhausted, he hurried into the kitchen to grab his bag and then made quick work of saying goodbye.

"When will I see you next?" Reese asked, his hands on his incredible hips. *OhJesusLordGod.*

"When do you want me?" Jude answered. *God*, did he sound pathetic. Reese's smile looked salacious. Thank goodness Kyla was tending to Mr. Matheson and wasn't paying attention. Reese followed Jude out front.

"I think I made that very clear," Reese murmured behind Jude as he followed Jude out the door.

Jude turned on him, and his anger got the better of him. "Don't play with me," Jude snapped. "I have no interest in coming between you and Jada."

Reese's eyes narrowed as he stepped forward and closed the door behind him. "There is no between me and Jada. This isn't about her. This is about you. And me. And the fact that every second I spend around you is driving me crazy. I can't stand watching you float across the room, picking things up with your graceful hands, or speaking to me in that infuriating tone of yours."

Jude stepped back at the emotion in Reese's voice.

"I—I'm sorry, Reese. I—"

"I can't stand it because I *want* you in front of me. I want your hands on *me*, and I want you saying my name over and over in anything but that damn tone. I want you, Jude. God help me, but I want you."

"Oh," Jude gasped and stumbled on the top step as he backed away. "Oh. Well, I...." What the hell was he supposed to say to that? He felt himself smiling. *Stupid.* "You never said when you want me back here," Jude said as his ears got hot. He backed two more steps down from the porch, but couldn't seem to break away from Reese's gaze.

"I never said I wanted you to leave," Reese joked. But that was all it took to cool Jude's mood.

"Yeah. You did. I'll be back after class tonight to check in. And please leave his bedroom the way you found it this morning."

Jude turned on his heel and walked with purpose toward his car, confident Reese was watching him the entire way. He tried to remain composed, at least until he was out of Reese's sight. Then he could fall apart.

NINE

O F ALL the insensitive, idiotic things Reese could have said in that moment.

Yes, he had asked Jude to leave, but only so he could be with his grandfather and care for him. Jude hadn't put up a fuss. Surely he had a place to stay, didn't he?

But then he'd stumbled over his words in front of his nurse friend. *Shit*. What if he didn't have a place to stay? What if he was out there...?

He'd find out that night, for sure. When Jude came back, he'd make him talk—about a lot of things.

Kyla was just about done with Grandpa's check-in when Reese returned, and she offered to sit with him if Reese had anything he needed to do.

"Actually if you wouldn't mind, I'm going to be out in the garage for a bit? I just need to pull down some boxes. Me and the old man got some music to make, ain't that right?"

Grandpa just grunted. "Been waiting on you. Nothing to do but fiddle with my balls while you're out prancing around on stage."

Kyla laughed and turned to Reese. "We'll be fine. You do what you need to do. I can stay until four."

That gave Reese a couple of hours to get the boxes down and orga-

nize the sheet music. When they moved to the cottage from the larger
house his grandparents had owned, the movers did a shitty job. And
Grandpa had never organized his writing. No more. Reese knew the
music his grandfather had written over the years was pure genius.

He was inspired by Grandpa's song about meeting a girl on a street
corner on a summer's day—the story of how he met Grandma. Reese
imagined a whole musical around their meeting. When he brought up
the idea to Grandpa, he was skeptical at first. It wasn't until Reese's first
musical, *Ruby in Red Plaid*, about a young man's sexual liberation in
the 1990s, became a huge sensation on Broadway that Grandpa began to
see the possibilities. Reese just hoped he hadn't waited too long to get
started.

JUDE PULLED into the parking lot of Santa Francesca Catholic High
School and took a deep breath. Color guard had been his life when he
was a teenager, and he'd been choreographing for their team for the past
two years. His old coach was getting close to retirement, and the
thought was that Jude would take over in a few years. It was a great way
for him to stay connected to his brother and sister, and it was a way for
him to keep dancing. Before he started working for Mr. Matheson, he
took dance classes a couple of nights a week at the community college.
Now he just worked at the school and took his nursing course. It was
enough.

"Mr. D! Mr. D!" Some of the girls bounded over to his car as he
climbed out. It was always a struggle to keep boundaries with the kids.
Some of the girls could get downright handsy, and not with just jazz
hands. Jude tried to put off a no-nonsense vibe, but it didn't seem to
matter.

"Are we really going to be competing at state this year?" He pushed
these kids hard because he had an especially talented group.

"If you continue to progress, we'll have no problem qualifying at
regionals. But we need everyone to work hard. To want it."

They giggled and ran off to join the group. As soon as the rest of the
kids saw him coming down to the field, they immediately followed their
captains in their stretching routines and then ran through their

program in its entirety. They tossed their flags and rifles in absolute symmetry. Jude expected perfection from the kids, and they gave him their all.

Practice lasted over two hours, and the kids were spent when they finished. The sky had been dark for an hour, and he knew it was time to let them go, but he'd wanted to work with them just once more on a particularly difficult combination. He pulled his brother and sister aside.

"You haven't been answering my texts, JJ," Brianna said with her hands on her hips, just like their mother.

"I know, sis. I've been out trying to find a job. I'm going to be back helping Mr. Matheson some—"

"After his grandson fired you? Why would you go back?" Bailey asked sullenly.

"Because I care about him. And because I want to make sure he's cared for in the best way possible."

"What about us? Do you even care about us anymore?" Bailey stormed off toward Tito Rommel's car as it pulled up. Tito Rommel waved at Jude, who waved back. Then he turned to Brianna.

"Don't worry about him," she said quietly. "He's just angry because Junior ripped up his AP Bio notebook. He'll be okay. But we do miss you. It's not the same when we don't get to see you regularly. Even if it's just at practice, you know?"

Jude hugged his sister and breathed deeply to alleviate the heavy weight of guilt that threatened to crush him.

"I'll hopefully have the money soon to move out. I love you guys so much. I hate not being able to have you with me, but I've been doing what I had to—"

"We know that. Bailey just forgets sometimes. Things were fine until Junior moved to our room. We'll be okay." She cocked an eyebrow at him. "Where have *you* been staying? I heard Tita Gemma saying you were staying with Tita Germaine, but I know you told me you couldn't stay there."

His little sister was getting to be too smart for her own good. "With friends, Bri. I'm fine, but I need to go. I love you, and I'll be over as soon as I can."

She hugged him tight, gave an extra squeeze at the end, and then waved as she ran off to the car.

Jude waited until each and every one of the forty-six kids was picked up, and then he climbed wearily into his car and started the engine.

When he pulled up at the cottage, he could hear the piano and Reese's singing. His heart stuttered. He had such a beautiful voice. Jude first heard Reese's music when he was in high school. He and his friends danced along during warm-ups at color guard practice. He'd bought Reese's CD and everything. It was probably still in his case under the front seat of his car.

But this music wasn't like his pop hits. His versatile voice crooned just like Michael Buble, or the original even—Frank Sinatra. Mr. Matheson had a great voice too, but Reese's was sort of magical. At least it had a magical effect on Jude.

He entered the house and immediately went to the kitchen to clean up the mess Reese was sure to have made. But he found none. He checked the laundry only to find that Reese had folded everything—sloppily but folded, nonetheless—in baskets next to the washer. He had nothing to keep himself busy with.

Jude went into the living room and watched Reese and his grandfather until they stopped playing.

"Jude, my boy. What do you think? Sounds pretty good coming out of this guy, huh?"

Jude could just nod. The music was great.

"Yeah, once Toby gets back and starts helping me piece the story together, we'll be golden. Grandpa, you remember Toby, right? My writing partner?"

"Oh you mean the fairy? Yeah. I remember him. Boy can sure sing."

Reese frowned. "Grandpa, he's not a fairy. He's gay. Say it with me. *Gaaaaaaay*. It's not a bad word, I promise."

Mr. Matheson snorted. "Whatever you call it. It don't matter to me as long as he doesn't try to kiss me again. Yuck."

Reese laughed. "Oh come on. It was on the cheek. Just for that," Reese said. He lurched for his grandfather and gave him a juicy smack of his lips on the top of his head. They both laughed as his grandfather put him in a headlock, but Reese went willingly.

Jude was puzzled by the interaction. Reese was certainly not afraid to challenge his grandfather, but he didn't exactly confront him either. It seemed Reese got through much of his life by joking.

Jude helped Mr. Matheson to bed at nine and loved that he seemed so happy. Reese was really good medicine for him. He was just intoxicating all around. Once Mr. Matheson was comfortable in bed he went straight to sleep, a testament to how much he needed the rest. Jude went back out to the living room and said good night to Reese.

"You'll be back in the morning, right?" Reese asked from the piano bench where he was still playing around with the music. Jude loved watching his long fingers dance over the keys, but he'd pulled his hair back into that ridiculous man bun again—ridiculous because Jude had to pinch himself to keep from staring at Reese's neck. "I was going to go surfing early, if that's okay? You'll be here?"

Jude realized Reese had spoken only when he turned away from the piano. A piece of curly hair hung down his forehead.

"Yes." But what was he saying yes to? He was fatigued and overwhelmed, and he needed to get out of the cottage. Fresh air would be a good idea—alone.

"Great. Thank you, Jude. Thank you for coming back."

Jude nodded, grabbed his backpack, and beat feet out the front door. He got to his car and could do nothing more than sit in the back seat and stare at the headrest in front of him.

He mulled over his options—the ones he was running out of. He'd been so exhausted that he actually dropped Mr. Matheson's dishes. He couldn't afford to make that kind of mistake again. Reese had seen his exhaustion as well.

It wouldn't do for him to continue sleeping in his car, but what could he do? Tita Germaine had her hands full. Tito Rommel and Tita Gemma were already supporting his younger siblings as well as their *lola*. His cousins all had roommates. At least if he were closer to the Matheson house, he could be there bright and early. That way he wouldn't be found out by his family.

He parked under a tree two houses down from the cottage, thinking it would keep the streetlights from shining down on him. He used a bottle of water to wash up and brush his teeth and then crawled into the cargo area of the Pathfinder. His back was bothering him from not being able to stretch out, and that morning he'd had a horrible crick in his neck that took most of the day to work itself out.

Jude lay there for at least an hour as he ran through his situation and his finances until he wanted to tear his hair out. His only solution would be to find a full-time position working a graveyard shift. That would allow him to work mornings for Reese, steal a couple of hours of sleep in a room he'd rent somewhere, and then be up in time for color guard and class. It wasn't ideal, but at least he could shower and have a place for his meager belongings until he could afford to get a real place for him, Bailey, and Brianna. He rolled over and attempted some breathing exercises to relax his body. Then he remembered Reese's parting words from that morning. *"God help me, but I want you."*

If only it were possible. Well, sure, it was possible. Jude could allow Reese to seduce him. He'd love every minute of it. One night exploring every inch of Reese's golden skin, losing himself in Reese's touch? Heaven. A beautiful distraction. But then what? Reese would go about his life with someone else, and Jude would be left feeling bereft. And he knew Mr. Matheson had no tolerance when it came to Jude's sexual orientation. He'd heard the man make many hateful comments over the years, but he loved him anyway. Jude kept to himself and they got along famously.

Jude had come out to his tita Germaine and his mother. They'd both been very understanding, but they cautioned him about reactions from his father and uncle, who held very strict Catholic beliefs. Jude had resigned himself to being alone other than the occasional hookup. What would be wrong if that hookup happened to be with Reese?

So many things—Reese's public persona, Mr. Matheson's beliefs, oh, and the fact that Jude didn't have casual feelings for Reese. At all.

Jude rolled over once more, yanked his blanket over him, and allowed himself to picture Reese's handsome face. Just once more.

TEN

T HE SOUND of someone pounding on the car woke Jude the next morning, and the first thing he saw was Reese's handsome face, which looked furious.

"Open up this fucking door right now."

The humiliation overwhelmed Jude. He turned away from Reese's angry face at the window of his Pathfinder and wondered if he could disappear if he just closed his eyes tightly enough. It could happen. He used to play that game with his father when he was a boy. He'd close his eyes, and his father would pretend he'd become invisible. Jude would laugh and laugh while his father looked all over for him.

"Jude, I swear if you don't open this fucking door, I'll break the goddamned window."

Jude supposed his disappearance wasn't working. Maybe if he just turned over and closed his eyes, the nightmare would disappear. Jude's watch showed five thirty. It was still very dark outside, but Reese's golden locks glowed with the light from the streetlight. There was no escaping his awful predicament. The jig was up.

Jude climbed over the back seat and opened the door, but he refused to speak. He kept his arms wrapped around himself to hide the fact that he was shaking uncontrollably.

"You mind telling me what the fuck you're doing sleeping in your car outside my house? Are you crazy?"

Jude tried to keep the tremor from his voice. "I'm perfectly sane. One could ask you what you're doing outside before dawn shouting at me."

Reese blanched, leaned closer, and rested his arm on the roof of the car. "Please don't tell me you've been doing this since I came home."

"Okay."

"Okay what?" Reese asked, his voice growing more tense by the second.

"Okay, I won't tell you that," Jude replied and bit his lip to keep the nervous laughter at bay. He might have lied when he said he was perfectly sane.

"Why are you smiling? You have been, haven't you? Dammit, Jude. Why didn't you tell me?"

Any trace of humor evaporated. Jude raised his eyebrow at Reese.

"What would it have mattered to you? You'd already made up your mind to move in. I was in the process of finding a place when you asked me to come back," he lied.

"But your family—"

"My family has their hands full. They're already caring for my brother and sister."

"You have siblings? Where are your parents?"

"In the Philippines. Reese, what are you even doing out here this early?"

"I was just going to run to the store and grab some coffee. We're out. And I knew you'd be here soon. I just didn't know you were already here."

Reese peered around the inside of the car, furthering Jude's embarrassment. He looked in the back where Jude had been sleeping and noticed all the neat piles of clothes and books.

"You know, most people who live in their cars are like trolls. Even your piles of clothes are color coded. Hey, you own jeans. I was beginning to think you only wore scrubs." He chuckled, and Jude's embarrassment turned to anger. He reached over to pull the door closed, but Reese blocked him.

"What do you think you're doing?" Reese asked, the humor fading from his voice.

"I'm leaving. What does it look like?" Jude tried to tug the door shut, not even concerned about smashing Reese's perfect hands. It would serve him right.

"The only place you're going is in the house. No wonder you've been so exhausted. You're going to come in, shower, and get in my bed."

Jude's eyes flared, and he started to argue, but Reese held a finger up to his lips.

"As much as I'd love to join you there, now's not the time. We'll just take turns. Now grab what you need. You're moving back in."

Jude pulled away. "You can't just order me around. You—"

Reese snaked an arm around Jude's back and pulled him in for a kiss so quickly that a very stunned Jude could only open his mouth to object before Reese's tongue filled it. Shocked, Jude tried to push him away, but Reese scooped his other hand under Jude's ass and pulled him forward to bring their bodies flush against each other, Jude's legs spread against Reese's hips. When Jude would have fought harder, Reese bit down on his lower lip and growled low in his chest.

Kissing Reese was everything Jude feared it could be—overwhelming, intoxicating, and probably addicting. Jude forgot about all the reasons he shouldn't be kissing Reese, slid a hand around his back, and pressed their chests impossibly close together. Jude couldn't help smiling when Reese moaned his appreciation. Reese may have started the kiss, but Jude met his enthusiasm, stroke for stroke. A sort of quiet chaos built between them as they each finally gave in to a chemistry that Jude didn't quite understand. How could Reese make him so angry, turned on, grounded, and upheaved all at the same time?

Reese pulled back, sucking gently on Jude's lip, eliciting a moan from him. The fight bled out of Jude and he knew he had a choice to make: walk away from the Mathesons and protect his heart, or give in to Reese and give up all control of his life. One involved continuing to sleep in his car and abandoning Reese in his time of need. The other choice.... There really was no choice.

. . .

REESE WANTED to dive back in and keep kissing that delicious mouth.
The moment he felt Jude give in, Reese knew every victory with Jude
would be just as sweet. His lips.... God, Reese could explore those lips
for an eternity and never completely know them. Jude was like a deep
well of mystery that Reese wanted to get lost in. What was it about that
quiet young man that made Reese want to roar?

He waited for a snappy comeback, but Jude seemed to have given
up. Or given in, Reese hoped. He wanted Jude desperately, and though
he knew the timing couldn't be worse, he didn't care one bit. There was
a reason the two of them had been thrown together. Reese knew Jude
would stand by him, and while he didn't consider himself particularly
manipulative, he planned to use the situation to his advantage. Who
knew what would come of an affair with Jude? Reese had a feeling that,
once they allowed themselves to experience a deeper level of passion
with each other, there would be no turning back. And Reese was ready
to move forward with that plan.

Jude looked around the SUV as Reese waited for him to accept that
he had no alternative. He was counting on Jude's exhaustion to spur
him forward, and in the end, that was probably what finally got Jude to
climb out of the car and shut the door.

"Did you want me to grab anything?" Reese asked, trying to keep
the triumphant smile off his face.

Jude just raised that eyebrow once more and then turned his back
on Reese, moving in that sensual way that had Reese panting after him.
He needed to cool his jets a bit. It wouldn't do to strip Jude down and
bend him over the first available surface. He'd have to be creative. And
there was Grandpa to consider. He knew Reese had a colorful love life,
and he didn't keep his opinions about it to himself. It didn't bother
Reese, but he had a feeling Jude would take the grumblings of the old
man personally. Reese could tell he was sensitive that way.

If only they were going into the house alone. Reese intended to feast
on Jude for hours... just as soon as he had an opportunity. As though he
heard Reese's thoughts, Jude turned and looked back at him as he
climbed the steps to the porch. *Oh, Jude, you're in so much trouble.*

Jude headed straight for the bathroom and closed the door behind
him. Reese peeked into Grandpa's room and was relieved to see him

sleeping peacefully. He usually woke around seven and wanted his breakfast and coffee soon after. Coffee. *Shit.* Reese looked toward the bathroom. Should he wait until Jude finished? Should he knock and poke his head in? No, that was a bad idea. Seeing Jude's body uncovered for the first time was a sight he yearned to savor, but he wanted it to be on Jude's terms. As much as Reese intended to orchestrate things in his favor, he'd only feel like he'd won if Jude gave himself freely. He wanted that to happen. And soon.

Reese prepared Grandpa's eggs and toast. The old man didn't seem able to tolerate his favorite breakfast meats any longer, but he still enjoyed the eggs with a little Tabasco sauce. He was eating less overall. Along with his increase in sleep, that meant his time was running out. Reese vowed to make the remaining time as enjoyable as possible for the man who meant so much to him.

He heard Jude shut off the shower as he slid the food into the warmer. Then he remembered that Jude hadn't grabbed anything from the car. He'd probably been too tired. Reese went to his room hoping to find some smaller clothes that might fit him. He was just pulling out some sweats and a long-sleeved T-shirt when he heard throat-clearing behind him.

"I didn't—"

"I was just grabbing some clothes for you. They're not as fashion forward as scrubs, but I think you'll be comfortable."

Reese turned to find Jude standing in a towel in the doorway and froze where he stood. Jude's torso was sculpted beautifully. He didn't have the kind of muscle tone you'd see on someone who lived in a gym. He was built more like the dancers in Reese's show. His chest was bare. The only hair visible lined his lower abdominal region and disappeared under the towel. Reese had to remind himself that he wanted Jude to give himself over and that removing the towel himself would be all kinds of wrong. He needed to hand him the clothes and leave. But Jude was absolutely breathtaking. Reese stared for several moments before his brain kicked back into gear.

"I'll just leave you," Reese stammered, his face hot. He placed the clothes on the bed, though he longed to join Jude there, naked against each other.

"Get some rest," Reese said in a husky voice. "I'm going to run to the store. If you can just—"

"Reese?"

Reese had been trying to leave the room with his sanity intact, but the tone of Jude's voice stalled him. He turned slowly.

"I won't be in your way. I'll—"

"I *want* you in my way. Don't ever do that again, Jude. This is more your home than mine. I don't ever want you doing without again."

The lust that had fueled their spontaneous kiss morphed into a determination within Reese to do right by the man who'd taken such good care of his grandfather. Reese fully intended to take care of Jude, no matter what happened between them. He owed him.

ELEVEN

J UDE LOOKED down at the clothes Reese had set out for him and shook his head. How exactly was he supposed to wear clothes made for a man at least six inches taller and forty pounds heavier? But he was too tired to complain. He pulled them on and laughed at the result. The shirt came down to his thighs, and the sweats required rolling if he didn't want to trip. Thankfully they had a drawstring, so he didn't have to hold them up. He lifted the shirt to his face and inhaled Reese's scent. His eyes rolled back in his head, and he groaned at the feeling that hit him low in the gut.

That kiss was quite possibly the hottest moment Jude had ever experienced in his life. He'd had lovers before—some casual flings with acquaintances and secretive encounters that were more to scratch an itch than to build any sort of relationship. There were too many factors working against that possibility. Jude got what he needed. He demanded to be in control, to set the terms, and he took what he wanted. But what he wanted from Reese was to give up that control. He wanted Reese to take control, and he wanted to allow himself to just....

Jude fell back on Reese's king-size bed, surrounded by Reese's scent. He stretched out and relaxed for the first time since he'd found himself homeless. He wouldn't allow himself to get used to the feeling, but for a nap, Jude would take the opportunity to recuperate so he could help Reese.

JUDE SLEPT like the dead and assumed he was dreaming when he felt gentle fingers in his hair. He snuggled into the touch and resisted the urge to open his eyes and confirm it was Reese. He wanted to continue the dream.

"You're so beautiful," Reese whispered as though Jude wouldn't hear him. Jude's heart fluttered. Could Reese really see him? In all the time Jude had been crushing on Reese, he never imagined the golden boy would ever notice him, much less return his feelings. But what he heard next changed everything.

"I know there are a million reasons why I shouldn't want this, but none of them matter when I look at you. You look like everything right to me. I want to make this right."

Jude wanted to reach out and take what Reese was offering, but he didn't want to break the magic of the moment, so he remained still and felt the bed shift. Reese's warm breath caressed his forehead as he placed a gentle kiss there. Then his weight lifted from the bed, and Jude heard his heavy footsteps leaving the room.

Jude opened his eyes and blew out a breath. *Wow.* The man was a true romantic.

He was right, though. There were a million reasons why they shouldn't even entertain the idea of getting involved. That thought spurred Jude into action. He needed to get up and do his job. That was most important.

It was close to noon by the time Jude entered the living room. Mr. Matheson was sitting in his chair watching *Judge Judy*, and sounds from the kitchen meant Reese was likely fixing his lunch. Then Mr. Matheson would sleep for at least an hour. He'd wake and want to walk out back. Then *Ellen* and supper at four. Then the news. Then another walk. Then bed by early evening. The routine was most important for him. Jude hoped that a couple of days back on schedule would help Mr. Matheson perk up. Jude didn't like the amount of sleeping he'd been doing. Not to mention him forgetting Reese. Jude knew how much pain that caused Reese, and he hoped there weren't many more of those incidents.

"Jude, my boy. What happened to your uniform? You look like a ragamuffin in them clothes."

Jude looked down at Reese's gigantic clothes and grimaced. What would he think?

"I, umm—"

"Old man, I got your grilled cheese here," Reese called out as he entered the room, but he paused when he saw Jude in his clothes. A sly smile spread across his face. It made Jude blush and turn around.

"Hot stuff. Bring it on over. And after I eat, we gotta play some music. You got my sheets outta the garage?"

Reese's smile faded a bit. "Got them out yesterday, remember? Let's play some music." Reese sat the plate down on the tray and placed it on Mr. Matheson's lap. "Jude, I made you one too. Have a seat."

Mr. Matheson frowned at Reese and then at Jude. He seemed to be trying to figure out what was different, and he didn't seem happy. Jude sank into the couch and felt swallowed up by the clothes, by the couch, and by his guilt. He had no business entertaining the thoughts he was having about Reese. Sitting in front of Mr. Matheson just hammered that thought home.

"I want to start going through these songs and piece together the best for the musical. I'm still playing with a title, and I know I want it to be something about a girl on the corner, but that just sounds wrong."

Reese handed Jude a tray with a grilled cheese sandwich, potato chips, and fresh fruit on it, which put Jude further out of his comfort zone. He wasn't a guest. *Why is he serving me?* Jude looked wide-eyed for Mr. Matheson's reaction—a frown.

"Why is he wearing those clothes?" Mr. Matheson's frown deepened.

Reese put his hands on his hips. "Because Jude is going to be staying with us," he answered.

"No, Mr. Matheson. I just needed a change of clothes. I spilled something earlier, and your grandson was nice enough to let me—"

"Grandpa, Jude is our guest. He's going to be staying with me so you and I have time to work on the musical."

Jude wanted to argue, but the more he spoke and the more Reese argued with him, the more Mr. Matheson looked angry.

"Well," Mr. Matheson said finally. "You should let him cook. He's better than you, son. He makes me that meat on the weekend, what do you call it? The stuff in the can I thought I would hate?"

"It's called Spam, Mr. Matheson. And I'd be happy to make it for you this weekend."

"You ate Spam? But you always said meat in a can wasn't real meat. You wouldn't eat the chicken salad I tried to make you."

Mr. Matheson ate a couple more bites of his sandwich and chewed slowly. He swallowed the food down, and his expression became defiant.

"Like I said, because Jude cooks better than you. He makes that spicy vinegar stuff that's so hot it makes my balls stick to my legs."

"Oh, God, Grandpa. Enough with the balls."

"What? You rather I talk about some pansy-ass shit? Men talk about their balls, son. It's a fact. Balls are a big deal, unless you're a fairy."

Reese groaned, looked to Jude apologetically, and stormed back into the kitchen.

"Maybe it's not too late to have you gelded, old man," he hollered. "I bet that friend of yours, Lefty, could tell you something about that."

"Why? 'Cause he was in the mob? Nah. The only thing he knows about losing balls is from the cancer. That's why he ain't an enforcer anymore. You lose a ball, you're washed up. I might be losin' my marbles, but I still got my balls." Mr. Matheson laughed at his joke and slurped down the rest of his iced tea. His attention wandered back to *Judge Judy*, and the frown set back in.

"Can you believe these two cream puffs? They're fighting over who should get their poodle. What kind of man goes on television with his gay lover and fights over a dog? Where are *his* balls?"

Reese stood in the doorway and frowned at the TV. "What does it matter if they're gay? The fact is, one of them didn't pay his share of the vet bills, so the other one wants custody. That shit happens all the time. It doesn't matter if it's two men, two women, or whatever."

"Well, don't get your panties in a wad. Hey, do you wear panties? I know you wear them tight pants on stage and you prance around with them dancer types. Back in the day, when I played with Frank and the boys, none of that crap went on."

"Bullshit, Grandpa. You don't think there were gay men in Las Vegas in the fifties and sixties? Need I remind you of Liberace? How you guys didn't know he was gay is beyond me."

Mr. Matheson grumbled in his chair and stood slowly. "Yeah, well...." He mumbled incoherently down the hall to his bedroom and shot an irritated glance at Reese, who beamed like he'd won a playground argument.

"Must you egg him on like that?" Jude asked as he took a bite of the sandwich. It was richer food than he'd been eating lately, but he was so hungry he would have eaten just about anything.

"Yes, I must. He needs to be put in his place now and then. I can deal with his backward thinking to a point, but he knows intolerance isn't tolerated in my house."

Jude ate slowly, uncomfortable with Reese watching his every move. He wiped at his mouth with a napkin and looked up to see Reese leaning against the doorway, smiling down at him.

"How do you want this arrangement to work?" Jude wanted to get back to business.

Reese's grin was infuriating. He never took anything seriously. Jude started to scold him, but Reese shook his head.

"I'm sorry. I was just enjoying watching you eat. I don't think I've ever—"

"Reese."

"Sorry. Uh, I'll take the night, you take the day? I'll get in some sleep early morning until maybe eleven. I work better at night, but I need to work with him on this musical in the afternoons when he's awake. You sleep when you need to. You'll take my bed, of course."

"Reese, you need your rest. I'll figure something out for a place to stay."

Reese's smile disappeared. He stormed around the edge of the couch and sat on the coffee table in front of Jude, resting his elbows on his knees.

"I'm willing to be flexible and let you handle Grandpa's care and call the shots about his schedule and shit. But I won't give in on this one.

This is your home. I never should have uprooted you, and I'm sorry. It was completely thoughtless of me, and I plan on making it up to you. I want you under this roof, and that's final. Understood?"

Jude slumped against the back of the couch and sighed. The whole situation was uncomfortable for him in every possible way. He was a private man. He couldn't deal with the way Reese watched him and scrutinized his every move as though they were playing the high-stakes poker that Mr. Matheson so enjoyed.

"You could have at least given me notice, you know," Jude said, unable to keep the smile from his face. He lifted his foot and rested it on the coffee table next to Reese's leg. Reese took that opportunity to pick up Jude's bare foot and begin to massage it.

"You're right. I was completely selfish and reprehensible. I should never be forgiven."

Jude wanted to moan at the feel of Reese's strong hands working the tension out of his foot. He'd been getting awful cramps in his calves from sleeping curled up and not eating his usual nutritious diet.

"Who said you were? Just because I'm letting you rub my feet doesn't mean I've forgiven you."

Reese smirked and hit a particularly sensitive spot in Jude's arch. He flinched and sucked in a breath.

"You're so tense. It's like you're carrying the weight of the world. What can I do to bear some of that weight for you? I want you relaxed."

It was Jude's turn to smirk. "Right. I think you've got enough on your plate. Your grandfather, this new musical. What's it about anyway, if you don't mind me asking?"

Reese set Jude's foot down at his side and bent to lift Jude's other leg. Jude smiled shyly and allowed Reese to pamper him.

"My grandfather told me a story once about when he met my grand-mother. He was in Las Vegas at the time, out on the Strip one afternoon on his way to a gig, and he saw her standing on the corner. He said she took his breath away. He asked her to join him for a cup of coffee, and she refused—said she didn't know him from Adam. How did she know she could trust him? He told her he played in Frank's band, and she didn't believe him."

Jude laughed at that. He could see the young woman thinking he made it up.

"Anyway, she finally agreed to see him play that night, but she showed up with her parents. They were all in town on vacation, and they agreed that a show was a great idea. Her family was very wealthy, and they happened to be staying at the hotel where Frank's band was playing. After the show her parents had arranged with the concierge to have drinks with Frank. The band wasn't usually invited to join in, so Grandpa had to stay outside the VIP section, watching Frank flirt with his girl. He was so angry. But what could he do? So he wrote her a song. When the bouncer wasn't looking, he snuck into the VIP section, sat at the piano, played the song for her, and sang his heart out. Her parents barely noticed, but she loved it. She asked Frank to keep her parents occupied so she could meet up with Grandpa, and the rest was history."

"That easy, huh? Seems like there would have been more obstacles." Jude slid down a little farther and allowed his foot to rest on Reese's thigh with his knee up. Reese bit his lip and worked his way up under the sweatpants to massage Jude's calf, where the real stiffness was, and Jude laid his head back against the couch letting out a small moan. "You may continue," he said, but Reese didn't speak. Jude opened an eye and found Reese looking very involved with his current activity. He slid his hands up Jude's leg and made long strokes that started behind the knee and ended at the top of his Achilles. Jude exhaled, and a shiver ran through him.

"Cold?" Reese asked.

Jude shook his head and said, "No. Just enjoying your hands."

Reese sucked in a breath and laughed softly.

"Tell me how he finally won over the girl."

Reese paused for a moment. "He finally wore her down, I suppose. Thomas Matheson has some serious mojo. Grandma claimed that, once he wooed her with his song, she was hooked. He wrote many tunes for her, over the years, and she said she never tired of listening to him play. Her parents weren't happy about their match, but as they'd been fans of Frank and thought Frank could do no wrong, how could they deny their daughter the pleasure of his piano player's company?"

"How indeed," Jude said, his eyes still closed. Reese's hands were warm and so large they could almost encircle his calf. When he switched back to Jude's other leg, Jude was putty in his hands. Both of his legs lay open and across Reese's thighs, and Reese continued to massage him gently, but with a quiet urgency. Jude's back arched involuntarily as he became more aroused. "I love to hear you play. You've got great hands," Jude whispered, his eyes opening to take in the sight of Reese's hands working over his body.

"I do. How's this feeling?"

"Hmmm. All right, I guess. For an amateur."

Reese pinched Jude's inner thigh and made him jump. Then he laughed and moved forward onto his knees. He slid his hands slowly up the sides of Jude's thighs.

"Tell me about you, Jude. Please? I feel like an idiot. In all the time you've been working here, I never knew more than your name and that you drove a shitty car. Which you do, by the way. I plan to rectify that."

Jude sat forward and slapped a hand on Reese's chest. "You'll do no such thing. I happen to like my car. It's come in quite handy the past couple of weeks. You'd be amazed at the storage capacity of the Pathfinder."

Reese growled and reached for Jude, who playfully shoved at him, knowing Reese was stronger and loving the feeling.

"You keep fighting me, and we're going to have it out," Reese said. Their chests were touching, and Jude's breathing was shallow. His mouth watered at the thought of another kiss.

"Is that so, Mr. Matheson?"

Reese brought his hand up behind Jude's neck, grasped firmly, and pulled his face closer. Their lips brushed together when Reese spoke.

"It is indeed, Mr. De La Torre."

Jude shuddered at the sound of Reese saying his name and at the feel of their lips together. He took the initiative and pressed a nervous kiss against—

"Reese, my boy. You bring me any of them JCPenney underwear yet? I got a card game tomorrow, and I don't wanna be sitting at that table with my balls flapping in the breeze."

TWELVE

WHEN GRANDPA called out from his bedroom, Jude scrambled back, pulled his knees against his chest, and looked incredibly worried. Reese didn't like the expression on his face. He wanted Jude back in his arms, but knew he had to be careful. If he pushed too much, Jude would leave. Or Grandpa would catch them, and he'd never hear the end of it. Even though Reese had bought the house, it was Thomas Matheson's home, and the old man assumed he was still in charge.

But at some point, he and Jude would be alone together. Reese shivered at the thought. He needed to figure it out and fast. If he really dissected his feelings, he would have to admit that Jude was a welcome diversion from a pretty devastating situation. It hurt to watch his beloved grandfather deteriorate further. It hurt a lot. Having Jude there was a lifesaver, a distraction, and a complication. He knew that, but he couldn't help himself.

Reese needed to have something positive to look forward to and focus on at all times. Usually it was his music, and while writing the musical was a passion project he'd waited a long time to work on, it was bittersweet. He'd be putting his grandfather's music in front of the world for the first time, and there was a strong possibility his grandfather wouldn't be around to enjoy the adulation.

Eventually "the biz" would be back in his face and his reprieve would be over. He'd fought long and hard with his agent and manager to have time off. They warned him that going into seclusion would hurt the chances for his next project, but he knew better. It was going to be a masterpiece.

FOR THE rest of the afternoon, Jude sat with Grandpa while Reese hunted around in the garage and pulled together the pieces of music he wanted to play with his grandfather. He brought them in just before supper and sat at the antique upright player piano in the living room. Grandpa insisted they keep the old thing so he could put on the rolls and just listen if he didn't feel up to playing.

"Are you guys ready for this?" he said excitedly. He couldn't wait to see Grandpa's reaction to hearing his old tunes again. Reese got comfortable at the bench and winked at his grandfather, who was sitting in his chair. Jude lingered in the doorway to the kitchen, his arms crossed over his scrub-clad chest. He'd changed out of Reese's clothes at some point, which irritated Reese for some possessive reason.

Reese laid his fingers on the keys, cleared his voice, and prepared to launch into the first verse when Grandpa stood up and made a clucking sound.

"That ain't the right beat. That's too bouncy. It's smoother—like a jazzy bit. Move your ass over. I'll show you how it's done."

That was secretly what Reese wanted, so he slid over and made room for his grandfather.

"Make room, son. My balls take up more space these days." The old man chuckled, and Reese groaned. He glanced back at Jude and found him smiling. Then he couldn't tear his eyes away from the sight. Jude's smile was filled with straight, white teeth and surrounded by full, dark lips. Those lips had tasted so good and were so fun to kiss. He could spend hours—

"Reese, my boy. Pay attention. Here. You play this part and sing it."

Reese did as the old man commanded and sang the lyrics he remembered his grandfather singing to him as a younger man. Reese had learned to play piano on a lot of the songs his grandfather either wrote or played himself. It felt good to belt out the tunes. He hadn't done much singing in a long time. For his last show, he played piano in the orchestra rather than conducting his own score. He didn't want that responsibility.

He hadn't used his vocal instrument much since rehearsals for the show eight months earlier. They'd done a four-month run on Broadway and then two months in London. It was grueling but fun, and audiences loved it both in New York and across the pond. He wanted to do it all again, but with Grandpa's tunes.

THIRTEEN

THE MATHESON men played piano, sang, and laughed for a solid three hours. Jude was concerned that Grandpa missed his evening meal as well as his programs, but he saw how much fun the two of them were having. Eventually they stopped, and Mr. Matheson stretched out his back and hands.

"That sounds great, son. This is going to be a helluva show."

"Thanks, old man. Hey, how about we head over to the diner and have some supper?"

Jude turned to go to the kitchen and finish the dishes from lunch, but Reese called him back.

"Jude, why don't you go change while I help Grandpa?"

Jude turned around and frowned. "I—"

"Come on, Jude my boy. They got some cute little waitresses at this place. I like to pretend I keep dropping my napkin. Works every time." He waggled his bushy eyebrows, and Reese made a disgusted face.

"What would Grandma think if she heard what you're up to?"

"She'd probably feel sorry for the poor girls. She used to say I was too much man for just her."

"I'll bet," Reese said as he rolled his eyes. Then he looked expectantly at Jude. "Well, come on. You know how he gets when he's hungry."

Jude couldn't help but feel like Reese was setting up more than just a trip to the diner. If he wasn't mistaken, it seemed like Reese was including him in their outing as though he were part of the family, which made any sort of intimacy on their part seem even more wrong. Either they needed to agree to be hands-off and continue as friends or give in to their feelings. Jude would continue to help him until.... When? Until Mr. Matheson had to be placed in a facility? Until.... But he'd grown to care so much for the older man that he was sure it would be just as tough for him when it came time to make those difficult decisions. He couldn't desert Reese.

Jude marched out to the truck and was about to open the door when he sensed Reese behind him. He turned to see what he wanted, and Reese pinned him against the door of the Pathfinder.

"Look, Jude. I don't know what I'm doing here. I promise I'll behave if you'll just—"

"Whatever, Reese. I'll go along with it. I'm frankly too tired to argue with you." Jude couldn't help laughing and shaking his head. It was absolutely crazy.

Reese grabbed him around the waist and nuzzled his neck. "And later on I'll tuck you in. You look really good in my bed." Jude tipped his head to the side to give Reese more access.

"And before you say anything, I pulled out the air mattress, and I'll be camping out in the garage. I'll be fine. It's finished in there. Anyway," he said nibbling on Jude's ear, "hurry up, would ya? I'm hungry." Then Reese strolled back to the house.

Jude was left feeling as though he'd just ridden out a tropical storm. What on earth was Reese playing at? Jude had never been pursued like that before. And yet he'd acted like one of those idiots who chased tornados or stood on the coast watching a hurricane approach the shore —in awe of its beauty and unable to look away despite the danger. *Huh. Hurricane Reese.*

He pulled a stack of clean clothes out of the back seat and figured he might as well have a couple changes of clothes since Reese seemed hellbent on having him there.

Shortly thereafter the three men left the house in Reese's Tesla. Mr. Matheson complained about Reese's car the whole way.

"I miss riding in a car with balls. This car has no balls. It's so damn quiet, you practically run people over in crosswalks. I like a nice rumble when I roll down the street."

"Grandpa, those days are over. We can't afford to keep polluting our environment with those beasts. Sorry. You're going to have to make your own rumble, just not on my leather seats. Got it?"

"Hey, sometimes you gotta let 'er rip." The Mathesons laughed together in the front seats, while Jude cringed in the back.

"I don't think I've ever heard anyone carry on so much about male genitalia and bodily functions. This is like an episode of *Beavis and Butthead*."

"You're always so damn proper, Jude my boy. Don't you ever let loose a little? Don't you Asians ever talk about your balls?"

Jude burst out laughing. "Mr. Matheson, it's one thing to discuss this type of thing with my family and another with my employers."

"See, that's where you've got it all wrong, Jude. You're part of the family," Mr. Matheson said, and he turned to offer Jude a rare smile.

It had been a long time since Jude had been in a family situation. He skipped most functions at Tito Rommel's house to avoid the constant barrage of "Where's your girlfriend? When are you getting married? When will you give us babies?" talk. He was closest to Tita Germaine and saw her all the time. But Tita Gemma was a gossip extraordinaire and always pushed for the latest and juiciest information. Jude had been content to hide out at the Mathesons'. Perhaps he'd been evading more than he thought.

"Well, I'm still not talking about my balls, if that's what it takes to be a part of this family."

Reese and Mr. Matheson laughed, and the remainder of the short drive was full of all kinds of potty talk. Reese parked in the lot behind the diner, and Jude helped Mr. Matheson out of the front seat. They had to wait outside for a few minutes while they cleared a table, so Grandpa said he wanted to go in and "use the can." Jude enjoyed listening to Reese imitate his grandfather. They laughed until their bellies ached and leaned on each other for support.

"Wow, same position, different man." Jude spun around to find Jada and a film crew behind them. Jada was standing with her arms crossed at her waist and despite what Reese had said, Jude felt guilty—as though he'd been the one to wrong her.

"What is all this?" Reese asked her through gritted teeth. He attempted to remain calm, but Jude could see the tension in his shoulders.

"Well since you refused to answer my calls, I thought I'd come find you. I know you love this ridiculous place. I should have known you wouldn't be here alone."

"Jada, what are you doing? Can I talk to you for a minute? Off camera?" Reese stuck his hands on his hips and glared at the cameramen. Jada held up a finger to the cameramen, approached Reese, and got up in his personal space.

"I told you they either wanted to interview us together, or catch us in a candid setting. You didn't set up the interview, so...."

"Did you really think I'd agree to this circus? My grandfather is inside waiting for us, Jada. For God's sake, have some fucking class." Reese turned, walked to the door, and placed a hand on Jude's back. "Let's go."

"I knew you'd hook up with him as soon as I was out of the picture. I can't believe you, Reese. I can't believe you treated me like this. You led me on for two years."

Reese froze in his spot and took a deep breath. He looked at Jude apologetically and sighed. "Can you please see to Grandpa? He should be finished. I'll deal with this."

Jude felt terribly uncomfortable for many reasons. He was angry that Jada was trying to drag their dirty laundry out in public. He was shocked that she'd insinuate that he and Reese were together. And he was confused. *Had* Reese led her on? What exactly caused their break up?

He wanted to stand by Reese and be supportive, but his presence was only making the scene worse. He offered a smile and wished it were appropriate for him to respond to Jada's accusation. There was a lot he could say about this scenario. Instead Reese opened the door for him, and he walked inside. Jude wanted to shield Mr. Matheson from the drama as best he could, and he was relieved when the hostess said she would seat them toward the back and away from the window. Mr. Matheson was just making his way toward the front, so Jude was able to intercept him and guide him to their table.

"Where's my boy?"

Jude wasn't sure how much Mr. Matheson knew about Jada. "He's wrapping up a conversation out front. He'll join us in a minute."

They sat down across from each other, and Mr. Matheson looked toward the windows where he could clearly see Reese arguing with Jada. The cameras were filming the whole thing. Jude and Mr. Matheson looked at each other and frowned.

"That little bitch. I should go give her a piece of my mind."

"I think that would make things worse for Reese. Let's just give him a minute."

He looked over his shoulder and frowned. How *dare* she put him through that.

"You been good to us, Jude my boy. I appreciate you helping my grandson out. I know I'm getting more forgetful, and it's getting harder to get around. Promise me something?"

Jude raised an eyebrow. "What is it?"

The old man sighed and took a drink of the coffee the server had just brought for him. Jude didn't remind him that he shouldn't have more coffee.

"Promise me that when I'm gone, or as good as gone, you'll take care of him? You're a good man, Jude. You're more than just a nurse. Reese is going to need somebody to help him make decisions, and I can't think of anyone I'd trust more."

It was heartbreaking—and unfair. Mr. Matheson was lucid. He should have more time with Reese. They should be able to make their musical together and enjoy their success. Jude leaned forward and placed a hand over Mr. Matheson's.

"I won't let him go through this alone. I'll do whatever I can for you both."

Mr. Matheson smiled. "Of course you will. Now where is that cute little waitress? I hope we get the one with the red hair. Her ponytail makes me think dirty thoughts."

Jude rolled his eyes and then straightened up as Reese joined them. He slid into the booth next to Jude with a tight smile.

"What did—"

"We'll talk about this later," Reese said hurriedly. "So, old man, where's the cute one?"

At that moment a very attractive woman approached the table with a big smile and a bigger pile of red hair.

"Tommy, why aren't you sitting in my section?" she purred. She gave Reese a big smile, and her eyes lingered over Jude with curiosity.

"Well, ma'am, these two eggheads were in charge of picking the seats. They don't know how things work."

She cocked out a hip and put a hand on his shoulder. "Well, they'll have to do better next time, won't they?" She winked at Reese. "I'm sure Sue Ann will do right by you. I'll catch you next time. Bye y'all."

She walked away from the table, and Mr. Matheson made no effort to hide the fact that he was watching her ass.

"Don't they complain about your harassment?" Reese laughed.

"Nah. Not if you tip well. Now, what was all that nonsense out there? Paparazzi catch up with ya? Too bad they didn't get my picture. I haven't been in the magazines for a long time."

Reese smiled, but his eyes looked stressed. "Trust me, old man. You'd want nothing to do with that bullshit."

"That diva bothering you, eh?"

"Grandpa," Reese admonished, "I don't totally blame her. She's got these producers on this show pressuring her—"

"She has no right to make such a fuss."

"Well, she had to put up with a lot of shit when those photos came out. People made up all kinds of stories. It had to have been embarrassing for her with all she's got going on. People thought I dumped her for a guy in my show."

Jude straightened in his seat. So *that* was what happened.

"Yeah, well, I still think she needed to be lowered a notch or two. It's not like you were messing around with that guy."

Oh. Boy.

Reese leaned forward and clasped his hands on the table. "But it was certainly possible."

Mr. Matheson fidgeted in his seat and frowned. "You young people today. Just go off with whoever," he said, waving his hand as though he were too uncomfortable with the idea to even say it out loud.

Reese wasn't going to drop it. He waved his hand, imitating his grandfather. "And...."

The older Matheson shrugged it off and looked around for the waitress. "Ain't she gonna come take our order? I'm wastin' away."

Sure enough, a blonde woman came over to the table, flirted a little less than the redhead, and asked to take their order.

"Gimme the liver and onions," Mr. Matheson said. Then he stared at Jude as though daring him to correct him.

"Ew. For real? That shit is disgusting," Reese said and scrunched up his face.

"It's like eating the filter," Jude said, shuddering. "Not to mention the carcinogens in fried food."

"Well, I ain't gonna live forever. I might as well eat what I like."

"Yeah, but now we gotta smell that shit all night," Reese said.

Mr. Matheson just grinned.

Reese and Jude simultaneously ordered turkey and avocado sandwiches. They looked at each other and grinned like a couple of teenagers, and Mr. Matheson rolled his eyes.

"All that healthy eating ain't gonna keep you alive forever."

"Yes, but it makes the life you have feel a lot better," Jude said quietly. Reese was watching him way too closely. He was also practically sitting in Jude's lap. Their thighs touched under the table. It felt too cozy.

"So Jude, my boy, how's the dancing coming?"

Reese looked at him sharply, and Jude blew out a nervous breath.

"It's good. We've got most of the program choreographed."

"And they use those scarves and ribbon thingies and rifles and swords and stuff?"

Jude laughed. It was good to know he remembered. "Yes, Mr. Matheson. That's right."

Reese was still staring at him. He wanted to elbow him or something to get him to stop. So he kicked him under the table.

"Ow. What was that for?" Reese had no clue how to be subtle.

"What the hell is your problem now? This boy of mine. Such a klutz. Remember the time you broke your arm playing football?"

Reese's good humor vanished immediately. "Grandpa, that was Dad. He played football."

"Oh, that's right. How could I forget? You were the one prancing around on the stage. Singing. This boy dragged his grandmother and me to every single one of his plays and crap like that. Piano recitals, yada yada yada."

"Come on, Grandpa. They weren't all bad."

Their food arrived and Jude watched the two of them reminisce about Reese's childhood performances. Jude learned that Reese had been quite the thespian in school. He'd attended UC Santa Bonita on an academic scholarship and he performed throughout his time there while he pursued a double major in Creative Writing and Theater. His singing career took off after he wrote a few hit songs for an up-and-coming pop star and she took him on tour with her. He was an overnight sensation with a hit debut album, and his life was changed forever. His song ended up in a movie, and Reese Matheson became a household name.

Reese slipped his credit card to the server as she walked by. Jude started to protest, and Reese grabbed his thigh under the table as though it were the most natural thing for him to do—right there, in front of his grandfather. Jude looked to see if Mr. Matheson had noticed anything, but he was finishing the last few bites of his liver and onions and making satisfied noises. When Jude looked back to Reese, he was startled by what he saw.

Pain. Sorrow. Reese had been cheery during their meal, but it seemed forced to Jude. Now he could tell for sure. Something awful must have happened with Jada. Either that or Reese had been more affected by his grandfather's memory slip than Jude originally thought.

Reese stood first and helped his grandfather out of the booth. The three of them slowly walked back to the car because it was obvious Mr. Matheson had overdone it. The sky was darkening much earlier since they were headed into late November. The weather would be cold soon, and as much as Jude felt uncomfortable being back in the house with

Reese there, he was grateful he wouldn't be sleeping in his car any longer.

They pulled up to the house, and Reese helped his grandfather inside. Mr. Matheson stumbled a little on the steps, and Reese caught his weight.

"You need to fix that step, son. It's warped or something."

Several times Jude had advised Mr. Matheson that he needed to start using some sort of walking aid. A quad cane was the best idea for him to keep his balance, but he would hear nothing of it. He was a vain man, and he didn't want to appear weak.

Jude offered to help him get ready for bed, and Mr. Matheson was very quiet—he didn't even make any ball jokes. Jude laid out his bedclothes and helped him with his toileting. Then he led him back to the bedroom.

"Thanks, Jude my boy. My grandson is coming home tomorrow. Have you met him? He's a great kid. Gayer than a fruit basket, but that's his business, I reckon. You should meet him."

"I'm sure I'd like that," Jude said as Mr. Matheson reclined on the bed. Jude covered him with the blanket and asked him if he could get anything for him.

"I miss my wife," Mr. Matheson said as he closed his eyes. He scrunched up his face, and a tear slid down his cheek. Jude used a tissue to wipe the tear away, and then he touched Mr. Matheson's hand.

"Get some rest, Mr. Matheson. Good night."

Jude sat on the edge of the bed until he was sure Mr. Matheson was asleep. He wiped at his own eyes and took a moment to collect himself before he went out to face Reese. He decided not to tell Reese about that memory slip. It would only make him feel worse.

FOURTEEN

REESE POUNDED on his keyboard, but the headphones contained the product of his rage so he wouldn't disturb his grandfather and Jude. His music sounded angry and hurt, like fury and tears that refused to be denied. He wanted to sing his heart out because he knew it would help quiet his rage, but he wasn't alone.

Out of the corner of his eye, he watched Jude slowly enter the garage and sit on the workout bench. He looked as distraught as Reese felt, so he finished the last few bars of the song he was working on and took off his headphones. He pulled the hair tie off his wrist and wrapped his sweaty hair up into a bun to get it out of his face, but one stubborn piece kept falling in his eyes. He blew it up and tried to smooth it behind his ear.

"You could use a haircut," Jude said quietly. "And a shave. And a really good night's sleep."

Reese barked out a laugh, and some of the tension finally bled out. He stood from the bench and stretched out his back. Then he trudged over to the mini fridge and pulled out a bottle of water. He offered one to Jude, who shook his head.

"I'm fine. Your grandfather is sleeping peacefully. I think he had a bit more excitement than he should have today."

Jude looked at him expectantly. What was he supposed to say? He really didn't want to go into what happened with Jada. How did he tell Jude that he had sacrificed his own privacy to protect Jude's?

"I should leave you. I just wanted to see if you needed anything," Jude said as he stood. He seemed unsure of himself.

"I do," Reese blurted out. "Please. Stay."

Jude lowered himself back onto the bench and waited patiently for Reese to speak.

"I'm sorry," Reese finally began. "I wish you hadn't had to deal with all that earlier."

Jude crossed his leg over his knee and raised an eyebrow. Reese paced back and forth in front of the storage shelves.

"Reese, you don't have to explain anything to me." Jude was trying to give him a way out, but Reese wouldn't have it.

"But I do. I don't want you to think I fucked around on Jada. I mean, I did have a couple.... But it wasn't what you think... I... *dammit.*" He stopped pacing and hung his head. "Look, Jada and I had an agreement...."

"Reese, you *really* don't need to explain anything. I'm going to—"

"I told her to leave you out of it. I told her she could film us having a fake fight if they didn't include you anywhere in the footage or use your name."

Jude stood and approached Reese. "Why would you do that? Why would you let her use you like that?"

Reese could see Jude was angry. He wanted to reach out and touch him and hold on to him for support, but it wasn't fair to take this any further unless Jude knew everything.

"Because I know your privacy is important to you. I don't care what she says about me, but I don't want you hurt because of me. I've already hurt you enough."

"Reese, you didn't know. What's done is done. But I still hate for her to hurt you."

"I'm not hurt." He laughed. "I'm irritated, but she can honestly do whatever she wants. Sure, I'd rather not be tabloid fodder, but I'm just happy to not have that stress. She was very high maintenance, and I guess I resented her for it. I think part of why I didn't just move in with

Grandpa in the first place was because she didn't want that. I brought it up back then, but she was like, 'Shouldn't he be in a home or something?'"

Jude narrowed his eyes. "That's a terrible thing to say. Your *lolo* should stay with you. Always. Family takes care of family."

"Lolo?"

"Yeah. It means grandfather. You know why my parents are in the Philippines? To take care of my *lolo* and *lola*. That's what we do. You don't put old people away. They're to be treasured. My other lola lives with my uncle here. She's got some health complications, but she's better being with family, and my auntie is able to care for her with help from her sisters. Reese, we'll take care of your grandfather together as long as we can. I'm here for both of you."

Reese didn't know what he'd done to deserve Jude's loyalty. He certainly hadn't been loyal when he sent him packing. But he sighed and gave in to the urge to touch Jude once more. He lifted a finger to Jude's V-neck T-shirt collar and traced the skin there. Jude let his eyelids drift shut and a small sigh escaped. But when his eyes opened, he was frowning.

"This can't happen under your grandfather's roof. I may have sinned in my life, but I'm not going to do anything to hurt your grandfather."

Reese couldn't help his lopsided grin. "If you were going to sin under anyone's roof, it might as well be this one. You *have* heard Grandpa's stories, haven't you?"

Jude rolled his eyes as Reese circled his arms around Jude's waist. Reese was determined to wear down his defenses.

"Reese," Jude breathed in warning. Reese could tell Jude was warring with himself. It was enough to know that he wanted him just as badly. For now.

"Fine," Reese huffed. He turned and made an exaggerated groan as he approached his mini fridge. "But you have to get drunk with me. I'll give you enough ammunition on the old man that *you'll* feel violated," he laughed. Then he pulled out two beers and handed one to Jude, who stared at it in disgust.

"Really? You drink Sierra Nevada? Who does that?"

Reese's mouth gaped open in surprise. "Jude... wait, what's your middle name?"

"Why?"

"Because it makes the statement stronger. Come on," he said, gesturing with his hands. "Lay it on me."

"It's Joseph. Jude Joseph De La Torre."

Reese's eyes flared. "That's a mouthful."

Jude raised that eyebrow, and Reese forgot exactly why they weren't naked yet. Oh yeah, because Jude was determined to be a saint. Like his namesake.

"Yeah, well, mouthful or not, I'm not drinking that piss."

"What's your poison, then? We're fully stocked here at Chez Matheson."

Jude snorted. "Don't I know it. I almost had to dispose of it all, a while back. Mr. Matheson wasn't fond of hearing that alcohol was a bad idea in his condition. He ranted and raved about it until I got him to agree that, once in a great while, he could have some, just not tie one on."

"Well, I'm going to tie one on tonight." Reese went into the house and grabbed a bottle of Jägermeister and glasses. Then he returned to the garage humming and left the door open a crack so they could hear the old man if he needed anything.

He set the bottle and glasses on the makeshift coffee table he'd set up in front of the old couch. It was a relic from his bachelor days. Who was he kidding? He was a bachelor once again. It didn't feel like it, though. Not with Jude around. He wouldn't admit it out loud for fear of chasing him off, but the idea of playing a little house with Jude was titillating. They couldn't share a bed, of course, but knowing he was under the same roof, in the next room....

"Feel free to get wasted," Jude said with a laugh as Reese poured the liquor. "I'll just have a bit. One of us needs to have their full faculties."

Reese handed Jude a glass and motioned for him to sit on the couch. He held up his own and cleared his throat. "A toast—to the old man and his balls. May they live in harmony and stay inside his clothes where they belong."

Jude clinked glasses with Reese and then sat on the couch and tossed back the shot. He made a face and licked his lips. "Wow. That's vicious."

Reese laughed and poured himself another shot. "That'll burn the hair off your balls."

"Not you, too. I can't take it. No more balls."

Reese threw back his second shot. He coughed and stuck his tongue out. Jude laughed and stretched out a bit on the couch as the warmth from the liquor tingled throughout his body.

"I guess he had to have some balls hanging out with Frank and the fellas... and the gangsters in Jersey where he grew up, and in Vegas." Reese moved over to the workbench and pulled out a cigar box. He selected one, sniffed it like a pro, and wiggled his eyebrows at Jude.

"Please tell me you aren't going to smoke that."

Reese laughed. "Seems fitting to be smoking the old man's cigars while drinking his booze. Actually the Jäger is mine. I never touch his brandy or scotch. Besides, I'm out of weed."

Jude dropped his head back and laughed. "You're a mess, Reese Matheson."

With a little less humor, Reese said, "Yeah, well, it ain't for lack of trying." He pulled a lighter out of the box, lit the cigar, and puffed on it as the tip turned to orange embers. He held it out toward Jude, but Jude raised both eyebrows.

"Nursing student, remember?"

"And? Come on. You gotta smoke this with me," Reese pleaded. He held it out until Jude gave up and reached forward to pluck it out of his hand.

"I haven't had a cigar since the last time my father was home. I don't recall that having a good outcome. I'm pretty sure I ended up puking in the garbage can."

Reese watched as Jude took a small drag on the cigar and blew out the smoke. He was surprisingly smooth.

"Nice. Not even a cough."

Jude handed the cigar to Reese, and then he leaned forward and poured himself another shot. "Maybe I learned my lesson last time." He downed the shot and blew out a harsh breath while Reese puffed on the cigar and let the aroma take him back to his early years when he used to sit next to Grandpa at the piano.

Reese walked to his keyboard and took a seat on the folding stool. He settled his fingers over the keys and began the melody for one of his favorite tunes. Jude's body language changed instantly. He leaned forward, rested his elbows on his knees, and with rapt attention, he watched Reese play.

Reese let the words to "I've Got You Under My Skin" pour out and effortlessly sang the lyrics to a tune that had more meaning then than ever before. Jude tapped along with his foot and smiled with abandon. Damn, if Reese knew that was all it took, just to sing to him, he'd have been singing for days already. One song turned into several, a couple of shots turned into plenty, and Jude was right there, watching and laughing with Reese.

"And Grandpa swears that Frank wrote that song about their adventures in Chicago. I still think he's full of shit, but he won't let it go. I know they were friends, and I know that the old man misses him and that life, but once he married Grandma and they moved out to the West Coast, he mainly did sessions work while he wrote his own tunes. Grandma's money kept them living well for a long time." Melancholy threatened to set in when the topic of his grandmother came up. He hated it when he became the sad drunk, and he refused to lay that shit on Jude. He stood from the piano and stumbled over to the couch, but he gave Jude plenty of room.

"Jesus. I certainly achieved my goal. I'm drunk."

Jude laughed at him again, and his laughter came much easier after a few drinks. Reese loved his smile and the musical quality of his voice. Jude was an enigma. He had a strong build—on the slender side with the exception of thicker thighs—and his ass... well.... Reese rested his arm over the back of the couch and then rested his chin in his hand.

"You could use sleep," Jude said quietly. His eyes darted toward the garage door that led into the kitchen. Then he looked back at Reese. "I should—"

"Stay. I promise. I won't... I just need...." Reese felt incredibly buzzed and gave up trying to speak. He crawled over and rested his head in Jude's lap before Jude could resist. His eyelids were heavy, but he didn't want to stop staring.

JUDE HAD no clue what to do with Reese's head in his lap. Part of him wanted to shove him off and storm out of there, but he'd be lying if he said he wanted to be away from him. He yearned to comfort Reese because he knew Reese was suffering in so many ways.

"Tell me a story," Reese said in a little-boy voice that made Jude roll his eyes. *Does he know how ridiculously charming he is?*

"Fine. Once upon a time, there was a prince who lived by the sea."

Reese smiled. "This sounds fun. Did he wear a crown?"

Jude snorted. "More like a tiara. Okay. Maybe he was a princess."

Reese pinched Jude's thigh and made him jump.

"Hey, do you want a story or not, princess?"

Reese snuggled into his lap. "More."

Maybe it was the booze, or maybe Jude just enjoyed the playful manner they were fast adopting with each other.

"The prince had a gift. He played the harp beautifully—"

"A harp? What the fuck? That's for princesses."

"Will you let me tell my story? I can stop right now if you want—"

"No. Please." Reese turned his head until his ear was resting against Jude's belly. He smiled up at him, closed his eyes, and sighed. "Go on."

Jude couldn't resist running his fingers through Reese's golden locks. They were so many shades of gold. All the time he spent in the sun had turned his hair a color most women would pay handsomely to replicate. On Reese it was natural, just like everything about him.

"A visiting family came to hear the prince play one afternoon, and they were spellbound—especially their son. He'd heard the prince was a spoiled brat who had everything he wanted, but he was shocked by the beautiful music the prince made. Being a soldier, the only thing the son had ever known was hard work and discipline. The music made him yearn for more.

"The boy knew that the harp player wanted to travel the world playing his music. But the prince had a kingdom to care for, so the boy volunteered to stay behind and protect the people in exchange for the harp player's promise that the prince would come back and play for him once he had traveled the world. Just for him."

Reese's face relaxed, and a snore escaped from his nose. Jude smiled and bit his lip. Reese was beautiful when he slept. Even the angry wound on his nose, which needed to be cleaned and rebandaged soon, didn't take away from his beauty. Jude pushed Reese's hair away from his face and wished he could kiss away the tension still in Reese's forehead. Sure, Jude had his own worries, but he'd always been good at planning ahead. He'd taken the month's severance that Reese paid him and put it away for a deposit on an apartment—which he intended to get as soon as he had a full-time job. At least that's what he planned before Reese asked him back. They still hadn't discussed his salary, or how long, or....

Reese turned over, buried his face in Jude's belly, and grunted when he bumped his nose. He brought his hand up and rested it on Jude's hip. Then he sighed happily and began to snore in earnest. Jude was trapped—in more ways than one. But for the moment, he'd let himself enjoy the feeling of being in Reese's space—no longer being just the help, but maybe, truly, a part of their little family.

Although family to Reese and Mr. Matheson was much different from what Jude was used to. Reese was right earlier when he'd said that Jude was a private man. He was. He needed to be. Reese might think Mr. Matheson would "get over" the two of them being together in any way other than friends. But Jude's family? His father and uncle? No way. The Church said it was a sin, so it was a sin. Period. Jude didn't think they'd go so far as to shun him or anything, but they would never accept it.

Jude looked at his watch. It was just after midnight. He figured he should get some rest so he could care for Mr. Matheson in the morning. He didn't want to disturb Reese, but he knew he should go to bed. He attempted to lift Reese's head.... No luck. Reese's long body barely fit on the old couch. His legs hung over the armrest, he'd wrapped a strong arm around Jude's hips, which effectively held him in place. Jude could push himself up and over the back of the couch. It wouldn't be graceful, but it would work in a pinch. He tried to angle his hip and slide out from the side, but Reese grumbled in his sleep and tightened his grip.

"Where do you think you're going?" Reese asked in a slurred voice.

Reese used some wrestling move, some maneuver—something—and Jude found himself pinned under Reese's greater weight. Jude's head was spinning a bit from the alcohol. Or maybe it was just Reese.

Reese smiled down at him, but his eyes were unfocused. It was enough to let Jude know that Reese was in the "lost inhibitions" stage of drunkenness.

"Reese, let me up. You need to slee—"

Before he could get out that last *p*, Reese's tongue plunged into his mouth in a sloppy but determined kiss. It wasn't like before—hot and possessive and lustful and genuine. This one smacked of hookup. Reese grabbed a fistful of Jude's hair and kissed him hard, using his pelvis to pin Jude in place. He reached clumsily down to Jude's pants and tugged on the button. Jude froze. He didn't want Reese like that. He wanted Reese to know exactly who he was with and why.

Jude pushed Reese's hand away, but it was back a second later. It took effort to get in a breath in order to speak. "Reese, let me go," Jude said quietly, and he hoped Reese wouldn't take it as a rejection of anything other than drunken sex. It took two more tries—his voice was firmer on the last one—and then Reese pulled back, stunned.

"Jude, I... I'm sorry." He hurriedly pushed up and off of Jude's body with a look of horror on his face. "I never meant to—"

"It's done. Let me up and go back to sleep. No harm done."

Reese's lids were still so heavy that Jude knew he'd be back asleep before his head hit the pillow. Pillow! He looked around and found a stack of pillows and blankets on a shelf by the washer and dryer. He grabbed them and was back to the couch in an instant. Jude made sure he was propped up enough that, if he got sick, he wouldn't....

Well, now he was worried. He had two Matheson men to be concerned about. Reese snuggled into the pillow, and Jude covered him with a blanket. But he had to get out of there before he curled up next to him.

"I'm sorry, Jude. I'm sorry," Reese mumbled in his sleep, and then he fell to snoring again. Jude's heart beat out of control. Things had almost just gotten critical. He had to be more careful. Reese had little to no impulse control, and while it excited Jude, he knew they had to be cautious. There was a lot at stake—namely one Thomas Matheson, who was depending on the two of them to care for him.

Jude entered the kitchen and cleaned up the last few dishes left over from the day. He swept through the living room, righted a few things that had fallen over, and took a few moments to dust the pictures on the wall. They were photos of Thomas and his wife, Ruby. She'd had the most beautiful red hair, according to Thomas, and he adored her fiery spirit. They would have been married for sixty years this year. Instead she went quietly in the night a year before Jude came into the picture.

Thomas kept his grief to himself most of the time, but Jude had seen him stroke her face in the pictures and become wistful, even teary. Then he'd sit down at his piano and play songs that he admitted he'd written about her.

Seeing such a romantic love played out in front of him made Jude wonder. Sure, his parents loved each other, but their marriage was practically arranged when they were young. They both came to the United States as preteens, and their families were close. His father described his mother as a beautiful flower that he'd been attracted to like a bee looking for pollen. His father thought he was so poetic, when it just sounded creepy to Jude.

His mother had loved to dance, and her children inherited her poise and grace. As long as he and his younger siblings kept up their grades, their father didn't care what they did and never questioned Jude's desire to dance and perform in the color guard. Jude didn't think his father actually understood him. He was always too busy working as a real estate agent to come to any of his performances.

His mother was always there. She worked for their family business, but she made it clear to his dad that she wouldn't miss a single one of his shows. Jude was grateful that his mother was so supportive of him, but it gave him even more of a reason to fear hurting her.

FIFTEEN

REESE GROANED as he woke on the sofa in the garage. He was completely disoriented. Was he back in college? Whose house had he crashed at? What time was it?

Jude.

Oh God, what have I done? Vague memories surfaced from the night before, almost as though he were recalling a dream rather than reality. He'd had Jude under him. He'd tried to undress him. He'd mauled the poor guy. How could Jude ever forgive him for that? He'd leave for sure, and Reese wouldn't blame him. He'd sworn to himself that he'd let Jude come to him—and then Jägermeister. And cigars. And singing. Did he really sing Frank tunes? "I've Got You Under My Skin" rang in his head. It was true, so very true. Jude was a sensation that Reese never wanted to go without. And then he'd tackled Jude and gone all porn star on him.

He tried to sit up, but his head spun wildly. He was so hungover. What he wouldn't give for a do-over.

"Good morning," Jude said with a smile as he glided into the room with a breakfast tray. He set it down on the coffee table and sat a cushion away from Reese. "I brought the best hangover cure I could whip up."

The tray contained a plate of fried eggs over easy, some hash browns, and what looked like ham, but was probably—

"It's Spam. It's fatty and will help protect your stomach from any remaining alcohol your body might be trying to digest. Some black coffee, some juice with vitamin C. I could give you ibuprofen, but I'd rather wait to see how you feel after this."

Reese held his head in his hands and fought the urge to groan. At first inhale the food smelled heavenly. Then his stomach lurched. No. He wouldn't throw up. He'd *man* up. And in what alternate universe was Jude speaking to him, much less waiting on him?

"I am such a bastard. I can't believe you're speaking to me at all."

He gathered up the courage to chance a glance at Jude and found him smiling in an "I-told-you-so" kind of way.

"I wouldn't call you a bastard. Perhaps a sloppy drunk? You definitely kiss better when you're sober."

Whatever expression Reese's face decided to make, Jude burst out laughing. Reese stood, only wobbling slightly, and stumbled across the room toward the kitchen.

"Aw, was it something I said? Reese-y poo can't handle a widdle teasing?"

Reese jerked around to stare at Jude in disbelief.

"Reese-y poo? Really? I thought that you'd be pissed at me. I'm so sorry for the way I acted, Jude. That's never how I want to treat you."

"I should hope not," Jude said as he moved toward him. He sniffed a little as he got closer. "That black licorice smell is much worse this morning. You should shower. I had Kyla bring a chair for Mr. Matheson. You should probably use it." He bit his lip, pushed into the house, and left Reese dumbfounded in his wake. What was going on?

Reese trudged into the house and only grunted at his grandfather as he made his way to the bathroom to unload and clean up the disaster zone he was currently inhabiting. Sure enough the shower chair was already set up in the stall. Jude. That sonofabitch was enjoying this. Reese deserved it, but turnabout was fair play.

He showered quickly, cursing at the seat in his way, and toweled off haphazardly. He looked at himself in the mirror while he brushed his teeth and saw a haggard sight. Reese never needed to work at his good looks. He didn't make a big deal of them either. But today he saw dark circles, almost like black eyes, and stubble in patches that covered the bottom half of his face. His once-healthy hair looked dead around the edges. He hadn't waxed his chest in a long time. It wasn't convenient in London, and since he'd been back, there'd been Grandpa. Oh, he'd love to explain that one to the old man. "Yeah, Grandpa. I let an Asian woman smear wax on my chest and rip it off, just to feel nice and smooth. I also shave my balls. How about that?"

"Uh, Reese?"

Jesus! He needed to remember there were no more private moments in this place.

He stuck his head out the door and grinned sheepishly at Jude.

"You're probably wondering—"

"Nope. Not at all. Didn't hear a thing. Look, I have to be at the school this afternoon, and then I have class tonight. Do you want me to run to the store? Cook you guys dinner before I go?"

Reese didn't let the smile leave his face. He sure smiled a lot more around Jude—maybe enough for both of them, although he could tell Jude had to fight to keep from returning the smile.

"What I want," Reese began, and his heart skipped a beat as he decided to put it all out there. "What I want is to take you out for some pampering... or dancing. Just out for a tiny little bit." He didn't want to look disappointed when Jude brushed him off, so he took that possibility into account. "But I bet you'd never come with me. I really don't think you know how to have any fun."

Jude raised both eyebrows, and his mouth fell open. "Are you serious? You think I don't know how to have fun?"

"I *know* you don't know how to have fun. Put it this way—you wouldn't know fun if it bit you right on the nose."

Jude crossed his arms and then peeked over his shoulder to be sure Grandpa wasn't listening. When he turned back, he lowered his voice to such a deep register that it gave Reese goose bumps. "I'll go out with you. Let me rephrase. I'll take *you* out. You have to trust me to pick the place. And you have to make arrangements for your grandfather."

Reese's mouth watered as he thought of what the two of them could get up to away from home.

"Deal."

"Tonight. Nine. Be ready to go."

Reese couldn't believe his luck. Maybe he hadn't screwed up as badly as he thought.

"Oh, and surfer chic isn't really acceptable, so wear something nice." Jude raised an eyebrow again and returned to the living room. Reese closed the bathroom door and looked back in the mirror. Despite his aforementioned issues, he felt good. The fog of the hangover lifted as his fantasies about a night out with Jude took over.

As JUDE pulled away from the Mathesons', he mentally kicked himself for allowing Reese to rope him into his ridiculous plan. What business did he have going out on a date with Reese? And where in the world could he take him? But during his freak-out, he hadn't stopped smiling.

He needed to let go of the guilt he felt over leaving Mr. Matheson for the night, that is, if Reese actually found someone to stay with him. Maybe he wouldn't and it would all be a moot point.

But what if...? Dancing. That's what they should do. Jude's friends had a place just outside of town that they went to on Thursday nights. People would know him, but they could avoid a ton of publicity because people at Incognito were good about protecting their own. Would Reese consider himself one of them? They hadn't talked about it. Jude assumed Reese was bi, but who knew how far that went? Curious? Established? The man could sure kiss. That much was confirmed.

Jude arrived at the high school before the kids came down to the field. He took the time to stretch thoroughly and wished he could fit dance classes into his schedule. He missed it. Having a tie to his siblings and to dance kept him satisfied for the moment. But there was no way to know how long he would be at his assignment.

Mr. Matheson was far more than a job. If Jude had his way, Mr. Matheson would never see the inside of a nursing home. In his culture grandparents were never sent away. Families took care of their own, and Jude was committed to caring for him as long as Reese allowed. He just didn't want any sort of intimacy between him and Reese to interfere. But he also didn't want Reese to get overwhelmed and listen to doctors who might advise him to put Mr. Matheson in a home.

The kids arrived, and Jude put them to work. He'd choreographed very difficult formations for their routine because this group had the talent to handle it. Like some sort of mad scientist, he loved watching his creation come to life before his eyes. He watched Brianna lead her group in an emotional, lyrical piece, and he spotted Bailey, across the field, struggling with his part of the formation. Bailey was stuck behind two girls who had very little coordination, but they were hard workers, and Jude had been able to camouflage them... to a point. When the group finished the program, Jude called Bailey over.

"You're doing great. Carrie and Donna will get it eventually."

Bailey shrugged his shoulders and lifted up the bottom of his shirt to wipe his face. He wouldn't make eye contact, and Jude didn't blame him.

"Listen. I heard about Junior moving in with you guys. I promise—"

"Just forget it," Bailey muttered. "It's not your fault Mom and Dad left us."

Jude's chest tightened. He could see why Bailey would feel that way.

"Bail, they didn't want to leave you guys, but they knew you'd get a better education here than in the Philippines. You have to know that."

Bailey nodded and chewed on a fingernail. "I know that. I just miss them."

Jude pulled his brother in for a hug and prayed he'd respond and not just stiffen. Bailey relaxed against him and tentatively touched Jude's back.

"My hours have eased up a bit. I'll have some more time. Can I come and take you and Brianna out this weekend, maybe?"

Bailey glanced over at his older sister. "She's going on a group date with some of her friends. Tito Rommel only let her go because there are more girls than guys going."

"And why aren't you going?" Jude worried about his brother and the amount of time he spent alone. The kid never smiled anymore. He'd always been quiet and let Brianna talk for him, but he never seemed depressed until recently. Their parents had been gone for two years and usually only came back one at a time, once a year, for a few weeks. This year they were both due back for the holidays, though, which should help. Jude just wished he could do something more.

"Because Brianna's friends are annoying, and the guys going are total douches."

"*Douches*? What gives them such a dubious distinction?"

Bailey sighed. "They're just fuckboys from the soccer team. I don't even know why she hangs out with them. She likes Troy and thinks he's 'different than the other guys.' She won't listen to me when I tell her he's a fuckboy."

Jude had really missed out on so much with them both. Since Reese was back and living with Mr. Matheson, Jude could negotiate more time off to spend with his brother and sister.

"Well how about I pick you up this weekend, and we'll go hang. You need anything? Clothes or shoes?"

Bailey shook his head. "No. I'm fine."

Jude knew he wasn't fine. But their break was over. It was time to get the kids back to work for another half hour, and then he needed to get to class. If he wasn't mistaken, Bailey had pushed himself a little harder in the last go around. Jude was determined to be there for him. He was pretty sure his siblings were straight, but he wondered about Bailey sometimes.

Class felt like it dragged on that night, and Jude was more distracted than ever. He should have been listening to his anatomy professor. Instead he thought back to the night before and how much fun he and Reese had—even the drunken kiss. *Wow.* Sometimes Jude cursed himself for how much he tried to do right. He could have had Reese in many different ways, but he was determined not to take advantage of the inebriated. And Jude still wasn't quite sure what to do with Reese's sexuality. He came on strong, and he kissed like he'd been down that road before, but had he? Just what expectations did the pretty white boy have?

SIXTEEN

JUDE DROVE too fast on his way back to the cottage, and he was way more excited than he had any right to be. He parked, grabbed his nicer clothes from the back seat, and ran up the front steps. Then he stopped in his tracks, suddenly unsure of himself. When Jude opened the door, Reese was laughing at something Kyla said, but he quickly turned very mischievous eyes on Jude. The man on the couch was not the same one he'd left that morning.

"Kyla agreed to stay with Grandpa tonight. He went to bed early."

Reese stood from the couch. He was wearing a pair of charcoal gray slacks and a pale-blue button-down that really showed off his tan. He'd shaved and probably had a facial. And he'd removed the Steri-Strips from his nose, which left behind an angry cut, but it looked like it was healing fine. The rest of his skin glowed.

But the most dramatic transformation had to be his hair. It was past his shoulders that morning—a big, wavy mess. Now the mess was cut back to a mop on just the top of his head, and it fell into his eyes until he pushed it off to the side. The rest was cut close to his scalp, and the effect was stunning. He could have been a runway model with his high cheekbones and pink lips. Jude opened his mouth to speak a few times, but he was too flabbergasted to make any sense.

"You dressed for going out, or do you need a moment?" Reese beamed. He clearly enjoyed making Jude speechless. With a frustrated groan, Jude stormed down the hallway toward the bathroom, ignoring the laughter from the living room. He set his things neatly in a corner of Reese's bedroom and then relaxed. From the look of Reese's wardrobe, which was strewn about the room, the confident Reese had been just as nervous—at least when he was getting dressed.

A quick shower and shave later, Jude was a bit more collected. Reese had set a game into play by daring him to go out that night, and Jude intended to come out on top... maybe even literally.

"You ready to go yet?" Reese said with a smile as Jude joined them in the living room. Kyla let her eyes travel up and down Jude, taking in his outfit in a way that assured him he'd done well. He wore a short-sleeved cream shirt with black pants—simple but flattering. And Reese's gaze expressed his approval.

"Don't worry about me. I don't work tomorrow, so stay out as long as you like."

Jude had known he was gay since middle school, but he never acted on it until after high school. Kyla didn't seem surprised at all that he and Reese were going out.

Reese held open the door for Jude, and they walked toward Reese's car.

"I may be letting you plan our date, but I'm driving."

Jude stopped in his tracks. "Reese, what exactly are we doing?"

Reese turned to face him and stepped closer. He kept his hands to himself, which seemed like a challenge.

"We're getting to know each other better? Blowing off some steam? I don't know. I just want to be with you, and you're so guarded while we're here. I want to see if you'll let down that wall."

"And then what?" Jude asked. He wanted to know what Reese expected. As attracted as he was to Reese, he didn't want to lose his job or be stuck in a sticky situation. "You don't have to make me any promises or anything. It's just, if this is just a need to get off, I'd rather you take care of that urge with someone else."

Reese cursed under his breath and shoved his hands into his pockets. "This is exactly why I want to get to know you better—want you to get to know *me* better. I don't just need to get off. I told you I want you, and I meant it. When two people enjoy each other's company, they choose to spend time together. Up until now you haven't had a choice but to spend time with me. I've been all up in your space. I wanted to see if *you* wanted to spend time with *me*."

The vulnerable tone of Reese's voice was at odds with the rest of him, but Jude could see hesitancy—and perhaps fear—in Reese's posture.

"I wouldn't have agreed to your crazy idea if I didn't want to spend time with you. I'm just trying to decide how much meaning I should give tonight."

Reese looked into Jude's eyes and finally stepped forward. He held a hand to Jude's jaw and lifted his chin. "Give it meaning. You might think I'm something I'm not, but I mean everything with you." He bent closer to Jude, but lingered inches away and waited for Jude to close the gap.

THIS KISS was real. It had meaning. Reese made sure of it. He didn't want Jude to think the night was about anything other than being close to him. Reese wanted to shut out the world—even his thoughts of his grandfather and his new musical—and just focus on the man in front of him who'd made him feel things he hadn't felt, honestly, ever.

Their lips brushed lightly, like a kitten would tentatively touch a thing of wonder in front of it. But Jude's moan spurred Reese on. He gripped Jude's back with his hand, dragged him closer, and made their kiss more insistent. It wasn't that "rip your clothes off and find a horizontal surface" kind of kiss, though. It was a meeting of two hearts that longed to share space.

When they finally came up for air, they were both smiling like kids with a secret. Reese hated to lose the feeling of Jude against him, but he wanted to take the next step.

"So... what did you plan for tonight, Mr. De La Torre?"

Jude exhaled and let go of all but Reese's hand. "I was going to take you to a place I know. We can be... us. We can...."

He seemed unsure, which made Reese wonder if that place was somewhere folks went to get off, like he'd mentioned before.

"I'll go anywhere with you. I'll do anything. But I don't want to share you, and I want it to be very clear that we're there together. This isn't just for tonight, Jude, if that's what you were thinking. Not to me, it isn't."

Jude looked him over as he scrutinized his words. "I want to be alone with you, but if we're around others, we'll be less likely to make this about sex. Maybe."

Reese laughed. "Yeah, maybe. Sometimes when I look at you, I think to myself that no matter what, I'm going to have you right there and then. But then I remember my manners." He laughed again and rubbed his face with his hand. He was maybe even a little embarrassed.

"Well, let's see how it goes with others around. Then, if we still want to be alone...."

Reese had an instant erection as the word *alone* passed Jude's lips. Couldn't they just go get naked?

"Fine," Reese said. He cleared his throat. "Point me in the right direction."

REESE HAD never been to Incognito before, and he thought the desert theme was a bit overdone. But once they were inside the bar, he didn't notice their surroundings. Jude took his hand, led him through a pack of men around the bar, and said hello to a few as they passed. Reese stood almost a head taller than many of the men. He was in good shape, but almost certainly not as good as those men were.

Jude moved through the bar and into the next room like a man on a mission. There was a large dance floor and a DJ, and the music was Latin flavored and loud. The clientele was well-dressed and very into their dancing. Reese felt a little intimidated by the quality of talent in the room—everything from men dancing close to their partners to groups of men showing off some serious skills. Jude led them into the middle of the floor, and the dancers parted to make room for them and then swallowed them up.

Jude raised an eyebrow when he turned to face Reese.

"You ready to move, or are you just going to stand there and let me work?"

Reese laughed. He wasn't a great dancer, but he'd never been one to pass up a turn on the floor. He stepped closer, placed his hands on Jude's face, and dropped a lingering kiss on his lips. Then he found his beat and went with it. Jude's eyelids grew heavy as he let the rhythm take over. Their movements were small in the beginning, but soon the magic of a dark room and heavy bass made them lose all inhibitions. They moved as one with their bodies pressed together and only separated long enough to watch each other with hungry eyes and lustful gazes.

Jude turned his back on Reese and pressed against him. Reese grabbed Jude and moved their hips together side-to-side, then in a circle. Jude brought his arm up around the back of Reese's neck as they moved, and Reese wrapped his arms around Jude, running his tongue and teeth down Jude's neck. Jude slid his hands around and gripped Reese's ass tightly.

Reese groaned, and their dance went on, getting hotter and hotter until Reese truly forgot they weren't alone. He turned Jude to face him and kissed him, and thrust his tongue in and out to let him know just how much he wanted him. Jude pulled back, breathless. He held a hand over his chest as though trying to control the frantic beating of his heart. Reese recognized the movements as they mimicked his own feelings. The music slowed enough that the couples around them began to sway together as though they were at a high school dance. Jude came enthusiastically into his arms, pressed his cheek against Reese's chest, and wrapped his arms around Reese's lower back.

Reese felt as though he held a prize against him, and he never wanted to let go. He marveled that Jude, who seemed so serious and reserved, could show so much passion. And it was there for all to see. Reese had thought Jude would jump out of his skin if he touched him in front of anyone else. He was elated to experience a different side of Jude, and he never wanted it to end.

Why couldn't they enjoy each other like this *all* the time? Grandpa would grumble, but he'd get over it. Reese found himself gloating and thinking that maybe he'd won—he'd found someone to share all the parts of his life, not just his career and everything that went along with it. With Jude as his plus-one, he'd have someone he treasured instead of a trophy. But reality came flooding back as his phone began to buzz in his pants.

Jude must have felt it too. He stepped back enough to allow Reese to bring the phone up and see that Kyla had texted.

I'm so sorry, Reese. He fell. I've called the ambulance, and they'll be here soon. He'll be okay.

Reese swallowed hard, and tears pricked his eyes as he turned the phone to show Jude. Jude nodded, grabbed his hand, and led him out of the small club. He held his hand out for the keys when they reached the Tesla, and Reese didn't argue. He handed them to Jude and let Jude open the door for him and close it once Reese was settled. He let himself in the driver's seat, adjusted it for his size, and turned on the car. Then he took hold of Reese's hand, brought it to his lips, and kissed him gently.

"Everything will be okay," he said quietly, although he looked resigned.

Reese was grateful to have the drive back to the house to collect himself. It could have been worse, but Reese felt horribly guilty. He watched Jude drive home and knew that, without him, he'd likely have freaked out, wrecked his car trying to get home in a hurry, and still been unprepared to deal with whatever he faced.

The emergency responders were at the house when they pulled up fifteen minutes later. Reese was out the door before Jude had the car turned off. He ran up the steps and into the living room in two strides. Thankfully he'd set up the room with enough space to allow for the gurney to be brought in. Grandpa was strapped on and getting oxygen.

"Old man, what happened?"

Grandpa pulled his oxygen mask down and cursed. "Goddamn, Reese. I can't believe I fell. I thought I had a good footing, but my damn leg went right out from under me. They're saying they think I may'a broken something, so they gotta take me in. Ain't this a bitch?"

Reese bit his lip to keep from crying. "I'm sorry I wasn't here, Grandpa."

The old man waved off his apology. "Wouldn't have mattered. Look. Bring me something to wear home, would ya?"

"Mr. Matheson, we need to take him now."

Reese nodded to the EMT and followed the gurney outside. Jude stood with Kyla on the porch, speaking softly. His eyes were wary as Reese approached.

"I'm going to follow—"

"I'm coming with you," Jude said without hesitation.

SEVENTEEN

JUDE WATCHED Reese pace the length of the waiting room. His level of agitation was clearly through the roof. Jude had already brought Reese some herbal tea from the cafeteria to help calm him, but he was inconsolable. Just when Jude thought Reese would collapse, he finally sat next to Jude in the hard plastic chairs and dropped his head back against the wall.

"I wish they'd tell us something," Reese said quietly, his voice full of emotion.

Jude took his hand in both of his. "He was lucid when we arrived. He wasn't confused. He didn't hit his head. Kyla said he didn't seem to be in a lot of pain. He just complained his ass hurt, and he was worried he sprained his balls."

Reese snorted and squeezed Jude's hand. He gave Jude a lazy smile. "That old man and his balls. I swear, I think I'd rather get castrated than deal with what he does."

Jude's eyes flared, and he covered his mouth. "But Reese, don't you...."

Should he even ask? Jude didn't even know where he stood on the topic of parenthood.

"Don't I what?"

"Mr. Matheson?"

Jude stood with Reese and followed as he approached the doctor.

"Your grandfather is resting. He has a hairline fracture of the femoral neck. It could have been much worse. He'll need to stay here for a couple of days for monitoring. I'm confident we won't need to do surgery. I understand your grandfather suffers from Alzheimer's and has a history of stroke, but no other major physical ailments, which is a blessing. We'll monitor to be sure no surgical intervention is necessary, and then we'll transfer him to a rehab facility where he'll stay until the bone heals. He's very lucky. If this were his pelvis or if there had been a head injury, we'd be having a different conversation right now. You really need to get him to agree to a walker or something similar for support long-term. Do you have any questions?"

The doctor had thrown so much information at Reese that Jude was surprised he was still standing. He gave a little tug on Reese's shirt when he remained quiet, and Reese glanced down at him, his eyes wide with horror. The color had bled from his face. Jude stepped in.

"Thank you, doctor. Can we see him tonight?"

The doctor looked at his watch. "They'll be placing him in a room shortly. You can visit him until they get him settled, and then he needs rest. The social worker will be in touch."

The doctor turned to leave, and Reese let out a whoosh of air.

"Please tell me that it's not as bad as it sounds?"

Jude squeezed his arm reassuringly.

"He's going to be okay as long as he follows directions, which we know will be difficult. But he'll make it through this. We'll take care of him. Okay?"

Reese looked despondent, so Jude wrapped his arms around him and held his trembling body. He'd faced so much loss, and much of it alone. Mr. Matheson had told Jude about Reese's parents—that they'd died in an accident after Reese finished college—and then Mr. Matheson had lost his own wife. How awful to lose those around you when you were so young.

Jude had experienced death. His lolo on his mother's side passed when he was just becoming a teen. The family rallied around his parents, and he remembered them celebrating his life. He'd been an important man—part of the agricultural movement in California along-side the famous Cesar Chavez. Many people were unaware of the Filipino contribution to the fight for farmworkers' rights, but his family was very proud of their heritage.

Reese gave one more squeeze and then let go. "Will you come with me to see him?"

Jude smiled. "I'll be wherever you need me to be. I'm here for you, Reese. I want you to know that. Not just as an employee. I love your grandfather."

Reese smiled a vulnerable smile. "I know you do. I know, and he knows. I can't thank you enough."

He brushed his lips against Jude's, apparently not caring that they had witnesses in the waiting room around them. Jude took his hand and led him to the nurse's station.

"Can you please tell me where I can find Thomas Matheson?"

The nurse escorted them back to a curtained-off bed. Jude snorted when he could hear Mr. Matheson flirting with the nurses.

"I'm going to be in this bed a long time. You sure you don't have time to—"

"Wherever you're going with that statement is going to be all kinds of wrong," Reese interrupted.

Mr. Matheson winked at the young Filipina nurse. She rolled her eyes and gave Jude a smile as she passed by. Mr. Matheson had his arms folded behind his head and lounged in what looked like a painkiller-induced euphoria.

"What am I going to do with you?" Reese asked as he bent down to press a kiss to his grandfather's forehead.

"Well you better make sure they have cute nurses on whatever floor I end up on. And can you bring me some of that Gold Bond? My balls are already sweating, and I ain't even in a room yet. Chafing is going to happen, you hear?"

"Lord, do I hear." Reese laughed and wiped at his eyes. Jude thought he saw relief there and was grateful Mr. Matheson seemed to be alert. Sometimes you just didn't know with him.

"The doctor said you'll be here for a few days, and then they'll—"

"Yeah, yeah, yeah. Rehab facility. Can you believe it? One lousy stumble, and I'm stuck in bed. You better bring that keyboard of yours over. We got work to do, son. I want that damn musical written so I can enjoy it before I finally kick the bucket."

Jude saw Reese's jaw clench at that statement.

"If they'll let me, you bet I'll bring it. We'll work every day, just like we've been doing. Just because you broke your damn femoral neck, or whatever the hell that is, you aren't off the hook, old man."

They laughed together, and Reese hugged his grandfather once more. They were so close, yet it was a different kind of closeness than Jude had with his family. There was more formality between Jude and his father, uncles, and grandfather. The women were all about gossip and guilt trips, but the men expected your respect.

The social worker came in then, and boy did Mr. Matheson's eyes light up. She introduced herself as Camilla Santiago, and she was an older Filipina, probably in her late fifties to early sixties. She had a dazzling smile and a beauty mark just above her lip.

"You look just like Marilyn," Mr. Matheson said from the bed. She nodded to Reese and Jude and then held out her hand to shake. Mr. Matheson took it in his and leaned forward to place a kiss on the back of her hand.

"Mr. Matheson, you're quite the charmer. I'm here to go over your admission." She turned to Reese and began discussing his insurance information. Thankfully Reese had made sure his grandfather had the best coverage. He insisted on it when his grandfather signed over power of attorney to him after his stroke.

Mr. Matheson leaned over and caught Jude's eye, waggling his eyebrows at the woman. Jude tried to send him a scolding look, but he couldn't help laughing. Even with a broken bone, his beloved charge was quite the charmer.

After a bit they moved Mr. Matheson to a private room, and he seemed to be ready for sleep. Reese assured him they'd be back in the morning to see him and make sure he didn't get thrown out for accosting the nurses. Mr. Matheson held up his hands innocently and then waved to them as they left the room.

The drive home was quiet. Reese stared out the window as Jude drove and tried to keep his eyes open. It was after 3:00 a.m. and the adrenaline rush that had fueled him throughout the hospital visit was wearing off. He pulled up to the cottage and shut off the car.

"Reese, I want you to take your bed tonight. You need your rest. I'll—"

"Stay with me?" Reese asked in a quiet voice. He didn't turn to look at Jude, but Jude could hear the pain and fear in his words.

They trudged up the steps, and Jude opened the door. He followed Reese to the bedroom and chuckled when Reese began to shove all of his clothes off the bed and onto the chair in the corner.

"I'm sorry. I'll clean that up tomorrow."

"No you won't." Jude laughed as he slipped off his shoes. "You really are a hurricane, you know that?"

Reese snorted. "Yeah. I suppose you're right." Reese kicked off his own shoes.

Both men paused with their hands on their buckles and laughed nervously.

"Umm," Jude said.

"Wow," Reese said.

Just a few short hours earlier they'd been ready to tear each other's clothes off. A lot had transpired. Jude wanted to be there for Reese, but didn't want him to think that anything had to happen.

"Reese—"

"You want me to go in the bathroom? Turn my back? This just got weird, huh?"

"It doesn't have to be weird, Reese. I won't.... This doesn't have to be anything."

"Okay. But it could?"

Jude smiled. The poor guy was a mess. "It could. But not tonight. You need rest. I'm pulling rank here."

Reese blushed and shook his head. "Yeah. Understood. But I'm kind of all over the place when I sleep. I just want you to be prepared."

Jude laughed as he made the first move by unfastening his pants and letting them slide down. He purposely left his black trunks on and hoped the message was clear. Then he unbuttoned his shirt, folded it with his pants, and placed them on a chair. Then he crawled into bed— with Reese watching his every move. *Could this be any more awkward?*

"As long as you don't start throwing elbows, we're cool," Jude said, trying to keep his voice steady as Reese unbuttoned his own shirt. How he wished he were the one doing it. He stared up at the ceiling and fought to gain control of his emotions as Reese climbed in beside him.

He wanted Reese, and he might be falling for the guy. He certainly cared about Reese's emotional well-being.

But he was hard as a rock.

And wide-awake.

EIGHTEEN

B Y THE time Reese crawled into bed, he was almost too tired to do anything but curl up to Jude's side and throw a leg over his —almost. Reese sighed happily at the feel of Jude's skin. An electrical current ran through him at first touch, but as he relaxed, it soothed him. He placed his left hand over Jude's heart and sighed happily.

"I haven't shared a bed with someone since before I went to London," Reese admitted to Jude. "When Jada threw me out, I was actually relieved. I didn't want to come home and pick up playing house with her. And she'd never have been there for me with what happened tonight." He tilted his face up to look into Jude's eyes. "I'm so grateful for you. I'm sorry this is how we're spending our first night together, but I'm not sorry."

Reese grinned sheepishly and felt a strange mix of shyness and affection for Jude. In the past Jude never seemed to take Reese seriously. Not that he wasn't respectful. He just seemed, well, more. More of a man than Reese. More mature, more serious and intelligent.

Reese wasn't an idiot by any means. He'd graduated with honors from college and hadn't reached his level of success by being an airhead. But when it came to real-life stuff, everything came easy for him, despite losing his parents. His grandparents had always been there for him, and while his grandfather still spoiled him, he also regularly schooled him on what it meant to be an adult. After Grandma died, Reese stepped up and took over care for his grandfather. He was proud that he'd felt prepared to do so. But even though he knew what to do, he still felt lost. He needed Jude's touch.

Jude slid an arm around Reese's neck and kissed his hair. "I just wish you didn't have to go through this. Maybe I'm sorry that we met under these circumstances... but I'm really not. Watching you care for your grandfather has shown me what a good man you are."

"You don't know how much it means to me to hear you say that." Reese leaned in to kiss Jude, but Jude pulled back.

"What's wrong?" Reese asked, his voice cracking.

"Nothing. I just don't want you to think I expect anything." Jude looked away, a frown on his face, and took a deep breath.

"I know you don't. But I—"

"You need some sleep, Reese. I know you want to be there for your grandfather. That means you need to take care of yourself too. *I* need to take care of you. That doesn't involve taking things any further tonight."

Reese exhaled and pouted. "Fine. I won't take care of what you've got going on under these blankets, then. You'll regret it in the morning, but that's fine."

He made an exaggerated production of rolling over onto his side. He'd felt the heat coming from Jude's groin and wanted to explore it—so much so that he thought about just going for it—but he stood by his desire to have Jude come to him. He smiled to himself when he felt Jude roll over and spoon him. Then he gasped when Jude pulled Reese's hips back against his and nestled his erection right in the sweet spot.

"I always knew you'd be a cocktease. Go to sleep, pretty boy." Jude kissed Reese's back and wrapped an arm around him, and Reese smiled so widely that his cheeks hurt. But he didn't dare move. He knew exactly how Jude felt and exactly how being close to Reese made Jude feel, and that was revelation enough for one night. He let himself slip into a much-needed sleep and dreamed about Jude dancing in front of him, next to him, against him....

. . .

THE SUN broke through the drapes and spilled light and warmth upon Reese's and Jude's bodies. Reese awoke in the opposite position he'd had the night before. He was pressed against Jude's back, and, having just awakened from a pretty steamy dream, his hips were slowly, rhythmically pushing into Jude's bottom. He paused when he realized he was dry humping a sleeping man, but then Jude reached his arm around, grabbed his ass, and pulled him closer. Apparently he didn't mind being woken up like that.

Reese caressed Jude's smooth chest as he pressed kisses onto his back. Jude moaned and pulled Reese's hips harder against his ass. Reese gasped at Jude's strength as his length throbbed against him.

Jude felt good under his hands, and his movements convinced Reese that he might have Jude right where he wanted him. He felt victory coming on. And then Jude grabbed the hand Reese had pressed against his chest and forcefully moved it to grasp his erection through the cloth of his underwear.

"God, I've wanted to touch you," Reese breathed. He bit down on Jude's shoulder and snaked his other arm underneath Jude's body to pull him even closer. They moved together, tentatively at first and then desperately. Jude thrust slowly into Reese's hand, and his whole body trembled. Jude turned his face into the pillow and moaned as his body went rigid. Warmth spread over Reese's hand through the material as Jude's erection jerked. Reese was so turned on that his release came right after.

"*Fuuuuuck,*" he groaned and pressed his forehead against Jude's back. They both breathed heavily, their bodies slick with perspiration. Reese held Jude against him, afraid that letting go would end the magic between them.

"I really don't mind that you hog the bed, especially if this is how you wake me up," Jude said once his breathing had settled. Reese barked out a laugh, kissed the back of Jude's neck, and rolled onto his back.

"What a great fucking way to wake up. Damn, Jude. I haven't—"

"Me neither. Wait. You've never?" Jude turned to look over his shoulder with wide eyes.

"No. I mean, I meant to say I haven't ever had morning sex, but I could get used to this. Why? Did you think...?"

"I don't know what to think," Jude said as he turned to face Reese. "I don't want to ask you to put a label—"

"Oh. Oh, yeah. Well... I like who I like. I want who I want. Gender doesn't matter to me." Reese felt his cheeks flush. "I like you a whole lot, Jude."

Reese loved Jude's satisfied smile. His sleepy face was incredibly sexy and so much more relaxed than he'd ever seen him.

"I'm glad to hear you say that. I didn't know what to think." Jude reached up and cupped Reese's cheek. "I'm really glad. I like you too. A lot."

Reese was relieved at Jude's confession. He was so hard to read, and given how they'd known each other previously, it made sense he might have been confused.

"So no morning sex either, huh?" Reese asked.

Jude shook his head. "No. No overnights. You?"

Reese ran a finger down Jude's chest. "Jada wasn't exactly a morning person," he said with a laugh.

Jude frowned as though he wanted to ask more.

"And she's the only one I've lived with. Anyone else, well, they were 'heat of the moment' adventures, not necessarily folks I wanted to stick around until the sun came up."

Jude smirked. "You're a curious man, Reese Matheson."

"Curious? I guess," Reese said. He rolled over to caress Jude's jaw. "What are you curious about? I know I'm curious about you, what you like, what you—"

Reese's phone buzzed from the bedside table. He scrambled to grab it before the call went to voicemail.

"Hello?" His face broke into a grin. "What's the matter, old man? Your balls getting cold in that hospital gown?" He winked at Jude and shook his head. Jude took that minute to crawl out of bed and head to the bathroom.

"I want my pants, but they said no. Can you believe this shit? Anyway, when you come, bring your keyboard, and let's play some music."

"Grandpa, I don't know if they'll let me. I'll ask when I come down there. Is there something else I can bring if they don't?"

Grandpa cursed under his breath. "Yeah. Bring some cards, I guess. It's high time I teach you how to play poker. Someone's gotta carry on the Matheson name."

"I'll bring the cards. Jude and I will be down soon."

"Oh good. Tell him I want some of them noodles. See if he'll make me some with the hot sauce."

Reese heard the shower turn on, and he smiled. "Sure. I'll tell him. Stay outta trouble, old man."

It was great to hear his grandfather's voice after the harrowing night they'd had. He started to have faith that everything would work out.

It was all going smoothly. Jude had taken him dancing, and he'd thought he'd finally be able to break through all that serious and stern crap and get Jude to loosen up. Boy, had he. Dancing with Jude at that club had been the best form of foreplay he'd had in forever. He'd never been so turned on just from watching someone dance and feeling someone move against him fully clothed. But everything about Jude had been different. Reese wanted to pull him out of the club, find some quiet corner, and take action—until he received the text from Kyla.

His chest tightened with worry when he thought about what could have happened. He could have lost Grandpa, or at the very least, Grandpa could have been seriously hurt. A broken hip could have meant imminent death for someone in Grandpa's situation, and as much as Reese told himself he understood what was coming, last night proved he wasn't ready. It was only Jude's calming presence that kept him grounded.

Again he wondered just what was it about Jude that had him so enamored? Reese didn't have a type, but he'd never dated someone so much younger before. He preferred the company of women his age or men a little older. Before Jada, he'd dabbled in all kinds of flavors, and she'd been the tastiest—the one who made him think he could settle down with a favorite.

And yet his eye wandered while he was on tour, and he knew for a fact that Jada had taken lovers while he was gone. He'd had two trysts with men over the entire two years they'd been together, and neither had involved anything more than heavy petting. A lot of men didn't know what to do with him. He didn't subscribe to any one sort of play, and he didn't fit stereotypes.

Jude defied stereotypes as well. Reese thought for sure he'd be more submissive in intimate matters, but he should have known by the way Jude took charge of situations that he'd demand to have his way. It was crazy exciting to Reese. He never knew what to expect, and he loved that. He loved to challenge Jude, push him to his limits, and watch as his more dominant side took over. That could open up all kinds of possibilities Reese had never experienced before. And he couldn't wait.

Reese climbed out of bed and hoped to catch Jude still in the shower. He knocked just as the water turned off, and he opened the door as Jude covered himself with a towel.

"That was the old man. He's already putting in orders for your delicious food."

Jude smiled. "I'll make him whatever he wants. Did you want to hop in here? I'll give you space," Jude said, his eyes traveling over Reese's mostly naked form.

"I'd hoped to join you," Reese admitted. Then he frowned at the chair. "Damn. I think we need to have this bathroom enlarged. I'm thinking a tub—"

"Reese," Jude began slowly, seeming unsure.

"What is it?" Reese asked. He almost slipped and called him babe. He wanted to. He wanted to be demonstrative as all get-out. He wanted to run outside and yell to anyone who would listen that he'd spent the night in Jude's arms.

"I don't know what I was thinking this morning. I should have... we should have talked about being intimate before anything happened. I get tested every quarter, whether I've been active or not, which I haven't been for a long time. I just don't want you to worry about anything."

Reese shrugged. "I'm not. I see how you take care of everything. Other than living in your car like a troll."

Jude raised an eyebrow and looked as though he were going to snap Reese with the towel, but must have realized that would leave him naked. Reese jumped out of the way and raised his hands.

"Other than that escapade, I know you take care of yourself and would be safe. It's been about six months for me, so I'm due. I'm going to take care of it."

He stepped into the bathroom and crowded Jude against the wall. "I don't want to be done with this. Please tell me you haven't had enough yet. Tell me we can—"

"Yes," Jude interrupted, his eyelids heavy. "I want more of you. I want you, Reese."

Reese bent to kiss him, and immediately Jude clung to Reese's back, whimpering softly. Their embrace was full of wonder, their eyes as open as their hearts were becoming. Reese could feel Jude questioning what was happening, just as he was. But he'd take Jude at his word that he wanted to explore what they could be together.

Jude's towel slipped, and he grabbed for it before it hit the floor. Both of them laughed nervously. Reese stepped back and ran his hands through his hair and stared longingly at Jude's well-kissed lips.

"I'm just going to let you... yeah," Jude said as he left the bathroom, grinning nervously as he shut the door behind him.

"*Great* fucking way to wake up," Reese murmured to himself.

After Reese showered, he and Jude had breakfast together with lots of blushing and flirting. Then they dressed to visit Grandpa in the hospital. Reese decided not to bring his keyboard until he got permission. Jude let him know it would probably be more appropriate once Grandpa was in the rehab facility. He explained once again that Grandpa could very well come out fine, that going to the facility didn't mean he would be there permanently.

"You think you can talk him into the walker?" Reese asked Jude.

"I'll do my best. He's been very resistant. I even brought up using a quad cane, and he wouldn't have it. Maybe now he will, especially if he thinks the alternative is a wheelchair," Jude said as he raised his eyebrow. He looked quite devious.

Just then Jude's phone buzzed, and he pulled it out with a frown. He answered as he walked quickly into the backyard. Reese's instinct was to follow, but he sensed Jude wanted his privacy. The easiest way for him to mess things up was to get too much into Jude's personal space. He watched Jude go from the relaxed state he'd been in that morning to standing on the back deck with his shoulders practically up around his

ears. Reese immediately thought he should bring over a massage therapist, cook Jude a nice dinner, bring him flowers....

That was all domestic shit. Wow. Was that what was happening?
Reese looked longingly out the window at the man he so desperately
wanted to be close to and thought, *yeah*. Domestic with Jude would be
pretty damn amazing.

Jude hung up the phone, and Reese watched as he took a cleansing
breath. Reese made himself busy as Jude returned to the kitchen. He
hesitated by the door.

"Umm... do you...? Would you be okay going to the hospital by
yourself? Just for a bit? I have something I need to take care of."

He stood with his hands on his hips and Reese noted his discomfort.

"Sure. I'll be fine. Is everything okay?"

Jude frowned and chewed on his lip. "I don't know. But.... It's, well,
it's a family—"

Reese held up a hand. "You don't have to tell me anything. I understand. But if I can help, I'd be happy to."

Jude dropped his hands, cocked his head to the side, and studied
Reese. Then he approached him and placed a palm against Reese's
cheek.

"You're *so* not what I thought you'd be." He pushed up on his toes
to kiss Reese softly on the lips and then disappeared around the corner.
"I'll meet you over there," he called. Reese heard the water run in the
bathroom a moment later and the sounds of tooth brushing. Jude was
back in minutes with keys in his hand. He seemed lost, like he wasn't
really sure what to do.

"Jude?" Reese placed a hand on his shoulder. "Whatever it is, I'm
here if you need me."

Jude looked up at him as though he wanted to spill everything.
Instead he nodded, chewed on his lip again, and left without another
word.

NINETEEN

J UDE CURSED as he took a corner a little sharply on the way to his brother's school. Bailey's counselor said she'd keep Bailey in the office until he could get there. Jude rushed in the front doors and took the familiar path to the counselor's office. He'd graduated just over four years before, but it felt like a lifetime.

"Jude," Mrs. Martinelli said as she shook his hand. "It's really good to see you. Please come in."

She gestured to the empty seat next to Bailey, and Jude sat down. Bailey wouldn't look at him, which pained Jude tremendously.

"I'm sorry to take you from work, but Bailey has something he'd like to tell you."

Mrs. Martinelli waited patiently at her desk for Bailey to speak. After almost a full minute of silence, Bailey mumbled, "I got picked up cutting school."

"Excuse me. What did you say?" Jude asked in a low voice. He shifted in his seat to look more closely at his brother. Bailey had lost weight or grown... or both. He didn't look high, but something was off.

"The police did a truancy sweep this morning, and they found your brother downtown, coming out of a coffee shop."

Jude raised an eyebrow in question at his brother.

Bailey said nothing. They sat in silence until Jude thought he'd gone deaf.

"Mrs. Martinelli? May I speak with my brother alone for a moment?"

She seemed uneasy about leaving them, but Jude figured she knew him and knew he worked with the kids. She stood up.

"I'll just be right outside if you need me," she said. She touched Bailey's shoulder on her way out the door. Jude turned to face his brother and planned to wait him out, but Bailey spoke.

"I know it was stupid, and I know I shouldn't have done it, but you have to let me explain."

"I'm waiting," Jude said after a moment.

Bailey looked down at his shoes. "You'll think it's stupid."

Jude sighed. "I will always listen to you, Bailey. No matter what. But you have to be honest with me."

"I was out trying to find a job. I thought if I earned some money, I could help, you know? Pay for an apartment. And we could move out. With Brianna. I'm just so sick of it there."

To Jude's horror, Bailey started to cry.

"Bail, no. Honey, don't cry." He knelt next to his brother's chair and breathed a sigh of relief when his brother accepted his embrace. Jude held Bailey while he cried and cried as though his heart were breaking.

"I'm going to fix this," Jude said. "Give me a week. Stick it out for a week, and I'll find us a place. Just the three of us. I promise."

Bailey looked up at him with dark eyes so much like his own. "I can't take it anymore," he cried, his lower lip quivering. "I'm always getting yelled at, always doing something wrong. Brianna's the star, and I'm the loser. My grades will never be like yours and hers. Tita Gemma tries to be nice to me, but...."

Jude hugged his brother tightly. He knew just how difficult it was for his younger brother to be compared to his older siblings. Bailey was the best dancer of the three of them, but academics were always hard for him. Jude would help. He would make it right. Until his parents came home.

Mrs. Martinelli came back in with a sad smile. "How're we doing in here?"

Jude stood and took his chair, moved it closer to Bailey's, and grabbed for his hand. "My brother is going through a tough time at home. I'm going to try to come up with a solution, but is it okay if I take him with me? For the rest of today? He'll be back tomorrow, I promise."

Mrs. Martinelli grabbed a pad of passes from her desk. "I think that's a great idea. Bailey, you give yourself a break today, spend some time with your brother, and see how you feel tomorrow. Okay?" She handed the pass to Bailey and shook hands with Jude. "I'm here if you need me. Either of you."

"Thank you," Bailey mumbled as he and Jude left the office. Jude nodded his thanks, and they walked quietly to the car and got inside. Jude sat for a moment before turning on the engine.

"I have a confession to make, Bailey."

Bailey turned to look at him with a frown. "You? A confession?"

"Yeah. I do. Okay? Look. You know I got let go, but then Reese asked me back because he needed help, right?" This was going to be much more difficult than telling Mom. Jude blew out a breath. "I'm staying with him, but there's something else I need to tell you."

Jude turned to look at Bailey and recognized the same crease in his forehead he saw when he looked in the mirror.

"I'm gay, Bailey."

Bailey blinked. "Okay. So?"

Jude blinked. "'Okay? So?' That's it?"

Bailey shrugged. "So, you're gay. So? What does that have to do with anything?"

Jude laughed loudly. "Wow. Yeah. It has everything to do with it. Umm... I'm kind of.... There's something...."

"I've never seen you act so weird. What? Do you have a boyfriend or something? Look, whatever it is, it doesn't matter to me as long as you're happy."

Now it was Jude's turn to cry. With everything Bailey had been through, he cared about Jude's happiness first.

"I love you, Bail. Seriously. I don't deserve you, but I love you. You're right. I have a... something. Reese. I don't know what's happening."

For the first time in a very long time, Bailey smiled. He beamed. "That's really cool, Jude. I'm happy for you."

"Thanks," Jude said as he wiped at his eyes. "The reason it matters is that I've been back staying at the house. But I'm going to find us a place. Okay? I promise. I'll make it work. Somehow."

Bailey put a hand on his arm. "Jude, I don't care if I have to sleep on the floor somewhere. Anywhere. Just please don't make me go back to Tito Rommel's. I hate it there."

Lord, what was he about to do?

REESE STAYED at the hospital through lunch and told Grandpa he'd be back in the evening. He wasn't sure why Jude hadn't made it there, and he was worried. He checked his phone a couple of times, but there was no word. Then he went home thinking he'd grab some food, but instead he just collapsed onto the bed. He smiled when he smelled Jude's cologne. He knew he should get up and change the sheets, maybe even straighten up their mess, but he was too tired. It felt empty without Jude there.

"Reese? Are you home?"

Reese woke to the sound of Jude calling from the living room. He popped up out of bed, and had to fight to keep from running out and jumping on him—which turned out to be a good move, since he wasn't alone.

"Heyyyy.... Wow, Jude, you didn't tell me you had a mini-me."

Jude looked as uncomfortable as Reese had ever seen him. And the kid was grinning like he'd just caught big bro in deep doo-doo.

"This is my brother, Bailey. Bailey, this is Reese Matheson."

"Yeah, I know," Bailey said. He walked forward with his hand extended. Reese shook hands with the kid and smiled at Jude.

"Let me fix you both lunch," Jude said hurriedly as he walked toward the kitchen. Reese recognized Jude's need to busy himself when he was uncomfortable. Reese and Bailey followed him in. Jude pulled out some pasta from the drawer and started water boiling. He found the rotisserie chicken Reese had picked up and sliced breast pieces off for each of them. Then he pulled fresh broccoli from the drawer in the fridge to steam... and was promptly out of busy work. The whole time Reese and Bailey sat at the table chatting about life.

"So you haven't actually started learning yet, even though you have your permit?" Reese asked Bailey.

Jude dropped a spoon loudly into the pasta bowl. "What? When did you get your permit?" Reese could hear the frustration in his voice.

Bailey shrugged. "A couple weeks ago, I think? Tita Gemma took me. Said she'd put me to work once I got my license."

Jude looked as though he'd just been kicked in the stomach. He turned to finish the food and called over his shoulder, "Bail, go wash up. The bathroom is down the hall."

"Sure. And thank you for lunch."

Reese couldn't hide his shit-eating grin. "You brought your brother over."

Jude turned to face him and crossed his arms. "I did."

Reese's face was going to break if he smiled any wider.

"He cut school to go try to find a job. His counselor called me and asked me to come down to the school to talk."

Reese's smile faded as his look turned to confusion. "Why would he do that?"

"Because he's unhappy living with our uncle. He had it in his mind that if he could contribute, I would take him and our sister and get a place of our own. Which I need to do. I'll continue working with you, Reese, and with your grandfather, but I need to find a place for them."

Reese folded his hands on the table. "Bring them here. We'll make it work. They can have my room. You and I can stay in the garage. We'll buy a bed." He nodded like he had it all figured out.

Jude shook his head and turned to the food preparation as Bailey came back to the room.

"So, are you my brother's boyfriend?" Bailey asked Reese.

Jude dropped the sauce-covered wooden spoon on the floor. "Shut up!" Jude snapped at his brother.

Bailey's smile dropped, and he put his head down, completely admonished.

TWENTY

REESE COULDN'T help but be amused by Jude's discomfort, but he figured he should be the adult. "It's a little early to be asking that question, I think. But I will say I care about your brother a lot, and I would hope you would respect his feelings in all of this."

Jude stood quickly and fixed Reese with a warning look. "We'll talk about this later," he said through gritted teeth.

Lunch was a quiet meal. The only exception was Jude asking Reese how Grandpa was that morning.

"Already getting in trouble. The pain meds seemed to be keeping him comfortable. He recognized me at least. That's always good."

Jude gave him a sad look. He returned to his food and wiped his mouth with a napkin. "I need to take Bailey home to my uncle's and tell him I'll be working out a plan to move into a place with them within the week. I appreciate your offer, Reese, but I don't think—"

"Just think about it before you say no. Please." Reese knew he was pushing his luck. Things were so new between them that it could be a catastrophe, but he trusted his instincts. And his feelings. He might be just getting to know Jude, but he *knew him*. Jude's actions spoke volumes about what a good person he was. Just the fact that he was

trying so hard to take care of his siblings while also taking care of Reese's
family....

Reese intended to take care of Jude, whether he liked it or not. If he
wouldn't move in there with the kids, Reese would find them a place
and make sure they were safe. The image of Jude sleeping in his car
flashed through his mind, and it pissed him off all over again. Angered
him. But he bit back a comment about the last time he trusted Jude
with his own housing.

When Bailey finished his meal, Reese pushed back from the table.
"Come on out back with me. Let me show you my private paradise."
Reese put an arm around Bailey's shoulders, ignoring Jude's ques-
tioning look, and led the boy out the back slider from the kitchen.

The backyard had sold Reese on the cottage, and his grandfather
loved it too. There was a deck that ran the length of the house. Grandpa's bedroom also had a slider, and that end of the deck was covered by
an overhang. Reese had thought putting a hot tub there would be a
great idea, but now he was more focused on the possibility of expanding
the place. Beyond the deck was a large area of lawn surrounded by
incredibly tall cypress and redwood trees. A wooden fence surrounded
the property, and an iron gate opened onto a set of stairs cut out of the
earth. They led down to a wide expanse of beach.

"Whoa," Bailey said. He took a deep breath. "This is amazing."
Bailey stepped down off the deck and onto the stone pathway that
stretched across the lawn toward the gate. Reese thought that perhaps
adding an in-law quarters out back might work. There had to be a way
to make the place livable for all of them.

"Hey, Reese? Do you surf?" Bailey spotted the small shed against
the back gate where Reese stashed his surfboards and wetsuits.

"That I do. When I'm not all over the place. I haven't been able to
surf much because I've been taking care of Grandpa, but now that
Jude's back, I intend to get out there. You surf?"

Bailey shook his head, his hands on the gate. "I haven't ever been.
I've always been kind of afraid of the ocean."

Reese reached over and pushed the gate open. "Let's go check it
out." They walked carefully down the steps, and Reese immediately felt
the call of the waves. It was the place he was most relaxed, and yet he

could feel tension coming from Bailey. They reached the bottom of the steps, and Reese slid off his Vans. He let his toes wiggle in the sand.

"Take your shoes off and stay awhile," Reese said to Bailey. "It makes walking much easier, and there's nothing like warm sand between your toes to wash the blues away."

Bailey looked unsure, but he unlaced his dress shoes and placed them on the bottom step. Then he slid off his socks, rolled up his navy blue uniform pants, and pushed up the sleeves of his sweater.

"There, now. Doesn't that feel better already?"

Bailey grinned at him and wiggled his toes. They walked across the wide expanse of beach toward the water. Bailey nervously watched the waves crash as they halted at the top of the dunes, just before the sand became damp from the path of the waves. Reese moved closer and let the water wash up over his feet. He really missed surfing. Perhaps in the morning....

Reese caught movement coming from behind him and noticed that Jude had joined them. Jude patted his brother on the back and then approached Reese.

"Hey," he said quietly. Reese looked down at him and smiled. He wished he could take Jude in his arms and kiss him right then, but he figured Jude wouldn't appreciate the display in front of his brother.

"Your brother is a great kid. I'm glad I got to meet him." Reese was even more in awe of Jude and the easy way he took care of his brother. He was naturally a caregiver. The nursing school was just working out the details.

"I only came out to him on the way over here."

Reese turned sharply toward Jude. "What do you mean? He didn't know?"

Jude laughed. "He must have. He barely reacted. The kid is much more sophisticated than I gave him credit for. He's such a great kid, and it's killing me that he's so unhappy."

Reese felt honored that Jude was sharing these feelings with him. As more and more of his walls came down, Reese fell harder for him.

"I meant what I said. Your family is welcome here, Jude. I know it would make you happy too. This is your home."

Jude raised an eyebrow. "And how is that going to work? Your grandfather will wonder why they're here. You and I are just... well, whatever it is we're doing. And my sister still doesn't know. I've only come out to my mother and Tita Germaine. My family is really Catholic, Reese. Like *really*. My uncles and father are very involved in the church community, and—"

"And what, Jude? You are who you are. They may not understand it, but you owe it to yourself to live your life the way you want." Reese was angry for Jude. Even though Jude seemed resigned to it, Reese wanted more for him.

"I wish it were that easy." Jude looked out over the waves, and his voice sounded far off. "I don't know if I'm willing to give up my family to be out. Up until now it was never an issue," he said with a humorless laugh. "I never had a reason to think about it. I just assumed I'd be alone, and that was okay."

"Please tell me you have a reason now," Reese whispered. His chest felt really tight suddenly. What if Jude was too afraid? He *was* really young. He might not be ready to make that move yet. Would Reese wait for him? Eventually Jude would have to realize he couldn't be alone forever... right?

Jude looked as though he wanted to say something, but then he turned and walked back to where Bailey was sitting. "We should probably get you back to Tito's."

Bailey's face fell. Reese thought maybe the kid would make some headway around the water. Maybe he'd let Reese teach him how to surf. Maybe—

"Thank you, Reese," Bailey said with a shy smile. Jude put a hand on his back, and the two of them marched back up the sand, their heads down as they walked.

Reese exhaled and tried to clear his mind. It wouldn't do to go after him and beg. Just like with sex, Reese needed to let Jude come to him, otherwise he'd worry that Jude was only trying to placate him.

But he needed to get some food and get back to Grandpa. Reese climbed the steps to the backyard and glanced back longingly toward the ocean. *Soon, my friend.*

Jude was just cleaning up. He handed a container of noodles to

Reese. "I put the bottle of hot sauce in the bag too. I'll meet you there as soon as I can."

Reese sat the bag down and took Jude's hands. Jude jumped a little and looked guiltily at Bailey.

"Bail, can you wait in the car, please?"

Bailey smiled at them and hurried out the door. When Jude looked back at Reese, he looked sad.

"I'm sorry I can't go with you. I'm sorry all this came up. I...." He paused midsentence. That tight feeling threatened to return to Reese's chest, and then Jude pulled Reese down for a kiss. It was full of longing, full of guilt.

"Hey," Reese said as he pulled back. "I know you have a lot going on. I'm not going anywhere. Okay? I want you in my life, and not just because you're wonderful with my grandfather. Just please, don't feel like *you're* alone in this either. I'm here for you too. I—"

Jude kissed him again—hard. And then he was gone.

TWENTY-ONE

REESE MADE it back to the hospital just as the physical therapist was leaving and the nurse was taking the old man's order for dinner. The physical therapist assured Reese that Grandpa had been up and to the restroom and was working really well with the walker. He had an impressive amount of upper-body strength considering his age and physical shape.

"And none of them Brussels sprouts, ya hear me?" Reese heard Grandpa shout. "You people tried serving me that when I was here before. They look like Martian balls."

"Jesus, Grandpa. I leave you alone for a couple hours...."

The nurse smiled and excused herself. Grandpa grinned at Reese, but he seemed off. "Can I help you?"

Reese swallowed hard and put on a brave face.

"Hey Grandpa, it's me. Reese. I brought you noodles from Jude just like you asked for." Reese endured his worst nightmare as he waited for his grandfather to respond.

"I know it's you, son. Come here."

Reese bent down to hug him and spent an extra few beats holding on and praying his thanks. Crisis averted.

"Jude made me soup? Where is he?"

Reese took a seat in the chair. "He's taking his little brother home. Then he'll be over. He sends his best."

"His brother is a dancer like him. He told me all about him. Sister, too. Showed me one of them tapes of their performance. They throw them plastic rifles and ribbons around. Kinda pretty, if you ask me."

Reese smiled but he wondered how Grandpa could remember all that about kids he didn't even know, but he couldn't remember the man he'd helped raise. He understood that was sometimes how the disease worked, but it didn't make him feel any better.

"His brother is a great kid. He brought him over today. Seems he's been having a rough time."

"Oh yeah? Jude never talks much about the rest of the family. I know they're Catholic, though. Must be hard."

Reese frowned. "What must be hard?"

"You know, him being gay and all." He gazed off toward the window. "Junior, I ever tell you about Las Vegas?"

Reese tried to breathe evenly and not react to the fact that now Grandpa thought he was his father.

"You told me about some, yeah."

"There was this one time me and the guys was coming out of the club after practicing all afternoon, and it was just getting to be dusk. It was fall, so it wasn't too hot."

"Sure, and you saw Grandma—"

"Grandma? Naw. This was before I ever met your mother. It was dusk, and I was just gonna have a smoke when I saw this gorgeous red hair."

Reese smiled. He loved the story about him meeting... wait... he said that was before Grandma? Reese decided to let the old man talk and didn't correct him.

"Anyway, this kid comes over, and I can't stop looking at his hair. I was dumbfounded. I had to talk to him. He couldn't get his cigarette lit, so I took a chance and offered him a light, asked him for coffee, and next thing you know, it's late and we're back in my room. The lights are out. That hair was so beautiful. He was beautiful. I never seen anything like him. We spent that one night together, and that was it. He was gone the next morning, and I never saw him again."

Reese's heart was pounding. Could that story be a real memory? Maybe he was confused. Maybe it was—

"I never told anyone before," he continued, looking up at the ceiling. "I kept it a secret even from my wife. I never told anyone, but I want you to know, Junior. I see your boy, and I just know he's gonna be like that one day. He's just like me. Anyway, then I met your mother, and she had that red hair, and I knew it was meant to be. I loved her so much."

He fell quiet then and stared out the window while the ground shifted under Reese.

Jesus! That was huge. That story changed everything. And what did he mean, he saw it in Reese? Reese had never been....

But he had. He'd loved singing from the moment he learned to make sounds, and his mother told him he sang before he could talk, and all the time. But he'd never really thought there was anything different about him until high school. He thought it was normal to want the boys and girls to like *like* him.

"Reese, my boy. I thought I told you to bring me some of them noodles."

Reese snapped back to reality with a jolt.

"Oh, right. Here." He took the container out of the bag and with shaky hands arranged everything on the tray. As Grandpa got to work, Reese plopped back in the chair. He wasn't sure how long he sat there before Jude came in. He shot Reese an apologetic look and smiled at Grandpa.

"Mr. Matheson, how are you feeling today?"

Reese noted that Jude wasn't wearing scrubs. In fact he hadn't worn them for some time. He was wearing a fitted black T-shirt and a pair of gray Levi's. Reese enjoyed seeing him in regular clothes. He felt exponentially better because Jude was there.

"Thank you for this soup, my boy. They was trying to kill me with this hospital crap. Hey, have you met my grandson, Reese?"

Reese fought to keep a smile on his face. "Yeah, old man. Jude and I know each other."

Jude shot him an apologetic look and then wandered over to look at his chart. He read through it and then asked if Grandpa was in any pain.

"No way. They must have me on the good stuff. I can't feel anything." He pushed his tray aside, and his eyes drifted shut as he pulled his blanket up to his chin. "Hey Reese? Sing to me, why don't you? I'd like to hear you sing."

Reese laughed. "What do you want?"

Grandpa settled back into the bed and shook his head. "Anything."

Reese glanced at Jude and launched into "Night and Day." Grandpa smiled and held up one hand to "conduct." His eyes fluttered shut again after a bit, and he fell asleep.

Jude sat on the edge of the bed and smiled as Reese finished the song. He clapped and reached forward to take Reese's hands.

"You know it's because of the pain meds, right? He's just foggy right now. He'll be back to normal when he's off of them."

Reese felt a tear slide down his cheek, and he realized he didn't even have the energy to wipe it away.

"He's the only person left in this world who knows me, knows my history. Some people know bits and pieces, right? They've shared part of my life with me. But he's the only one who's been there since the beginning. I know it sounds petty to think of it this way, but when he's gone, or he doesn't remember me anymore, it's almost like my history is gone. Like I won't exist."

JUDE COULDN'T bear to see Reese in so much pain. He walked over to his chair and wrapped Reese in his arms to allow him a small moment of peace. Reese clung to him weakly, as though the events of the past two days had drained him of strength. Jude vowed to take care of him tonight—to be sure he got rest and a good meal.

"How did it go with your uncle?" Reese asked him when he pulled back and looked up at him.

Jude ran his fingers through Reese's hair and shrugged.

"I just told him Bailey wasn't feeling well and that I picked him up from school. I need to talk to our parents before I speak to Tito Rommel. It's very unusual for Filipino children to leave home unless they're married, despite their financial situation. The only reason I didn't get more flack for leaving was because I was coming to live with

Mr. Matheson. They still fought me about it and said I belonged at home. I had to tell them the only way I could have the job was if I lived there."

Reese ran his thumbs along Jude's lower back. Jude loved how affectionate Reese was, but it was strange for him. He was frightened someone would catch them, but didn't totally care. So what? They were in California, right? It was 2016.

But it was different for Reese. He could be with whomever he wanted, and no one would question him. Jude lived under a different set of rules, and not just because he was a semicloseted gay man. As a person of color, he had more to worry about.

"So your parents and your uncle may not allow Bailey to leave with you, is that right?"

Jude nodded. "I don't know what's the right move here. I love him, and I want him to be happy, but I don't want to take him away from our family either. And I don't want him to think he's coming to live in some party, you know? I won't be able to watch him closely because I'll be working and going to school."

Reese nodded. "And I don't want to pressure you because I know you have enough of that, but if you both move in with me, I'll be there to help out with him too. I like the kid. I never had a brother. It would be kind of fun for me, you know? And Grandpa would love to have someone else to mess with. Oh... but the ball jokes. I don't know. Maybe you're right."

Jude snorted and bent down to kiss Reese's forehead. Reese closed his eyes, tilted his head back, and presented his lips for Jude's taking. And who was Jude to deny him a kiss?

It was so easy, being intimate with Reese because he was loving and open about his feelings. Jude realized how much he had come to crave his touch, his kisses. It felt like the most natural thing to do, to kiss Reese. But it was one thing for *him* to live with Reese. His family would flip out if he brought Bailey over there to live with nonfamily, not to mention the fact that Reese wasn't just his employer, but was, for all intents and purposes, his lover.

His lover. He wanted that so much, to be lovers. He wanted to share every part of himself with Reese, but how did he get past all of their obstacles?

None of it mattered when they kissed.

"Excuse me," a woman called from the door. Jude pulled away from Reese, his eyes wide. Camilla, the social worker, entered the room with a big smile.

"It's nice to see you two. How is Mr. Matheson?"

Reese reached for Jude, but he pulled back to stand behind Reese's chair. "Umm... he's okay. He says he's not in any pain."

She smiled and touched Reese on the shoulder on her way to stand next to Mr. Matheson. "I wanted to talk to him a bit more about the rehab facility. He doesn't seem very comfortable about going."

Reese shifted in the chair to lean forward. "I think he's afraid he won't come home if he goes. He knows I want him at home, but he's afraid he won't be well enough to return."

She nodded and touched Mr. Matheson's hand. "It is very frightening to be in the hospital. The fact that you're here visiting will give him hope. I see so many older men come in alone, and no one is here to see them. It's easy to lose hope when you're alone."

Jude placed a hand on Reese's shoulder and gave him a reassuring squeeze while Camilla talked to them about the place he would go next and how long they might expect him to be there.

"I'm guessing six weeks, he'll be there. He's very lucky this break was so slight. If they had to do surgery, that would have really laid him up. He'll be good as new in six weeks."

Reese slumped a bit. "Six weeks? Can't he heal at home? What if we got him a hospital bed set up in the living room? Jude? Can we do that?"

Jude wanted to do just that, but they'd have to have a physical therapist come to the house, a daily nurse....

Camilla smiled at Reese. "Such a good man. Let's see how he does. We can talk to the doctor."

Reese thanked her, and she took one more glance at Mr. Matheson and then said her goodbyes.

Jude turned to Reese. "I would do anything for you, you know that?

But we also want to be sure he's getting the best care. See what the doctors think. I'll support you however I can." Jude looked down at his watch and frowned. "Hey, I need to run out for a bit. I have rehearsal for the kids and then class. My final is on Tuesday, and I think I'm going to drop my class for next term. You need me with you. It's just a few extra months. I—"

"I don't want to ask that of you, Jude. I appreciate it, though. I do. Hey, if you can give me these next few months, I'll pay for you to go to school full-time until you finish. Okay? I swear. Consider it part of your benefits. You've sacrificed enough for the old man. He'd want that too."

Jude bit down on his lip. With two or three full-time semesters, he could probably finish, and he'd be licensed. Then he could focus more on work, on his siblings—and dare he think?—have a future with Reese.

"That would mean a lot to me, Reese. Thank you. It feels very weird, though. I don't like taking from you. I feel like we're blurring some lines here."

Reese shrugged and stood up. He stretched his arms out wide, and his back cracked. "It's no different than any other employer offering it as an incentive. But I get it. What if you weren't my employee? Consider yourself working just for the old man?" Reese closed the distance between them and wrapped Jude in his arms. "Consider yourself my partner, my boyfriend, not my employee, Jude."

Reese's eyes were full of hope. Jude tried not to panic. He pushed up on his toes to kiss Reese gently on the lips. "I'll see you when I get back tonight."

And then he ran.

TWENTY-TWO

"**B**OYFRIEND? WHAT in the ever-loving name of all that's holy is he doing asking me that?" Jude shouted once he got in his car. Did Reese have any idea what asking him to be his partner would mean to him? Did he not get how incredibly impossible the whole situation was?

As Jude pulled up to the school, he intended to talk to Brianna, but he got stuck behind an accident and was almost late. He jumped out of his car, ran down to the field, and smiled when he saw that Bailey was leading the group in warm-ups. The kid was so talented. He really should be dancing with a troupe somewhere. Perhaps Jude could arrange that for him. Someday. First he needed to find a place for them to stay. He needed to talk to his parents. He needed to be there for Reese. He needed to clear his mind.

Jude danced with the kids and completely let go of his worries and allowed himself a precious two hours to just escape. When practice ended, he called his brother and sister over. He needed to come clean with Brianna since he'd told Bailey, but he had no idea how she'd react.

"Hey, guys, umm...." Oh, it was so much harder to tell his baby sister. She always looked up to him. How would she feel?

"She knows, JJ."

Jude froze. He looked to his sister and found her smiling expectantly at him. "It's not like I hadn't wondered. But do Mom and Dad know?"

Jude felt like someone had ripped the ground right out from underneath him. Everything was going to change as a result of his admission. It wasn't as though he were going to change for his family, but he never wanted to hurt them.

"Mom knows. Tita Germaine knows. Look. It's time I came clean with everyone, but I want to be the one to do it. Okay? They should hear it from me." He gave a pointed look at his little brother, who shrugged.

"How could I not tell her the juiciest news ever?" Bailey grinned like a fiend, and Jude just wanted to smack him silly. How could he be so entertained?

"While it might seem like great gossip to you, Bail, there are people who will be hurt by this news. This is not a game."

Bailey pouted. "I know it's not a game, but it's not the end of the world. Reese totally loves you, man. You guys can be happy together. The family will get over it."

Brianna turned on her younger brother then and grabbed his shoulder. "They most certainly will *not* get over it, Bail. I know you haven't been to church since Mom and Dad left, but did you forget that while the Catholic Church might be accepting of gay *people*, you have to remain celibate? I mean, who cares that the new Pope is awesome and tolerant and everything. Our family is very conservative. There's no telling what Dad and Tito Rommel will do when they find out. And when are you going to tell them?" she asked Jude.

"I... I don't know. Everything is happening so fast." Jude had to sit down. He felt like he was going to pass out. He'd tried so hard to keep a tight leash on his life, on his emotions. Staying in control and keeping it together had been his survival mechanism. Suddenly it was total chaos. Complete pandemonium. Hurricane Reese seemed to be ready to lay waste to every part of his life.

"Hey, are you okay?" Bailey put a hand on his shoulder and crouched next to him.

"I don't know. Look. This is for me to deal with, you two. Please let me be the one to tell our family. As for Reese, he... he doesn't understand anything. He thinks if we're together, that's it. He doesn't care who knows it. He doesn't have to worry."

Bailey giggled. "I can't believe that *the* Reese Matheson is your boyfriend. How crazy is that?"

Brianna giggled too, but she looked to Jude to make sure he wasn't totally losing it. "He's so *hot*." She covered her mouth as though she'd just blurted out a national secret. Jude couldn't help but laugh with them.

"Yeah, well, he may be hot, but he's—"

"A great guy. He really loves you. I can tell," Bailey said. "Don't worry about our family. They love you too. What? You think they're going to like, kick you out of the family? There's no way. I bet Tita Gemma will be all excited. She'll have more stuff to brag about to all of her friends. 'Oh, my nephew? He's so handsome. Do you know his boyfriend is a superstar?'"

"Speak of the devil herself," Jude said as he noted that Tita Gemma had just pulled up in her Chrysler to pick up the kids. The momentum was going, and he really wanted to just get it over with.

"I'm going to follow you," he told Bailey and Brianna as they grabbed their things. They looked at each other in shock and then looked at Jude.

"*Now?* Like you're going to tell them now?"

"Yeah, Bailey. Because if I wait, your big mouth will probably blab it all over town."

Brianna elbowed Bailey, and he gave her his most innocent look.

"I'll be right behind you." Jude walked to the car with them and leaned in to give Tita Gemma a kiss.

"Is Tito Rommell home? I need to talk to you both."

"He should be home. Yes. Is everything okay, dear?"

"Yes, ma'am. I just need to speak to both of you."

She looked worried, but he didn't give her time to ask questions. He waved to his siblings, who stared at him with wide eyes, and then he hurried to his car. He texted a friend from class to be sure he could get the review notes, and then he texted Reese.

Not sure when I'll be home. Time to tell my family. See you soon.

Then he prayed.

. . .

REESE RECEIVED the text from Jude and tried not to obsess over it. Was he really telling them? Seriously coming out to his family? It was a huge step, one he knew Jude had only partially made up to that point. He felt a little guilty knowing he was likely doing it because Reese was so damn pushy, but in the long run, it would be better for him. Reese came out as queer and then pansexual while still in high school and didn't care who knew it. Luckily he'd never suffered any adverse effects from it— other than Grandpa's smartass comments. He hoped the same would be true for Jude.

He felt empty returning to the house alone. Not seeing his grandfather in his chair or having Jude there... he couldn't stand being without the two men who meant the most to him. So he decided to call number three and see if he was back from his trip.

"Well, hello darling. It appears you've been up to no good lately, if TMZ is to be believed. Do I need to come over? Bring the vodka?"

Reese laughed. His songwriting partner and best friend was always way over the top, but he had an amazing storytelling ability and understood Reese—his music and his desires.

"Yeah. Get your ass over here. I need to have a few drinks, and I need to bend your ear."

"Sounds like trouble in paradise. Grandpa okay?"

"He's in the hospital. He's okay, but yeah. I'll tell you the rest when you get here, so get here."

He hung up before Toby could ask any more questions. Then his stomach growled and he figured he'd better eat something before he started drinking.

He'd asked Jude to be his partner—somewhat clumsily—and the guy had practically run away. Reese knew it was too soon, but he couldn't help how he felt. Maybe Jude thought he was just upset about his grandfather, or maybe Jude imagined that Reese just wanted *someone,* and it didn't matter who. But none of that had anything to do with it. Reese wanted Jude in his life permanently, and that was it.

Toby must have driven like a madman, because he arrived from

Santa Monica in less than twenty minutes, despite commuter traffic. He flung the door open and marched right into the house.

"Where are you, you big blond surf god? I *adore* this place. We could have such fantastic beach parties. We could go all Frankie and Annette *Beach Blanket Bingo* insanity!"

Toby found him in the kitchen finishing his leftover pasta and kissed him on the cheek. Then he thunked down a jug of booze and a carton of orange juice. "You talk, and I'll pour," he said gesturing over his shoulder. Toby's domestic goddess within must have known exactly where Reese kept the glasses. He poured them both stiff screwdrivers and opened the fridge to look for something to use as a garnish.

"Forget it. Just come sit. You're making me dizzy."

Toby never hid his flair, opting instead to dazzle the rest of the planet with his odd clothing choices. He embraced his color blindness and often put the most interesting combinations together. That day's ensemble included a pastel-pink polo with maroon pants rolled up to show yellow socks with his ankle boots. He worked it, though. You had to hand it to him for that and the recently bleached blond hair slicked back from his forehead.

"How was Fiji, or Bali, or wherever the hell you went on vacation?"

Toby had been gone for what seemed like weeks. He hadn't noticed how long it was because of his current upheaval.

"Hot. Moist. Lots of rain. So what's the scoop? What's going on with Jada?"

Toby appeared to be avoiding a subject, which would have alarmed Reese had he been in a clearer state of mind. Instead he let it go.

"History. I got back from London, and she threw me out. Thank God."

Toby clinked glasses with him. "Hallelujah. That girl was more drama than me, and that's saying something." He walked over and lifted a lock of hair off of Reese's forehead.

"What the hell did you do to your face?"

Reese felt his cheeks go red as he thought about his slip in the shower. So much had happened since then.

"So if it wasn't her that made you finally cut that beastly hair," Toby said, "who can I thank?"

Reese smiled and took another sip of his drink. "I'm so far gone I need a defibrillator."

Toby paused with his hands on the table, seemed to pick up on Reese's gloomy mood, and made a *tsk-tsk* sound.

"I'd say you were in rebound love if you had something real with Jada. I know, I know. You thought you did, but honey—"

"I know. I've heard the Toby Griffiths sermon on this topic many times, over the past two years. Heard you loud and clear." He laughed and took another sip. But he concentrated on not getting drunk, because Jude would be back. He didn't want a repeat of the other night.

Toby sat back, crossed an ankle over a knee, and propped his arm over the back of the chair. "Someone has got you all tied up in knots, my dear. I recognize *this*," he said as he waved a hand in an elaborate circular motion. "But I've never seen it on you before. Who is she?"

He'd called Toby for a reason. The guy was a soap opera waiting to happen, but he knew his shit. He knew people. He was a genius— Mensa candidate and everything. He'd been all-but-dissertation in Psychology when they met at UC Santa Bonita. He was the same age as Reese but so much more accomplished. They'd said, "Fuck it all," and started writing music together and then the musical. Toby was Reese's yang... or yin. Something. He'd see through all of Reese's bullshit.

"*His* name is Jude. You've met him. He's Grandpa's caregiver."

Toby squinted at him before his eyes about jumped out of his head. "You mean that beautiful Filipino boy who works here? Oh *gawd*. Tell me everything. I'm pretty sure I've got a boner by proxy."

So he did. He told Toby all that had transpired, including his drunken attempt at seduction. At which point Toby hooked his fingers around Reese's glass and slowly slid the drink away from him.

"So you're in love with him," Toby said, cutting through all the bullshit.

"Desperately," Reese finally admitted out loud. "I love him like I never thought possible. And he has no idea what to do with me." He barked out a laugh.

"Who would? My friend, you are a grade-A disaster when it comes to relationships, and yet, you're the greatest catch of them all. No one I know loves deeper, cares greater, or gives more of himself than you. And you're hotter than the sun. But you're *so much*. And he's, what? Twenty? Twenty-one? Barely? He's just a baby, although he certainly seems like he's got his shit together."

"He's twenty-two, and he's not totally out. Not to his whole family. And he seems to think it's going to be a major problem. You know me. I don't give a shit about what anyone else thinks, but I don't want him hurt."

"Of course you don't. Oh, honey. I want this for you. But you're a fucking bull in a china shop. I don't see you having the grace to pull this one off."

"Then tell me how, oh guru of all things," Reese said sarcastically.

"Have you hooked up yet?"

"Well, uh—"

"Oh, shit, Mr. I like who I like. You have no idea what you're doing, do you?"

"I really fucking don't. I just want him." Reese dropped his head onto the table, and Toby patted him as he would a child.

"Oh, cheer up. Maybe he'll, I don't know, see past all of that and love you back. It could happen."

Reese looked up at him and groaned. "Now can I finish my drink?"

Toby picked up Reese's glass and made a performance of walking over to the sink and pouring it out. "Enough booze for you. You need a clear head. Now, when is our boy expected back?"

"I don't know. He said he needed to tell his family. What do you think that means?"

Toby smiled. "I think it means little Jude is stepping the rest of the way out of the closet. This is a good thing. But are you ready for a whole ginormous Filipino family?"

Reese cocked his head to the side. "What do you mean?"

Toby rolled his eyes at him. "What do you *mean*, what do I mean? You know he has a big family, right? Do you know anything about Filipino culture?" When Reese shook his head, Toby sat on the kitchen table cross-legged in front of him. "Well, first you should know that they likely won't be super ecstatic about his change in status. They're all about keeping the kids home until they're married, and then they want babies."

"I'm okay with babies. I'd love to have a baby."

"Wrong plumbing, babe."

"I know that, dumbass. But seriously. I love kids. I'd love to be a father."

"That's good. No, I know you'd be great. But. Then there's the Catholic thing. What about marriage? What about your grandfather? Like, what are *your* thoughts about all of this?"

Reese sat back and put his hands to his head. "I think I've got a headache. Pass me some Advil, would ya?"

Toby reached behind him to the pill basket where Grandpa kept his meds. He handed Reese the pills and his own glass. Reese popped the pills in his mouth and tried to wash them down, but the vodka made him choke. He started coughing, and Toby pounded on his back.

"Cough it up, honey. You'll survive. Now come on. Why don't you play some music for me."

He jumped down off the table, and Reese followed him into the living room. They both sat down on the piano bench.

"Before Grandpa fell and landed himself in the hospital, we'd made some progress. I've got three songs so far that I want to include in the show. I think they're all a part of his journey with the girl on the—"

Reese stopped in his tracks. The story. Grandpa had admitted to having a homosexual encounter with a boy back in his Las Vegas days. Reese hadn't been dreaming. The story about meeting Grandma on the street corner hadn't been the whole truth. It didn't change the way he felt about their love story, but there was a whole other story taking shape in his mind. He needed to think on it more before he told Toby about it. They were still at the songwriting stage, anyway.

"You going to finish that thought or leave me hanging on to your last syllable? You know, this haircut looks fabulous, by the way. Ernie do this for you?"

Reese nodded absently as he played the opening notes to the first song. He hummed along until he got to the chorus.

That fire, you there with that fire
My heart longs to be warm beside you.
But that fire, you keep that fire
Away from me

How long must I wait
To be warm next to your fire?

He played it through again and smiled to himself when Toby started bouncing a leg, tapping his fingers, and with his other hand, making curlicues with his finger in Reese's hair. It was just something Toby'd always done while they worked together. He thought nothing of it until he heard the door open behind them and turned to see Jude with a hurt look on his face.

"Jude. It's good to see you, darling. Come on over here and see what Reese's got cooking."

Toby had the wisdom to stand from the bench and gesture for Jude to sit down where he'd been, dissolving the thick tension in the room. He had a knack for reading a situation and making it better. He always had.

Jude shut the door, moved slowly to Reese's side, and carefully sat down on the bench next to him. Toby moved behind them and placed his hands on both of their shoulders.

"Now play it again, Reese. This time I'm going to add in the harmony."

TWENTY-THREE

J UDE'S STOMACH hadn't yet released the knots that had formed when he walked in and found another man playing with Reese's hair. He recognized him from previous visits. Toby had flirted with Jude, but he didn't reciprocate because he felt it would be highly improper. Reese obviously missed it all because he'd been doting on Jada at the time.

But if Jude were honest, those knots had been there since Bailey admitted he'd told Brianna that Jude was gay—which led to his visit with his aunt and uncle and a phone call with his parents.

He cursed the fact that he'd shown his family how to use Skype so they could video call each other while his parents were in the Philippines. That meant everyone got the news all at once, which was better, he guessed, than his parents finding out from his aunt and uncle. But oh, what a nightmare.

"You don't know what you are saying, JJ."

"You're too young to know how you feel."

"But what about grandchildren?"

"JJ, the church teaches us that...."

They were relentless. Jude finally gave up trying to answer. It didn't matter anyway. They had their own opinions, and none of them were happy about the situation. But at no time did anyone mention disowning or disgrace, so he counted that as a partial win.

There was nothing more he could do that night, so he lost himself in Reese's soulful voice and enjoyed the way it mingled with Toby's to make a joyful noise. Their cadence mimicked the singers from his grandfather's era, but with a few more vocal theatrics. Toby's voice climbed to an incredible height and then dropped back down to join with Reese's.

"That is some beautiful shit right there, Matheson. We're going to slay them with this show." Toby made a production of checking his watch. "Oh, look at the time. Darlings, it's been real, but I have a date." He air-kissed Reese's cheeks and then gave Jude a wink. "Make sure you get some beauty rest, you two. Exfoliate. Invest in a mask, Reese. Those circles under your eyes are causing me to fret. Good night and good luck."

Once he was out the door, Reese shifted on the bench and turned to look at Jude. "Please tell me it wasn't awful."

Jude laughed and rubbed his hands on his thighs. "I wouldn't exactly say awful. Grueling maybe? Exhausting? Uncomfortable, like a bad case of hives?"

Reese stood and straddled the bench. "Here. Turn around. Let me." Jude turned his back to Reese and relaxed into his touch as Reese began to massage his shoulders. Surprisingly it was a little easier to talk like this.

"My parents decided to come home for Christmas. They're going to stay for six weeks this time, probably letting Tito Francisco get a taste of caring for my grandparents full-time. I think they're going to see how it goes, and if Tito Francisco is okay with it, they're going to stay for good. That will be great for my brother and sister."

"How do you feel about them coming home? How did they take it when you told them?"

Jude slumped a little, his body so wrung out from talking that he could barely hold it up.

"The short version is they're very concerned about me. My mother knew, of course, but she had to pretend like she didn't so as to not upset my father. He cried, Reese. He cried and said he must have sinned to have a son like me, but that he'd pray for me and pray on what to do."

Reese wrapped himself around Jude from the back, and that was the only thing that kept Jude from breaking down. Then he thought about what Tita Gemma said, and he laughed.

"What? Oh God, Jude. I promise it will be okay, I'll—"

"No, it's okay. I was just remembering what Tita Gemma said. She wondered if it was true what they said about white men and their big feet and hands."

Reese snorted behind him. "Wow. Okay."

"Yeah. And you're coming to dinner with me Sunday night. That was an order from my tito. He didn't say much, so I don't know how to prepare you for any of this."

Reese turned Jude to face him. "I'm coming to dinner?"

Jude nodded, worried. "Please. They want to meet you and make sure I'm not mentally ill—that we're really in a relationship together."

Reese smoothed a hand over Jude's hair and smiled. His eyes fluttered closed. "*God*, that sounds so good to me. Come here."

Jude was pretty sure that was the last coherent thing that was said between them. Reese's kiss was like a potent drug. It drained all the worry out of Jude, as well as his need to be in control. He wanted to be closer to Reese—skin-to-skin. He whipped his shirt off and then tugged at Reese's while climbing onto his lap. They couldn't get close enough to each other in that position, so Reese lowered them to the floor and had Jude's pants unfastened, it seemed, before his back hit the hardwood. Reese's eyes grew darker with lust as he tore away at the last barriers between them. He used those giant hands to caress Jude until he thought he'd climb out of his own skin. Never had he felt so frantic and desperate with a partner.

Then Reese replaced his hands with his lips and tongue. "I want to taste you," he said. Then he swallowed around Jude's cock until Jude cried out for relief, but Reese would provide none. He demanded and demanded from Jude, and Jude cried out Reese's name as his body shuddered and trembled. Reese took all of him and groaned his own pleasure at Jude's release.

. . .

REESE WRAPPED himself around Jude and savored every shiver in Jude's body, elated he could give him such pleasure. They kissed deeply, and Jude moaned against Reese's lips. Jude felt so good, so right, and Reese wanted him again. But Jude was exhausted.

"I love you, Jude," he whispered. "I love that you let me love you."

Jude sucked in a breath, and Reese immediately knew he'd stomped all over the moment in his desire to be completely open with him. When he started to speak, Reese shushed him.

"Don't. I'm sorry. I shouldn't put that kind of pressure on things right now."

"Don't fucking tell me don't, Reese. I love you too. Don't stop the pressure. Don't stop any of it. I don't want to stop."

Their kisses grew heated once again, and they moved clumsily across the floor and down the hall to Reese's bed, where they spent hours touching and kissing each other. When Reese told Jude he'd been tested that morning, Jude's man-in-charge persona took over, and he pulled Reese underneath him.

"Jude, I...." Reese said. He was desperate to be closer to Jude, but for Reese it was unfamiliar territory. He looked up into Jude's face and decided with certainty that he'd give him whatever he wanted. Jude must have seen hesitation in his eyes, and he paused.

"We don't have to if—"

"I want to, I just. Wow...."

"Don't worry, pretty boy," Jude said with a teasing smile. "I got you."

Reese tried to relax and let Jude work some magic with lube and his amazing hands. Reese's eyes rolled back in his head, and he groaned. "Fuck, babe. You telling me it gets better than this?"

Reese watched in awe as Jude carefully rolled on the condom and then winked at him. "Yeah, babe. It gets better than this."

And when Jude slid inside his body, Reese knew for sure that Jude was everything he'd never known he wanted and everything he'd ever need.

Jude made love to him tenderly, taking care with each thrust until Reese reached the point where all rational thought was gone and only pure ecstasy remained. It was more intense than any sexual experience he'd had to that point and the most fulfilling. Jude didn't stop until they were both completely spent.

Reese was grateful for the loving way Jude tended to him afterward. They held each other and shared many "I love yous" that night, their worries temporarily forgotten.

TWENTY-FOUR

WHEN THEY arrived at the hospital the next morning, Grandpa was more lucid—and ornery. Reese breathed a sigh of relief to see him up with the walker, assisted by the physical therapist as he moved around the room and grumbled about the chill.

"The least you could do is give me the dignity of wearing my damn underwear. My balls are smacking me in the kneecaps. My ass is flapping in the wind. No dignity, I swear. I used to have a nice ass, a long time ago. Everyone told me so. Now it moves like laundry on the line. Oh, hey son, come in here. Do you see what they're doing to me?"

Reese approached and hugged his grandfather, who seemed as strong as ever, if a little wobbly. "Damn, it's good to see you up and around."

"That's because you're facing my front. They won't let me wear my underwear. And where's your keyboard? I want to work on them songs."

Reese was elated his grandfather was so with it. When he noticed Jude speaking softly with the physical therapist, he assumed they were talking about the kind of care Grandpa was getting, but then the guy put a hand on Jude's arm and they laughed together. It gave Reese a sick feeling, and a slap-in-the-face reminder of what broke him and Jada up. He could see now why she would flip out over a simple laugh shared between two men. Reese would bet on the fact that Jude had slept with that guy before, and that was a bitter pill to swallow, especially after the night they'd just shared. But then Jude caught his eye and winked at him, which caused all of the air to leave Reese's lungs, along with any anger or jealousy. God, he was in love with Jude, and that wink did plenty to reassure him.

"Jude, my boy. Maybe you can talk some sense into these people. I want my damn underwear."

"Mr. Matheson," Jude began with that musical voice Reese was so mesmerized by. "It's hospital procedure. If I were working here, I'd have the same rules. Now, once you get to the rehab facility, you'll be able to wear them. Maybe. I would think."

Grandpa *hmphed* at Jude and kept walking his circle around the bed and toward the bathroom. "Well, at least I don't have to pull them down to go sit on the crapper." He left his walker outside the bathroom and shot them irritated looks as he closed the door.

"Make sure you use the handles, Mr. Matheson, and call for help if you need it," the physical therapist called to the closed door. He approached Reese with his hand out.

"I'm Roberto Valdez. I've been working with your grandfather."

Reese shook his hand and could certainly tell right away why Jude might have been attracted to the guy. He had killer hands—soft, strong, with a light dusting of dark hair on the backs. Very sexy. But Reese wanted Jude's. He let go and reached out to grab Jude's hand and squeezed it tightly. Jude smiled up at him, and Reese felt his heart thud wildly at the fact that he was letting him touch him in public and seemed just as happy about it.

"Thank you for taking such good care of him. I apologize for the litany of remarks you've had to tolerate about his balls, though."

Roberto ran a hand over the back of his neck. "Yeah. Well, he's certainly given me one less thing to look forward to about aging. Please let me know if you have any questions. I think he'll be able to be transferred in a couple more days. He's doing tremendously well. We'll take X-rays again tomorrow and determine a plan of action."

Reese smiled and thanked him as he left, and the air circulated a bit more freely through his lungs.

"I'm so glad to hear that," Jude said quietly. He linked fingers with Reese and gave a tug. "You okay?"

Reese nodded. "Can I tell Grandpa? Can I tell him you're mine? I'm really fighting the urge to tell every soul in this building, for starters. After that I might go stop traffic, break into a little song and dance."

Jude chuckled and rolled his eyes. "Hmmm. I'd like to see the song and dance, but can we change the tune for a bit? I'm just afraid.... I care about him so much, and I know that he doesn't particularly approve—"

"That's right. I haven't told you yet—"

The toilet flushed, and Grandpa shouted for assistance. Jude beat Reese to the door and opened it to find Grandpa shakily trying to pull himself up from the seat.

"That leg feels like it weighs about ninety pounds. Give me a hand, would ya?"

Jude supported him as he stood and kept an arm around his back and a hand supporting his arm as he reached for the walker. Reese loved watching them together, but he also felt helpless. He knew he was stronger than Jude, but he was nowhere near as graceful. The last time he'd really had to help Grandpa, he'd given the poor man bruises on his arms from his grip. He felt awful about it.

"Reese, will you give me a hand getting him into bed? I just need you to watch the other side." Between the two of them, they got Grandpa in bed, and he immediately closed his eyes. He was breathing a little heavily, which concerned Reese, but Jude got him all tucked in and fixed his pillow.

"You boys are so good to me. Thanks for coming by. Hey Jude? Will you bring me some of that chicken you get from that Joy place? It tastes so good. Reese, you gotta try it. Them Filipinos sure know how to cook."

Reese couldn't help thinking of how good *Jude* tasted. He gave him a salacious smile that his grandfather missed because he'd started to doze off. Jude rolled his eyes at him, but he thought he noticed a little pink tinge to his cheeks. Maybe?

They stayed for a few more minutes, and then Reese gestured for

Jude to join him. "Why don't you take off for a bit? I know you probably have school stuff or other things to do."

Jude smiled at him. "Thank you, Reese. You're so thoughtful. I think I'll go home and cook for Mr. Matheson, and maybe I'll get a little studying in. I'll be back soon," he said. His eyes darted around, and then he placed a kiss on Reese's bottom lip. Reese couldn't help the satisfied moan that slipped out.

"Maybe you should take a nap, too," Reese said in a low voice, and his lips split into a wicked grin.

Jude smirked. "I seem to recall you fell asleep first last night." He looked Reese up and down, raised an eyebrow, and left the room with a wave.

God, Reese was in love.

TWENTY-FIVE

THE NEXT two days Jude was perpetually nauseated. He dreaded dinner with his family, and he wanted to shake his fist at the injustice of it all. He was in love. *Finally*. And it was reciprocated by a wonderful man. He should be ridiculously happy, and yet he was in a near panic. His careful grasp of control had unraveled. He'd let Reese in, he'd let his family have a piece of him that he'd previously kept to himself, and he couldn't undo any of it. Reese was ecstatic, and when they were alone, it was easy. But their alone time had an expiration date.

Mr. Matheson would come home, and then *he* would become their focus, their priority. Reese also had his musical to work on, and Jude assumed that meant Toby would be spending a lot of time at the house.

Reese overwhelmed him, which was easy to do since Jude had mostly kept to himself since high school. For two years it had been work, color guard, school, repeat. Moving out had meant less time with his family, and he was okay with that, except for being away from Bailey and Brianna. He'd always been the doting older brother, and not being with them on a daily basis was rough.

Jude reached out to the only person he knew would understand.

"Jude, why didn't you tell me about Reese? I'm pouting over here, you know."

Tita Germaine had always been there for him, and she understood just how hard the situation would be.

"Well, one minute we were dancing around the issue, then he shoved his tongue in my mouth. Next thing I know I'm saying 'I love you, too.' But Germaine, Mr. Matheson and his no-filter will never stand for us being together under his roof, and let's not even talk about our family."

Germaine snorted. "Gemma's already saying, 'He's so handsome he turned my nephew gay.' No reality with that one."

"Like he's some sort of gay sorcerer? That's rich. He is sort of magical." Jude sighed and thought of the few nights they'd spent together. "He's crazy, though. He's ready to jump into this with both feet and no safety rope. He's talking about forever, and I'm still trying to catch my breath."

And he was. But it wasn't just physically that Reese was overwhelming. So far he'd talked of buying Jude a car, supporting him while he finished school, and he even had some crazy ideas about adding onto the house so his brother and sister could stay with them. He'd backed off a little when Jude raised an eyebrow at him... or maybe he could just sense Jude was ready to bolt.

But then they kissed, and everything else faded away. Their intimacy had been somewhat innocent until a few nights prior. Jude had wondered how much experience Reese had had with other men, and he was pleased to discover he could be Reese's first in some way. Reese's curiosity and passion were refreshing. He never made Jude feel like a hookup, and he was eager to please. It was unnerving how much Reese gave of himself, and he was open to anything. He didn't act or react like any of the men Jude had been with before.

"So what do you think is going to happen Sunday? You do realize that's in, like, two days?"

"Twenty-two hours, thirty-seven minutes, and seventeen seconds, but who's counting?"

What *was* going to happen? What would Tito Rommel say? Would he make Reese feel uncomfortable? Jude doubted that was possible since

Reese seemed to be the picture of confidence—the kind of guy the saying "water off a duck's back" was written about.

"I would tell you everything will be okay, but remember what it was like when I brought Paolo home?"

Germaine's husband was from Spain. They'd met in nursing school and were married a year later, no thanks to Tito Rommel. He'd only been her brother-in-law, but he had a say, and he hadn't been happy. Thankfully Germaine convinced Paolo that they should stay in Santa Monica rather than move back to Spain. Jude would have been lost without her. But at least Paolo was Catholic. Reese didn't even have that going for him, as far as Jude's family was concerned.

"Yeah. What a horror show. Well, the cat's out of the bag, *que sera sera*, and what have you. I won't completely go mental until probably four hours before we go over there."

Germaine sighed. "I'll be there to hold your hand. Your other hand. Because I'm sure Reese will have a tight grip on one. He's a good man, Jude. When are you going to tell Mr. Matheson? Because you should. It will be worse if he hears about it or—" She paused for effect. "Catches you in the act."

"And knowing Reese? That's not unrealistic."

THAT NIGHT Toby was over again late, and he and Reese were so involved with their music, that Jude stayed in the kitchen and studied so as not to interrupt. He also needed to give himself a little breather. His final was that week, and he wanted to ace it. But it was more to prepare himself for the possibility that he wouldn't be able to concentrate after dinner the next night.

Jude gave up his studies and went to bed without eating. He was frightened, which made him angry. He didn't like feeling out of control. It was his life. He should be able to do what he pleased. But he couldn't bear the thought that his family would be hurt by his decision to be out and with Reese. Going to sleep angry was never a good idea, but Reese and Toby were still banging away on the piano, so it wasn't like he could do yoga or meditate or anything. He tried focusing on Reese's voice, took a deep breath, and smiled to himself. That voice was heavenly.

Reese claimed to not be a spiritual person, but listening to him was a religious experience for Jude. It seemed surreal that he was in Reese's bed, much less his life, but for whatever reason, he was, and it was what he wanted more than anything else. So no matter what happened with his family, he intended to stay. He deserved to be happy. He did.

He finally drifted off and only vaguely remembered Reese joining him in the wee hours, snuggling up to his back and kissing his neck. It felt like a perfect dream, and when he woke, he assumed it was a dream, since Reese was nowhere to be found. Jude sat up and rubbed his face. Had Reese never come to bed? Had he chosen to sleep elsewhere?

He wandered through the house and cleaned up enough glasses and half-eaten snacks to rival a frat-house party, and he chuckled to think that would be his life if he stayed with Reese. He might as well don an apron and be ready to serve. *Kinky.*

As he entered the kitchen, he noticed a slip of paper propped up against a full pot of coffee.

Hey Jude
　　I promise I won't sing you the song
　　I've gone out surfing
　　I won't be long

Can't wait for tonight
　　Can't wait to say
　　How much I love you
　　And "Who cares if we're gay?"

Okay, I know you do
　　But I solemnly swear
　　To be on my best behavior
　　And show them how much I care

. . .

You're it for me
  And I promise you this
  A lifetime of love
  Sealed with a kiss

Love, Hurricane Reese

Jude wiped happy tears from his face as he laughed at Reese's corny rhyme. He *was* a hurricane, and Jude had told him that many times, but he loved him anyway. Jude poured himself a cup of coffee and walked out onto the back deck with a shiver. He couldn't believe Reese would be out surfing on such a chilly day, but he claimed he barely noticed with the wetsuit on.

Jude walked to the back gate, stood on the cliff overlooking the beach, and tried to spot Reese in the water. There were three or four people on boards facing the horizon, waiting patiently for their next ride. As a swell approached, Jude spotted Reese turn toward shore and paddle smoothly. Then he was up, crouched low on his longboard, flicking his curls out of his eyes. Jude sucked in a breath as Reese gracefully rode the wave toward the shore and then fell off as another wave joined the one he was on and knocked him sideways. He didn't breathe again for several seconds until Reese's head popped up next to his board and he climbed back on.

He repeated that four more times over the next hour. Then he jogged up the beach from the water carrying his board, and Jude's mouth watered as he watched him move, the wetsuit clinging to his long limbs and broad shoulders. Reese's lips broke out into a huge smile when he noticed Jude. He climbed the steps carefully, and Jude grabbed for his towel before he reached the top.

"That was either the scariest thing I've ever watched or the most beautiful. You're amazing," Jude said quietly.

Reese bent down to kiss him and then shook out his curls and splashed him with freezing water. Jude sputtered as Reese went to grab for him, and he took off running through the backyard with Reese's laughter echoing behind him. When he turned at the back door, he saw Reese unlock the shed and gently place his board inside. He then watched with appreciation as Reese unzipped his wetsuit from behind and began to peel the black material down his arms and chest.

"Go get the shower warmed up," he called to Jude.

"And miss the show?"

Reese laughed and continued the slow process of freeing his limbs from the suit. He grabbed for his towel and wrapped it around his waist.

Jude shook his head.

"Really?"

Reese then expertly reached under the towel and managed to finish undressing without showing a hint of anything inappropriate. Didn't matter to Jude's libido. As Reese turned to walk up the path to the deck, Jude went into the house and hurriedly disrobed. He hopped in the shower, yelped a little as the cold water hit him, and waited anxiously for Reese to join him. Moments later Reese's big hands were all over him. Jude moaned happily.

"You feel so good, Jude. I want you."

Jude smiled against Reese's lips. The feeling was so mutual. "I want you too, but we all know you and showers are a bad mix."

Reese growled playfully and chased Jude into the bedroom. They fell on the bed laughing, still wet and steamy from the shower. Jude took his time exploring every inch of Reese's tanned skin. He loved the soft curls on Reese's chest and had forbidden him to manscape. It added a delicious friction when they moved together.

Reese had received a clean bill of health, and Jude decided he wanted to give himself fully to his lover. He'd never allowed that level of intimacy with a partner, but everything with Reese was different, and he wanted more.

Reese was nervous at first. His hands shook as he caressed Jude and asked him what he needed to feel good. Jude never knew that talking about the mechanics of sex could be so hot, but a lustful haze soon came over Reese's handsome face, and Jude loved letting go for once. He faced Hurricane Reese naked and unafraid.

Reese's strength and size were a lot to take, and Reese soon lost control in his excitement. All Jude could do was hold on for the ride as the storm took over. Reese came with a roar as he thrust hard into Jude's body and dug his fingers into Jude's shoulder and hip. He collapsed on Jude's chest with a grunt.

"Oh, God," Reese said as he pushed himself up when Jude struggled to breathe. "God, I'm so sorry. I hurt you, didn't I?"

Jude chuckled, but he winced as they separated. "Hurricane Reese," was all he could say as he tried to catch his breath.

Reese removed the condom. He moved to Jude's side to caress and kiss the tender areas where he'd held on too tightly. "I didn't mean to hurt you," Reese said sadly.

Jude placed his hands firmly on either side of Reese's face. "I'm fine. I'm actually sort of flattered."

Reese sat up a little and scowled at him. "How can you say that? I never—"

"You didn't hurt me, babe. I just wasn't fully prepared for the Category Five. Maybe next time we can lower it to a Category Two or One, or maybe even just a tropical storm. Maybe I need to build up to the Category Five."

Reese dropped his head on Jude's shoulder and barked out a laugh. "I know I'm a disaster." He ran his fingers down Jude's torso and made Jude hiss when he gently scored his tender flesh with his nails.

"Let me commence with search and rescue."

Jude was swept away once more as Reese used everything at his disposal to bring on an orgasm more powerful than the first. He had to hand it to him. Reese might be a natural disaster, but he was thorough and attentive when it came to cleaning up his mess.

Jude felt closer to Reese than he'd ever felt to another person in his life. It was crazy for him to be so in love. He had no way of knowing what the future held for them, but he'd given himself to Reese in a way he never had with another lover, and he trusted that Reese would truly hold his hand through the ordeals ahead.

IT TOOK every effort Reese had to pull himself out of bed to dress and head to the hospital. He wanted to stay wrapped in Jude's arms for days, but their reality consisted of larger priorities than themselves. Jude would go with him to visit Grandpa, and then they would go to dinner at Jude's uncle's for what he assumed would be some sort of vetting process.

Reese wasn't a fool. Jude's family would find every reason in the world to try to keep them apart, but he knew how he felt, and he knew Jude felt just as strongly for him. Jude was more open than ever that morning, and Reese treated that vulnerability with care. He never wanted Jude to second-guess whether Reese would take care of him. He'd agreed to dinner so he could put on his best smile and reassure them that Jude was in a great place. He knew what he was up against, but he wouldn't be deterred.

Grandpa was in rare form when they arrived, and the three of them laughed and laughed. Reese brought along the four-track recordings that he'd made with Toby the night before. Grandpa was overjoyed.

"Yes. That's exactly it, my boy. You two got it just how I imagined."

They talked briefly about the story, but Reese didn't let on he was having different ideas for his project. His feelings for Jude and Grandpa's confession about the real person he met on the corner in Las Vegas, had him marinating a whole new plan for the course of the musical. He had run it by Toby, and Toby was wild about the idea.

"We may not find anyone with the balls to produce it, but dammit, we need to write this musical." His best friend was a smart man—a talented man—but he had no idea just how driven Reese could be.

Before he knew it, it was nearing four o'clock, and they were expected at Jude's uncle's by five. Jude grew increasingly quiet as the afternoon progressed. When they said goodbye to Grandpa and explained where they were going, Jude looked ready to jump out of his skin.

"*You're* going with him to dinner? Why's he taking you?"

They'd been over it. Jude wasn't ready for Grandpa to know. Reese wanted to tell him everything, but he respected Jude's wishes. This time.

"They want to make sure Jude's not living with a psycho and his crazy old man. I probably won't be able to do much to ease their minds, but I hear the food will be phenomenal."

Jude barked out an unexpected laugh, and Grandpa looked at him as though he'd lost his mind.

"You sure you want to take this guy? I could probably get a day pass. I'd appreciate the food more, that's for damn sure."

Crisis averted. Grandpa kissed them both on the cheek and waved to them as Camilla entered the room. Reese and Jude traded looks when Grandpa rubbed his hands together.

"You comin' to discharge me, pretty lady?"

She laughed and sat on the edge of his bed. Reese thought she was being awfully cozy with one of her clients, but hey, he couldn't deny Grandpa's mojo, and Grandpa perked up whenever she was around. Good for him, and God bless her.

"Ready to go?" he asked Jude quietly.

"Maybe they need someone to help out on the floor tonight. I think I'd rather change diapers and give sponge baths than go to Tito's."

"Oh, babe. It won't be so bad. What can they possibly do that's so horrible?"

WHAT COULD be so horrible? Jude knew Reese would find out all too quickly just how, ah, *involved* Jude's beloved family could be.

Brianna met them at the door with a pale face and wide eyes. "Tita Giselle, Tito Mario, and Tito Joseph are here. I thought it would be bad with the usuals here, but they brought in reinforcements."

Of course they'd invite everyone. Jude's coming out was huge news. Bailey sat in the corner of the front room playing video games with their cousins Marlon and Isaiah while Junior pulled his hair. Through the wide doorway, Jude could see his uncles sitting in the back room—Tito Rommel at the head of the table, Paolo and baby Antony, Tito Mario, who was married to his auntie Giselle, and Tito Joseph, his mother's older brother.

If Jude's father had been there, he would have held the seat at the opposite end of the table because he was the oldest in the family. He and Rommel were brothers who married sisters, which made Jude's family interestingly interconnected. His dad, Marvin De La Torre, would be there soon, and the whole conversation would happen again. Jude wanted to turn and leave, but Reese's giant body blocked his exit.

"Hello, sweetheart," Tita Gemma said, barely glancing at Jude because she was too busy smiling up at Reese. "Introduce me to your special friend."

He heard a snicker from Bailey in the corner, and Brianna scolded, "Tita!"

Jude kissed his auntie on the cheek. "This is Reese Matheson, but I guess you already know that."

She held out her hand and gave Reese a grin that was almost creepy. "It's a pleasure to meet you. You're even more handsome in person. Giselle, come meet Jude's special friend, Reese Matheson. You know, the one that's on the radio?"

Giselle came out of the kitchen with a glass of wine and did a double-take. "Reese Matheson. He sings that song... what is that song... Brianna?"

Brianna rolled her eyes. "Tita, just say hello."

Giselle held out her hand and fluttered her eyelashes. Jesus. Were all of the women in his family going to flirt with his boyfriend? He gave Reese a side-eyed glance and sighed.

How could they not? Reese was truly an Adonis. He'd decided to go a little dressier than his usual surfer chic, and the effect was mesmerizing. He wore black slacks and a maroon sweater with designer loafers. The clothes draped off him as though he were a damn runway model. It was disgusting how good he looked.

Jude also wore slacks, but he paired them with a traditional barong dress shirt. Reese seemed surprised, but said he liked it. Jude was trying very hard to please his uncle, just like any child would. It shamed and angered him. He was old enough to be taken seriously as a man.

Jude's cousins Christian and Adrian came over and shook hands with Reese, and their smug smiles demonstrated how incredibly happy they were to not be in the hot seat that night. They were older than Jude by a couple of years and had already been busted numerous times for their wild behavior, yet neither had gone so far as to come out as gay and bring home their boyfriend for the family to meet. They were off the hook for at least the next year.

"Why don't you boys go say hello to your uncle, Jude? I'll bring you a drink. Reese, would you like some wine?"

Reese blushed at the attention. "No, thank you. I'd love some water."

Gemma pouted a little as she turned to Jude.

"I suppose you won't be having any wine either. Why does no one want to drink my wine? Germaine still abstains, the boys would prefer beer...."

"Tita, I prefer the taste of your delicious dinner," Jude said, trying to keep her from a full-on tantrum.

"Oh, you hush your mouth, Jude Joseph. You go in and say hello to your uncle."

Great. The moment I've so been waiting for.

Jude glanced over his shoulder at Reese, who was looking around the house with a huge smile on his face. Jude tugged on his sweater to get his attention.

"This place is like a shrine. I've never seen so much idolatry outside of a church or a museum."

"Yeah. Well, I warned you we were headed into the Catholic stronghold. Now please stick close to me, or they'll—"

"Reese, I wonder if you could help me in the kitchen? You're so very tall. Won't you come help me get this platter down?" Too late. Tita Gemma had her claws out and was going to have her way regardless of how Jude felt about it.

Reese raised his eyebrows at Jude, and Jude nodded.

"Coming," Reese said with a smile. He sauntered off toward Gemma's voice. Jude proceeded to the back room. Alone.

"Hello, Tito Rommel." With all of his strength, Jude tried to appear confident.

"Jude," he said, and he looked him over as they shook hands. "You look well. How is Mr. Matheson?"

"As good as can be expected. He'll hopefully be transferred to a rehabilitation facility tomorrow. The physical therapist says he's doing well."

Rommel appraised him skeptically. "He will be there for a long time?"

"Hopefully no longer than four to six weeks."

"So what will you do while he's there?" Tito Joseph asked. Jude glanced at Paolo, who was busy playing with baby Antony and would be

no support. Christian and Adrian entered the room behind and took
their seats at the table, determined to be spectators to whatever was
about to go down.

"I'm, umm... finishing up my class this week. I'll probably try to
pick up some temporary work at the nursing facility. I've got to finish
up the choreography with the color guard before Christmas break." He
wanted to ask what the interrogation was about, but then Tito Joseph
asked Christian about his job at a subsidiary of Google, which led to a
discussion about the latest technology.

Jude was able to sit down and listen rather than continue his confession. But Tito Rommel kept one eye on Jude at all times to let him
know that their conversation wasn't over.

WHILE REESE retrieved the platter, Jude's aunt Gemma gave him the
third degree. "So tell us about you and Jude, Reese. How long have you
been boyfriend and girlfriend? Wait a minute. Who's the girlfriend? Not
our Jude. He's never been girly before."

Reese tried not to laugh. It would have been adorable if he weren't
speaking with grown women and if he weren't speaking about something so serious.

"It's been a fairly recent development," he answered, only slightly
meaning to sound coy.

"I told you he wasn't dating that Kyla girl," Jude's aunt Giselle said,
and Gemma raised an eyebrow that looked eerily similar to Jude's.

"Of course he wasn't. She's seeing that young black man from the
Costco."

"The one who helped us out to our car? Oh, he was very
handsome."

Reese was enchanted by the women and their banter. They
continued on for another fifteen minutes about Kyla and her boyfriend
and had all kinds of crazy ideas about why she was dating him. In the
meantime he was ordered about the kitchen to grab things off of high
shelves and cupboards, and then finally he was asked to gather up the
rest of the men and join the women at the table.

Reese walked into the back room and paused in the doorway. Jude looked very much like he had that day on the couch when Grandpa nearly caught them in an embrace. Jude's eyes darted around the table at the other men as they spoke animatedly in a mixture of Tagalog and English. A young man Reese hadn't met yet was seated next to Jude. He noticed Reese first and elbowed Jude, who jumped as though he were startled. He looked to Reese with wide eyes and then stood suddenly. He walked around the table toward Reese, grabbed his arm and walked him down the hallway. He pulled him into a room and closed the door. Jude looked pale.

"What's wrong?"

"We should go. I... you should go."

"What on earth is going on?"

Jude chewed on his bottom lip. "I don't think this is going to be a very comfortable dinner. For you. Or me for that matter."

Reese reached for his hand, but Jude wrapped his arms around his midsection.

"Jude, I don't care. I—"

"JUDE, ARE you ready to come eat? You and your friend?"

Tita Gemma stuck her head in the room and looked as though she were disappointed to not have caught them doing something naughty.

"We'll be right there." Jude gave Reese a warning look and shook his head. Reese had no idea what they were walking into. He just looked stupid handsome and smiled as though he hadn't a care in the world.

"It'll be all right. I love you," Reese whispered to him. Then he brushed past Jude and grabbed his hand on the way by. Jude pulled his hand back, but he worried he would hurt Reese's feelings, and he was angry that he felt he had to. Reese glanced back with confusion in his eyes, but they proceeded.

The rest of the family had taken their seats and deliberately left Jude and Reese to sit across the table from each other.

Everyone held hands while Tito Rommel said grace. There was the usual chit-chat while people served themselves chicken *adobo* and *pancit palabok*, but once people dug in, the voices dwindled, and everyone prepared for the inevitable showdown.

"So, Reese. What are you doing for work these days?" Tita Gemma asked.

Reese took a big drink of water and smiled as he swallowed. "Spending time with my grandfather. He and I are working on cataloging the music he's written over the years, and I'm working on a new musical with my songwriting partner."

"That sounds lovely. What is the musical about?"

Reese wiped his mouth with a napkin and grinned at Jude across the table. "It's about two kids falling in love back in the early nineteen sixties in Las Vegas."

The women all swooned. "That sounds very sweet," Tita Giselle said. "I love the music from that era. So glamorous. And the dresses, like Jackie O!"

Jude looked around the table and found his uncle staring at him intently. Jude's appetite for his tita's cooking was gone in an instant.

"Jude what are your plans now that Mr. Matheson is no longer living at the house?"

The food in Jude's stomach turned to lead. "I'll continue to spend time with him in the rehab facility, and I'll be looking for some temporary work until he comes home."

"Jude?" Reese asked and frowned at him. Jude shook his head, warning Reese not to interject.

"You'll make arrangements to move back here as soon as possible. Your parents will be returning soon. With Mr. Matheson in the rehab facility, there's no longer a reason for you to be living away from home."

Jude's mouth seemed to lose the ability to rebut. He refused to look at Reese.

"Tito, I don't want to put you and Tita Gemma out."

"Nonsense. We're family. There is no question."

The table was deathly quiet. Until Reese spoke.

"Jude lives in the cottage. It's his home. Why would he need to leave?"

Jude wished Reese would just be quiet. He had no idea what kind of land mine he was stepping on.

"It is no longer appropriate for him to live there. My nephew should be living with family until the time when he decides to get married. To a woman."

Reese's face turned red, and he gripped the edge of the table. Jude wished he were playing that childhood game once more—that he could close his eyes and no one would be able to see him.

"Jude is an adult, Mr. De La Torre. I understand that family is important, but Jude is a part of my family too. He should be allowed to live where he wants."

A few throats were cleared. Chairs squeaked as bodies squirmed. Reese and Tito Rommel locked eyes, and the power struggle was on.

"Mr. Matheson, family means something different in our house, and it doesn't involve two men playing house, especially not where my nephew is concerned."

"Rommel, don't be rude to our guest." Tita Gemma didn't particularly care for conflict, but she didn't object very hard. The situation was too scintillating for her to put her foot down.

Reese sat back with a shocked look on his face. "I can't believe you would be so disrespectful to your nephew. Don't you care about what makes him happy?"

"It is not appropriate for him to live there... with you... in this situation."

"Appropriate, huh? But it's fine for him to sleep in his truck? Which is what he was doing before so he wouldn't put anyone out."

"Reese!"

Jude's whole life was out on the table right then, and he felt helpless to stop the awful conversation.

"Jude, what is he talking about?" Tita Gemma asked softly. Everyone looked to one another.

Germaine frowned. "Jude? You were staying with Christian, right? That's what you told me?"

"He wasn't staying with me," Christian said. "I thought he was staying here."

Tita Gemma shook her head. "Jude Joseph De La Torre, you answer right now. You weren't living in your truck."

Jude shot a glance at Brianna and Bailey. Their eyes were full of guilt and sorrow. He wanted to be strong in front of them, but he didn't want them to hurt any longer.

"Reese, may I speak with you in the other room?" he asked as he stood from the table.

"Jude, this subject isn't over. You—"

Jude gave his uncle an angry look and told him in Tagalog to please give him a minute. Rommel sat back and grinned in a way that let Jude know he fully expected his word to be law. His family argued all around him, but he was determined to put an end to this. He stormed into the front room and waited for Reese to join him.

"Jude, I'm sorry, I didn't—"

"That wasn't your place to tell them."

"Dammit, Jude. I'm sorry, but I love you, and I want to take care of you. I don't care what they think. You belong with me."

Jude's eyes burned with tears as he looked at the one person who'd given him more happiness than anyone. He braced himself for the pain that would come.

"Reese, my brother and sister need me. I can't go against my uncle. Not right now."

Reese's eyes bugged out. "So you're *leaving*? You're going to leave me because your uncle doesn't approve? *Jesus*, Jude."

"I will still be there for Mr. Matheson. I will—"

"Jude, I love you. I need you with me."

Jude hated that he had anything to do with the pain in Reese's voice.

"I'm sorry, Reese. I just can't. You don't understand my family, my—"

"You're right. I don't understand how you can choose that intolerant, religious nut over me."

Anger pulsed through Jude as he narrowed his gaze at Reese.

"I think you should go."

Reese blanched. He looked as though he wanted to apologize, but then he looked over Jude's shoulder and his indignation was back.

"Is everything all right, boys? Please come and eat your food."

"Thank you for inviting me, Mrs. De La Torre. I'm afraid I won't be staying for dinner." And with that Reese turned and walked out the door.

All the air rushed from Jude's lungs as though he'd been hit with a sledgehammer. He tried to breathe normally but he couldn't seem to get enough oxygen. Then he felt his tita's hand on his shoulder.

"It is for the best, dear. You're too young to know what you really feel."

The pain was so intense that Jude felt he'd crumble if he opened his mouth to speak. He turned to face her, and her comforting smile returned his anger to the surface.

"I thank you, Tita Gemma, for taking care of my brother and sister while my parents have been gone. I understand it has been a sacrifice on your part. But you and Tito Rommel have no right to say what is best for me."

She jerked back and gasped. "Jude. How—"

Jude turned from her as Germaine entered the room.

"Will you take me to get my truck?" he asked her.

Germaine nodded, grabbed her purse, and gave her older sister an ugly look as she followed Jude out the door.

As they climbed into her car, silent tears began to flow down Jude's cheeks. She reached over and squeezed his forearm.

"I'm so sorry, Jude. This is all just awful. What are you going to do?"

He looked out the window and tried to compose himself. "I really don't know."

TWENTY-SIX

REESE WENT from Jude's uncle's house straight to the hospital to see Grandpa. He knew it might not be the best place for him in his current state, but he had to see the old man.

"Reese, what's wrong?"

Reese said a silent thank you to whomever was listening. His grandfather was coherent and knew who he was.

"Grandpa, I think I just fucked up. Royally."

Grandpa patted the side of the bed. Reese pulled the chair close and rested his elbows on the bed next to him.

"Tell me, son. What happened?"

Reese couldn't fight the tears. He blurted out the whole tale, how he'd decided he wanted Jude, how he'd pursued him relentlessly until he gave in, the happiness they'd found together... and then his disastrous declaration at dinner. Through it all, Grandpa held a concerned crease between his eyebrows and kept his hand on Reese's arm. He gave a little pat when Reese ran out of steam.

"My boy, Jude is a special man, but you can't expect him to just give up his family, to go against them, to be with you. You can't force him to choose. He won't choose you."

Reese buried his face in his arms and felt all of the weight of the past few weeks crash down on him like a brutal wave. If he'd been surfing, he might have paddled his way out of his mess, but all he could do was hold on to the life preserver his grandfather offered him and ride it out.

He stayed for another hour or so talking to the old man and then got the details of his transfer from the night nurse. Grandpa would be moved to the rehab facility in the morning and would be there for a minimum of four weeks, depending on how his fracture healed. Reese was determined that Grandpa wouldn't stay there a minute longer than necessary, and he began to think of all he needed to do to make the house more accessible for the old man.

Reese went home and poured out all of the alcohol so he wouldn't be tempted to drink himself stupid. He couldn't hide from the pain, and he needed to do something, so he organized his workspace, went to sleep early. Before exhaustion pulled him under, he texted Toby the plan for the next evening.

Be ready to work. We're going to plow through this shit and get this story down. Everything has gone to hell, and the only thing that will make it better is music.

Toby would understand. Toby would know what to do.

WHEN HE woke the next morning, Reese made calls to contractors and got someone out that very day to take measurements for the planned addition. The guy gave him a reasonable estimate, and it seemed like they were on the same page, so Reese accepted the bid. He told the contractor it was a time-sensitive situation and he wanted it done as soon as possible. The guy seemed to accept the challenge and promised he'd have a whole team there the next day.

Reese spent a few hours with Grandpa after he was settled into the new facility and got permission to bring a keyboard in so he could work with him daily. He liked the head nurse at the facility, and she and Grandpa hit it off well. Camilla even came to see him before Reese left that evening. She had definitely taken more than a professional liking to the old man, and that made Reese breathe a little easier. At least he knew Grandpa was getting some attention from someone other than him. He'd worried about him going to rehab and being alone.

That night he told Toby the short version of the story, and Toby was not pleased. "Hurricane Reese strikes again," he said.

They began a routine that consisted of Reese checking in with the contractor in the mornings, spending the day at the facility with Grandpa, and then nights with Toby in the garage. It was the only part of the house untouched by construction—that and his kitchen—but he had little interest in food. He hardly slept, which was fine by him. He hated going to bed without....

The music had a new intensity as Reese played it over the next two weeks, and the tone of the story began to feel more impassioned and profound. Gone was the desire to portray an innocent love story on a high note. In its place, *The Boy on the Corner* developed into a heart-wrenching tale of a pure love robbed of a future by a society that didn't approve. But he couldn't get to the happily ever after no matter how hard he tried. How could he? He wasn't complete, not in his heart. He longed for the man he couldn't have and poured out that desire and anger in his story.

Toby wisely took the hints when he tried to pry, and Grandpa also gave up trying to talk to him about Jude. Reese just couldn't go there without tears, and he had to take care of everything, so he had no time to break down. He felt as if he were constantly a few steps from curling up in bed with Jude's clothes and staying there until the pain went away or he was too weak to move.

JUDE PASSED his final with flying colors and enrolled full-time in school for the next term. There was no reason to crawl toward his goal. He needed to provide for himself, so he got a job working from ten at night to seven in the morning at the rehab facility where Mr. Matheson was staying. He started late enough that he didn't have to worry about running into Reese, and he could spend time with Mr. Matheson when he was mostly sleeping so he didn't have to talk to him about Reese. Oh, the old man tried in the beginning, but Jude's raised eyebrow put an end to that. Mr. Matheson mumbled something about them both being "stubborn as mules" and then let it go.

Thanksgiving came and went, and Jude still hadn't been over to speak to his aunt and uncle. He knew that once his parents returned in time for Christmas, he'd have to go there, but he was determined to steer clear until then. So he picked up his brother and sister from school each day and either rehearsed with them or took them out to eat—anything to spend time with them. Bailey was mostly quiet. He'd tried to apologize in the beginning, even asked after Reese, but again, Jude's eyebrow shut him up.

During the week Jude arranged a system where he crashed at Germaine's during the day while she and Paolo were at work and the baby was in day care. When the baby had a fever, Jude offered to take care of him, and he never put the little guy down. His baby cousin was precious, a chubby brown angel whose eyes lit up when Jude held him. He realized just how desperately he wanted a family. He missed Reese so much the pain was tangible, but he was resigned to the fact that he was destined to be alone. It just wasn't in the cards for him to have a family of his own, much less one with the man he loved.

The weekends were a little more difficult. Kyla referred him to another facility where he picked up a few shifts during the day, but he had to sleep in his truck again overnight. He didn't want to park anywhere near his friends or family, though. He couldn't take another family discussion about him. And it was only temporary. He'd be able to rent a room somewhere soon.

Jude spoke to his mother several times to find out when they were arriving and what the plan was. She felt terrible about what had happened, but Jude was done with discussing his relationship. His mother assured him that they'd bring Bailey and Brianna to live with them when they were back and settled, and there would be room for Jude as well.

He thanked her, but there was no way he'd go back home. His father hadn't spoken to him since he heard what happened at Tito Rommel's, and Jude understood. His father would come around or he wouldn't. But with his parents taking care of his siblings and their tuition, he could finally plan a life for himself. Alone.

TWENTY-SEVEN

"**D**AMN, THAT sounds fantastic."

Toby clapped his hands as they completed a run-through of the musical together. They'd finished writing it two days earlier and had been playing it through the past two nights.

"Thank you so much, Toby. You really helped me work this out. I'm grateful."

"You've created a thing of beauty, my friend." Toby's sad smile let Reese know that he understood just how bittersweet the situation was.

"*We've* created a thing of beauty. You made it great. I couldn't have done this without you."

Toby tried to play off the praise, but Reese was insistent. Toby had been with him through so many adversities. He was grateful he had his best friend at his side.

As happy as he was, however, that they'd written the perfect ending, Reese was still without *his* happily ever after. He'd run into Jude twice at the rehab facility, and all they'd managed were awkward hellos. It killed Reese to walk away, but he didn't know how to make it right.

Kyla would work for him once Grandpa returned home, which the doctor assured him would be the week of Christmas. Kyla assured Reese that Jude was okay, that he was living at his aunt Germaine's apartment and working full-time. She always seemed like she wanted to say more, but she refrained.

The addition was scheduled to be finished in time for Grandpa's release. Just one more week, and Reese would have him back. It couldn't arrive soon enough. Reese wanted to wait until Grandpa was home to play the musical for him, but it was killing him to not be able to share it.

Toby and Reese met with their agent, Arthur Frye, from Slade Artist Management, and they gave him recordings for the show to review. After just a sampling of the songs, he went bananas.

"Do you boys know how friggin' amazing this is?"

"Yes," Reese answered confidently. "Now it's your job to get things moving."

"That could take some time," Arthur backpedaled. "I'm not sure, in this current climate, ah... how well—"

"Don't fuck with me," Reese said as he stood up. "This current climate is *exactly* why a musical about two boys falling in love needs to be made. We can't go around being afraid. There are too many young people denying themselves a chance at happiness because of ignorance."

Toby and Arthur stared at him in horror.

"What?" Reese shouted.

Toby walked Reese over to his chair and handed him a tissue.

"Well for one, I think Arthur's a little shocked by your outburst, and two, your tears are a bit disconcerting. Let's just take a breather. Arthur? Do you still have that whiskey?"

"No. None of that. I'm not drinking, Toby." Reese rubbed his hand over his face to wipe the tears away. They were completely unproductive.

Toby sat back down and placed a hand on Reese's arm. "I think we need to do a little guerilla work with this show. I have a plan, and it's going to involve getting a little more exposure than you're used to, Reese, but it's important, nonetheless."

Reese listened carefully to Toby's brilliant plan and tried to climb out of his Jude-less funk.

. . .

JUDE HAD just wrapped up his day shift at the nursing home when Germaine called his cell.

"You've got to put the TV on. Go to NBC."

Jude hurried into the break room and turned on the TV in the corner. He flicked through the channels until he found *Ellen*—and Reese's handsome face.

"Oh God."

On the screen was a scene Jude never wanted to relive—Jada and Reese arguing in front of the diner.

"Reese, you should have told me. You should never have led me on."

"Jada, I know it's hard for you to understand, but being pansexual means I'm not just going to choose one or the other. I loved you, I may love another woman or another man, and it doesn't matter." Reese looked so handsome that day, but the exhaustion showed clearly on his face.

"So this thing with *beep*—"

"Please keep his name out of it. He's a good man who doesn't deserve to have his reputation tarnished because of me."

Jada feigned heartbreak. Her overacting was just as good as any other reality-show diva Jude had ever seen.

"It's just hard to say goodbye, Reese, after what we had and knowing you're going home with him."

The scene cut to Reese and Toby sitting on Ellen's couch. Jude covered his mouth.

"So, Reese, this was about two months ago, correct? And since then you've been—"

"Working on the musical, yes. I'd originally planned to tell the story of how my grandfather met my grandmother, but then I decided there was a more important story to tell."

"So *The Boy on the Corner* is your new musical. Tell us what made you decide to change the story?"

Reese linked his fingers together between his knees. "Love, I suppose. I fell in love, and we couldn't be together because, well, a lot of reasons. But the bottom line is that there's a large portion of our society that doesn't understand, that isn't willing to accept that love is love, and I want to show them that it is what it is. It's beautiful, just like any love story. I want to start a conversation with this show. I want people to realize that when two people love each other, it goes beyond politics and religion."

Ellen smiled. "I think that's a splendid idea. So when will the show open?"

Toby and Reese smiled at each other. "Well, we've decided to produce the show ourselves and we'll be holding a grand opening in time for Valentine's Day," Reese said, his mischievous smile plastered on. "We've started a crowdfunding page, and you can donate on our website. We've got some investors, including Blackened's singer Danny Black and his lovely wife Jesse Martin-Black, who is one of the leading Broadway-style dance choreographers on the West Coast. She's handling the choreography, and we're already in preproduction. We wanted to share it with people now because we want them to send us their beautiful love stories. We want to honor all of those people who came before us who had to fight to be with the person they loved."

"And we'll be compiling those stories into print, and the proceeds will go to the GLSEN organization to help young LGBTQ students feel safe in school," Toby added.

The audience cheered loudly, and Jude ignored the wetness on his cheeks. Onscreen, Ellen smiled at Reese and Toby. "And this show would like to be among the first to announce that, not only will we be sponsoring *The Boy on the Corner* and the book, but we'll be debuting a song from the show here, today, just for our audience."

The crowd went wild over Ellen's announcement. Reese and Toby walked over to the performance area, where a piano was set up, and Reese sat down to play while Toby stood next to the piano with a microphone. Jude immediately recognized the song as one they'd worked on back when Jude was still living with Reese, and his heart felt as though it were breaking through his rib cage.

When the song was finished, Toby and Reese stood, bowed, and hugged each other. Jude was overcome with emotions he had a hard time sorting out. He was grateful Reese had Toby, heartbroken that he wasn't there to hold Reese's hand, and excited for their endeavors.

How wonderful that they wanted to help LGBTQ youth. Jude never had to worry for his physical safety, but that was because he never shared his feelings, and he didn't stand out when he was a kid. He knew he would never have been accepted by the staff at his school as they preached the Catholic belief that gay sex was a sin. Jude was able to accept that God still loved him, but he'd love him more if he quit having fantasies about men and if he never acted on his feelings.

Well, he'd acted on those feelings. And he'd fallen in love. Now he wasn't speaking to half of his family. That made it hard to believe he was doing the right thing, but it was also hard to believe that the people who loved him would stop loving him because he shared that part of himself with them. He was still Jude, right?

He texted Germaine.

I'm so happy for him. Thank you for sharing with me.

And then he headed out to his truck to find a place to park for the night and let out the rest of his tears.

SOME TIME in the wee hours Jude woke with a start when he heard scratching noises outside the truck. He'd parked in the lot behind the rehabilitation hospital so he could maybe sneak in and see Mr. Matheson in the morning before Reese showed up, but it was really dark. The light must have gone out in the parking lot. Jude sat up just as a crowbar came crashing through the passenger side window of the Pathfinder.

"What the *fuck*?" he yelled, startling the person whose arm was opening the door from the outside. "Get the fuck out!"

Jude scrambled over the back seat and grabbed for the guy's crowbar, but someone grabbed him by his scrubs, pulled him out of the car, and threw him on the concrete. All he remembered from that point was boots—several of them—pummeling his back and his midsection. One caught him under the jaw. Then he heard shouts and was grateful when the would-be robbers ran off into the night. He rolled over onto his back as his co-workers came to his aid.

Well, shit.

TWENTY-EIGHT

REESE CALLED the rehab facility and asked them to tell Grandpa that he would be in late that day because he needed to do another interview and because he and Toby had to look at possible venues in Santa Monica and Hollywood. He hated it that he was being torn away from Grandpa already. His hiatus hadn't been nearly long enough, but once they finished the show, there was a sense of urgency that the story needed to be told.

When Grandpa heard the songs later that afternoon, he was overwhelmed. He couldn't speak through the emotion for several minutes.

"This is beautiful, son. You said everything I never could." And that mandate sealed the deal. It was time, and the world was going to hear his manifesto, even if the person it was intended to celebrate was no longer in his life.

Reese couldn't bring himself to contact Jude. His sane brain told him he was stupid for asking Jude to choose him over his family, but his heart still hurt. And it was more than that. He'd thought Jude would stand by him, and when he sent him away from his uncle's home... well, Reese's ignorant pride wouldn't let him acknowledge that he was just as guilty of breaking a promise. He'd told Jude he'd be there for him, take care of him and support him, and for that he felt terrible. He just had no idea how to repair the damage from the latest pass of Hurricane Reese, so he threw himself into the musical. He hoped and prayed that Jude would hear and understand... somehow.

When he arrived at the rehab facility that night, it was after ten o'clock, but Grandpa was still awake. Camilla had just wrapped up a visit with him, so he knew the old man would be in a good mood. He thought he should give them a few minutes to themselves, so he told them he was going to grab a cup of coffee and he'd be back. As he headed toward the cafeteria, he saw a familiar figure in scrubs. A wave of fear, love, anger, and confusion passed through him as he realized that the guy moved all wrong to be Jude. His shoulders were pulled up and tense, and he walked with a limp—definitely not his Jude.

"Not every guy in scrubs looks like him," he muttered to himself, but as the guy turned the corner, Reese's heart stopped. Reese ran after him, ignoring shouts from the nurses' station. When he caught up, he grabbed the man by the arm, and Jude yelped. Tears filled Reese's eyes as he looked into Jude's beaten and bruised face.

He brought his hands up to cup Jude's jaw. "Oh my God. What happened to you?" He couldn't hold back the sobs as he attempted to pull Jude into his arms, but Jude pushed him away.

"What are you doing here?" he asked around a swollen lip. Reese's sorrow turned to anger in a flash.

"Who did this to you? What happened, Jude?"

Jude looked around and pulled him into an empty room. He wrapped his arms around his midsection and Reese noticed one of his hands was bandaged. Jude didn't speak. He just looked at the floor and seemed to try to get his breathing under control.

"Jude. Please. What happened?" Reese asked in a softer voice when he realized that yelling at him wouldn't help.

"I got robbed."

That was it. He said nothing else. Reese shifted his weight on his feet and tried to be patient, but when Jude offered no other explanation, he had to fight the urge to shake him.

"Robbed? Where? Have you been to the hospital? Did you file a police report?"

"In the parking lot. Yes. And yes. Now can I get back to work, please?"

The whole time Jude wouldn't look at him. It hurt Reese to see his beautiful face so damaged and his body twisted in obvious pain.

"You shouldn't be at work. You should... you need to lie down, get some rest. Why don't you go—" The fury inside Reese rose to an unprecedented level. "You were sleeping in your fucking truck again, weren't you? Goddammit, Jude!"

Jude finally raised his gaze, and he looked just as furious.

"It's of no concern to you," he bit out through clenched teeth. "Get out of my way. I have a job to do." He shoved past Reese, grabbed his cart in the hallway, and winced as he pushed it ahead of him.

Reese stood frozen. It was all his stupid fault. If he hadn't pushed things.... But he had, and he put Jude in danger. He couldn't go after Jude, but there was something he could do. He took out his phone.

"Hello, Germaine? It's Reese. I'm sorry to call so late. I got your number from Kyla."

"Yes, Reese, what can I do for you?" Her tone gave Reese no clue as to how she felt about him. He hoped she wasn't angry.

"I need your help."

Twenty-Nine

REESE WENT back to his grandfather's room to find him sleeping. He kissed his forehead and grabbed his coat on the way out. Then he went to meet Germaine. If he were going salvage the mess and make sure that Jude was taken care of, he needed the help of Jude's family, so he needed to understand where he'd gone so wrong.

Germaine and Paolo were very gracious to meet with him so late at night. They offered him a drink, but he declined. He hadn't touched the stuff since the night he'd mauled Jude, and he didn't intend to. They sat on the couch with tea instead, and he began to explain himself.

"It's important to me that he be safe, more than it is for us to be together. I don't think he'll allow me to do anything, but I want to help."

Paolo took Germaine's hand. The couple were about the same age as Reese and very affectionate. Reese tried not to let it affect his determination. He still ached inside from the loss of his partner, and that was never going to go away.

"I knew he'd been sleeping here while we were gone. We told him that was all right. He's been so helpful with baby Antony. Any time we asked him where he was staying during the weekend, he refused to talk about it. He just said not to worry, he was being safe. I told him I wouldn't talk to Gemma and Rommel about it if he promised me he wouldn't sleep in his truck again. It's difficult to judge what's my place. He's an adult, but he's my nephew. He's so levelheaded and responsible, but he's stubborn. And now he's angry. I've never seen him so angry before."

Reese tried not to hang his head in shame. He'd given up trying to make excuses for his behavior at dinner. He was out of line. By trying to get Jude to leave with him, he insulted his family and his religion, for God's sake. He did what any typical privileged white male would do in the same situation. He forgot about anyone other than himself and his needs.

"So how can I—"

"Marvin will be home in two days. It might be good if you go talk to him. My brother-in-law is a reasonable man, much more so than his brother. He loves Jude very much, and he's very proud of him. He'll be heartbroken to know that his son has been doing without to take care of his younger siblings. You do know that Jude has been paying for their school tuition so they can continue attending the Catholic school?"

Reese cleared his throat and took a moment to get himself together. Paolo excused himself, and Reese appreciated the gesture.

"I had no idea," he said to Germaine. "He's so private. I feel like I got to know him, the man inside, but he kept all of the details from me. And now I feel like I'll never know...."

Germaine reached across the table. "There's always a way, Reese. My nephew is a forgiving person, and he loves you. Don't give up hope."

SO THAT was how Reese found himself back at Gemma and Rommel's home three days later. Germaine assured him through texts that Jude was working and wouldn't be over. Reese knocked on the door and did something ironic. He prayed.

THIRTY

CHRISTMAS EVE was normally a big party for the De La Torre family, but that year things were more somber. At least Jude's mood was somber. The rest of his family planned to celebrate the homecoming of their eldest brother and his wife. Jude planned to pay his respects, and then find someplace to hide out—because that's what he'd been doing. He didn't want anyone else to see him with bruises, but there was no way he could escape at least one holiday evening. He tried. He picked up a double shift at the rehabilitation center on Christmas Day, but no one needed to be covered on Christmas Eve.

Mr. Matheson had moved home. Jude had run into Camilla, and she told him he'd been discharged the previous morning. She beamed with pride that he'd healed so quickly and said she was planning to visit him for the holiday to bring him some Filipino food. Jude hid his pain from her, but couldn't keep it all in. After she left he took a walk out back and cried. The man who had come to be like his own grandfather was now out of his reach, and who knew if Jude would ever see him again?

As he approached his uncle's house for what he hoped would be a quick visit, he planned out what he would say and how long he would stay. He raised his hand to grab the front door handle, but it was yanked open from inside by his enthusiastic mother.

"My boy is here." She held on to him for so long, he had to gently extricate himself as his bruised ribs screamed from the pressure. Her smile held until she saw his face.

"My God. What happened to my beautiful son?" Tears filled her eyes immediately as she pulled him toward her to get a closer look.

Jude cursed inwardly and wished he had mad makeup skills so he could have covered the bruises and avoided discovery, but makeup had never been his thing.

"I'm fine, Mama. I was in the wrong place at the wrong time."

And thankfully he'd finally gotten his window fixed. The next night he slept out there he wouldn't freeze his ass off. His insurance said they would pay for his computer and his stolen textbooks as well, but he hadn't backed up his work, so he'd lost everything he'd done for his classes so far. Of course it could have been a lot worse. That's what he kept telling himself to keep from total despondency.

"You are not fine. Marvin, JJ is here. Come see what's happened."

Jude groaned as he found himself surrounded by worried family. They all fussed over him as they pushed him into the dining room and placed a plate full of food in front of him.

"I'm fine, I'm fine. I just surprised some guys as they were breaking in. That's all. It's taken care of."

His father entered the room, and Jude automatically stood to accept his father's embrace. He couldn't help the small gasp as his father squeezed tightly. And then the family shoved ice packs and bottles of painkillers his way, moved him to the couch, and forced him to put his feet up while his mother held his plate for him. It was all too much, but it went a long way to make him feel accepted—something he wasn't sure he'd ever feel again.

The room emptied casually, and soon it was just Jude and his parents, although he knew without a doubt that at least three or four family members were in the hallway right outside, waiting to hear what was said.

"I'm sorry to come to you like this," Jude began. "I wanted to see you and welcome you home, but—"

"Reese came to see me," his father began.

Jude's mouth dropped open, but he snapped it shut and hoped his parents hadn't seen his reaction.

"And?" Jude asked finally. He was tired of dramatic conversations. He just wanted to work and be left alone. He didn't have it in him to keep up the façade that he was doing all right.

"And I told him I was grateful that he had provided a home for you for the past two years while your mother and I have been away. We never wanted to be gone for so long, but I never worried while you were living with Mr. Matheson. I've been so proud of you for taking on such an important task for Reese while he was unable to care for his grandfather himself."

Praise from his father always meant a lot to Jude. He just wished he hadn't disappointed him.

"Mr. Matheson is back home now." Jude tried to keep the emotion out of his voice. "Reese has hired someone else—my friend Kyla—to work with him, so I'll be continuing on with the jobs I have now and going to school."

"That's wonderful, JJ! Isn't that wonderful, Marvin?" Jude's mother left Jude's side only long enough to lean forward and pat his father on the hand. He sat in the armchair next to the sofa to the side of Jude and his mother. The men stared at each other for a long time, until his mother obviously couldn't stand it anymore.

"That Reese is quite a looker. He sang karaoke with us, even. It was so much fun. But not the same without you here, my son."

Jude couldn't picture that. As much as he loved to hear Reese sing. Karaoke?

"I'm glad you got to meet him. Now Germaine tells me you've found an apartment? That was fast. When are you moving?"

His parents looked to each other and then smiled at Jude. "We'll move the day after Christmas. The movers will bring our things from storage. The apartment has two bedrooms and is close to the school, so Brianna will have no trouble getting to school."

Jude frowned. "Where will Bailey be? You can't leave him here. He—"

"Reese explained that he's added on to the cottage so there's a bedroom available for Bailey with you until we're able to get a bigger place. You can go back to your home."

Jude sat back against the couch with a huff. "What are you even talking about?"

His father smiled. "Reese is moving out so that you can come back home and continue to work with Mr. Matheson. His grandfather misses you, and Reese thought it would be best."

"Oh *Reese* thought so, did he? Look. I just want everyone to stop trying to make decisions for me. Is that too much to ask? I love you both, and I appreciate all that Tito and Tita have done but—"

"JJ, we thought you'd be happy! And it's so nice of Reese to offer this. It's only until we can afford a bigger place to live. We've been out of work for a long time, and we need to catch up financially. At that time Bailey can come home. We'll have room for you then too, until you—"

"Until what, Mama? I get married? I'm not getting married. You need to accept that. I have." He stood from the couch, suddenly needing an escape route like he needed his next breath. "I'm sorry if that means you have to wait for grandchildren, but I'm not ever getting married. Is that understood?"

"JJ, sit down." Marvin's tone was stern, but compassionate. "I will ask you not to speak to your mother that way. I understand that you've been through a difficult time, so I'll let it go. This time."

Jude felt like the world's most terrible son. He started to apologize, and his mother shushed him.

"Of course you can get married. You can do whatever you want, and that means whatever *you* want. Your father and I may not totally understand the choices you are making, but we love you and we'll support you."

Jude took a calming breath and counted a few beats.

"If it were a choice, that would be so much easier. It's not a choice. My only choice in this matter is whether I continue to hide that part of myself from my family. I am who I am, and that's not going to change. I'm gay. I was born gay. It was nothing anyone did or said that changed me. Reese did not *make* me gay, if that's what you think."

"Don't be ridiculous, JJ. Your mother and I may have been gone for some time, but we aren't completely in the dark. You're our son. Whatever you decide to do with your life is between you and your God. Only he can judge, and I don't worry that he'll judge you. You've done nothing but give to others your whole life. You're a child of God, my son, and I believe he will love you regardless of whether you marry a man or a woman."

Who *were* these people? Had he really gotten it so wrong? He hadn't imagined the response he got from his uncle.

"What about Tito Rommel? He doesn't agree."

"He is not your father, and he'll have to go along with my wishes. My wish is for you to be happy, son. I still don't know how I feel about all of this. It took me some time to come to accept, although I don't wish this life for you because I know it will be difficult. I also know you're one of the strongest people I've ever known, and I'm proud to be your father."

Jude couldn't hold back his tears. His father reached forward, placed a hand on Jude's knee, and gave him a reassuring squeeze.

"Now I want to play cards. Who's coming to play cards with me?" He stood and smiled down at his wife and son. Then he turned and left the room.

Jude went into his mother's embrace without hesitation. It was still okay to cry with Mom. Jude knew that, whatever his age, his mother would always hold him as though he were still a child. When he could breathe normally, he sat back and reached for a tissue to clean himself up.

"Are you better, son?"

Jude nodded, and his mother smiled.

"That's good. Now, just because Reese has arranged all of this for you, it doesn't mean you have to go. You need to do what's best for you —whatever makes you happy. Your father and I want that for you."

Jude was happy to be sitting next to his mother, having the conversation openly. Finally. It had been a long two years without her and his father around on a daily basis to help him navigate his life and continue to present him with advice. He hadn't realized just how much he missed them.

Jude spent another few hours with his family, who did an excellent job of avoiding the topic of Reese. Jude wanted to be free of decision-making and responsibilities. He just wanted to be a child again. As the evening wore on and Jude's eyelids grew heavy, he pretended he'd disappeared and no one could see how exhausted he was, how much weight he'd been carrying, and how much physical and emotional pain he was in. He tried so hard that he let his eyes close and burrowed into the couch, just for a short nap, he told himself. He'd leave when everyone left for midnight mass. Just a few minutes of rest....

JUDE WOKE the next morning to his phone buzzing. He reached across to the coffee table in his uncle's living room and picked it up. It was a text from work.

We don't need you today, after all. Thank you for offering. Merry Christmas.

Left with nothing to do, Jude allowed his body to rest. Bailey and Brianna shared the pull-out couch across from him. Jude smiled at their sleeping figures and let his mind drift back to Christmas mornings of the past when they'd been in their own home with their parents.

Jude would usually be the first one up, and he would wait patiently in front of the lit tree for the others to join him. They'd often sleep later that morning because of the days of predawn *Simbang Gabi* masses that led up to Christmas Day. And then Jude and his younger siblings stayed up late the night before, waiting impatiently for the rest of their family to come over so they could spend the day eating and opening presents.

Bailey sat up and rubbed at his face. His hair stuck up all over. He frowned and looked around until his gaze landed on Jude, and a big smile spread across his face.

"You stayed," he said.

"I did. You're stuck with me." Jude sat up and smiled when he realized his mother—or someone—had covered him with his favorite quilt. It felt soft under his hands, and it encouraged him to stay put and relax.

"So you talked to Mom? Are we going to Reese's house?"

He looked so hopeful, it killed Jude to disappoint him. But before he could answer, Brianna smacked Bailey in the face with a pillow.

"You're so loud. I'm trying to sleep here." She rolled off the sofa bed, trudged across the room, and plopped down next to Jude. She linked fingers with him and rested her head on his shoulder. "It feels right with you here," she said softly.

"It feels right having Mom and Dad here," Jude said, and he kissed his sister's hair. Being surrounded by his family's love did a lot to heal Jude's bruised and broken soul.

"They really do want you to be happy, JJ. Mom and Dad had a big fight with Tito when they got here and Dad got the real story."

Jude frowned. "What do you mean, the real story?"

Bailey snorted, and Brianna shushed him.

"Tito tried to tell them he was forcing you home because you were sleeping in your truck, but Tita said, 'Oh no you don't, you old fool. You don't want people talking about your gay nephew living in sin.'"

Jude shook his head at Brianna's story. Of course Rommel would be concerned about appearances.

"Yeah," Bailey said. "And then she said, 'I think it's wonderful that Jude found somebody, especially that handsome Reese Matheson. You know he used to have a girlfriend? I saw her on that new show. Maybe it was our JJ who turned *him* gay? He is very handsome too. And such a good dancer.'"

Brianna laughed, but then she leaned in closer to Jude. "Please don't stay in your truck again. I couldn't bear it if anything happened to you."

Jude hugged her to him and was reminded once more of how amazing his siblings were. "Hey, remember when you used to teach us dances for Christmas morning?" Bailey climbed off the couch and hurriedly removed the blankets, folded the bed back into the couch, and made a space for an impromptu performance. Brianna got up and shook off her sleepiness so she could dance with him. They sang along to "All I Want for Christmas is You" and busted out antiquated moves that made Jude cringe.

"Come on and join us, JJ."

Jude pulled himself off the couch and stretched, pleased to be warm and not smushed in the back of the Pathfinder.

"This space isn't exactly big enough for us anymore, you guys." He spun around, moved side to side, and nearly bumped a lamp off the table. Brianna laughed at his clumsiness, and he turned to face them. He mirrored their moves and admired how much both of them had grown in their dancing ability. Color guard was good for them. He was happy he'd been able to keep them involved with it. It made it all worth it.

As they started in on their second dance, Mom and Dad joined them from the kitchen and applauded. The family shared hugs and then sat together chatting on the couch. Jude was glad he hadn't gone to work.

While the family feasted on sweet spaghetti and *lechon*, Jude almost felt at home. When his phone buzzed in his pocket later, he reached for it without thinking. His heart dropped when he saw Reese's name on the screen, and when he pushed back from the table to answer the phone, his uncle shot him a scolding look.

"Hello?" he answered as he left the room and caught his mom's questioning glance.

"I'm sorry to interrupt your Christmas Day, Jude."

Just the sound of his voice made Jude's head swim with emotion. Was there any way he could ever have both parts of his life in harmony?

"You aren't interrupting," Jude lied.

Reese sighed into the phone. "I...."

They didn't speak for several moments. Jude wanted to tell Reese that he'd be right there, or for him to bring Mr. Matheson over and let their families figure out how to deal with them together. Then he remembered he was supposed to be angry with Reese.

"What did you need, Reese?"

He wanted him to say "you."

"It's Grandpa. He took off again this morning—"

"Oh no. Did you look—"

"I found him. It's okay. I was in the shower, and I'd forgotten to reset the alarm. He was just at the corner store trying to buy some noodles. He was arguing with the guy that he didn't want Cup O' Noodles, he wanted Jude's noodles."

Jude chuckled. "What can I say? The man is addicted to my cooking."

"It's good to hear you laugh," Reese said softly.

I miss you. I love you. Ask me to come home.

"I thought I would see if there was any way you could bring him some noodles. He seems really off today. I—"

"Yes. Yes, of course I will. I'll bring it over right now."

Reese was quiet. "Thank you. I'm sorry to bother you."

How could you ever think you were bothering me? What happened to wanting me in the way? What happened to us?

"It's no bother. I'll be there soon."

With his heart pounding in his ears, Jude hung up the phone. He went back into the kitchen and interrupted his mother and aunties, who had apparently been waiting for him.

"We packed food for you to take to the Mathesons."

Tita Gemma handed him two large bags full of containers. There were sweets, meat, *lumpia*, and a hot container of noodles.

"You should hurry," his mother said with a smile. "Don't want that to get cold." She kissed him on the cheek and smiled. "Go to your heart," she whispered only for him to hear. He smiled and took the bags from her.

"Can I come too?" Bailey stood behind him with an eager grin.

"Yes, Bailey, go with your brother," his mother said. She shared a knowing glance with Bailey. Apparently they'd worked out some sort of deal. It probably involved surveillance.

"Sure. Don't spill."

The De La Torre women shooed them out of the kitchen. Tita Germaine gave him a finger wave and a knowing smile.

The drive over only took fifteen minutes because traffic was light on the holiday. Bailey messed around with the radio dial and hummed along to a Christmas station. Jude could tell he wanted to talk, and he was grateful that Bailey respected Jude's need for quiet right then. He was too much of a mess to try to hold a conversation.

When they pulled up, Bailey hopped out of the truck, grabbed the bags from the back seat, and left Jude to gawk at the way the house had changed.

Was it even the right house? He checked the numbers, and sure enough, it was the Matheson cottage. But a giant new structure jutted out from the front of the place. Jude slowly climbed down from the truck and studied the addition in awe as Bailey bounded up the steps. Jude hurried to catch up as Bailey pounded on the front door.

"Not so loud. Mr. Matheson might be sleeping."

Reese opened the door, gestured for Bailey to go inside with the bags, and patted him on the back as he passed. Bailey pushed past him into the house and that left Jude standing awkwardly on the porch.

"Hi," Reese said, and a sad smile formed at the corners of his mouth. He was wearing a bulky dark sweater and jeans with holes in various places on the legs. They looked authentic, as if those jeans had traveled many of life's miles with Reese. His eyes were bloodshot, and he had dark circles under them. He was still incredibly beautiful to Jude and always would be.

"My aunties sent enough food for an army. I hope you're hungry."

Reese stepped back and held the door open for Jude. All Jude wanted to do was to curl up against Reese's broad chest and wrap his arms around his wide back. He wanted to be held, wanted to find that comfort once again. As he stepped closer, Reese backed up to give him space. It hurt.

Jude tried not to laugh when he got a look at Reese's feeble attempt to keep the house neat. There was nothing on the floor, but every surface was covered in clutter—from used dishes to magazines and books, to papers strewn about that appeared to be sheet music.

"He's in his room. He's got an adjustable bed now and a flat screen. He says it's more comfortable for him to watch TV that way. He seemed really down this morning. I'm sorry to take you away from your family."

Jude turned to face Reese, but Reese looked away and blew out a breath.

"I'll just, umm... tell him that you're here."

He walked over to a set of double doors that apparently led to the new bedroom. Jude heard him speak softly, and Mr. Matheson's grumbly voice answered. Reese returned to the room a moment later.

"He'd like to see you," he said. "I'm just going to fix him a bowl."

Jude nodded and watched Reese walk with hunched shoulders into the kitchen. Jude took a deep breath and entered Mr. Matheson's room.

"Quite the nice place you've got here," he said. He put on a brave smile.

Mr. Matheson was watching a giant flat screen with *National Lampoon's Christmas Vacation* playing.

"I love Chevy Chase. That guy has some balls. You ever see *Caddyshack*? Classic stuff."

Jude took a walk around the room admiring all the touches Reese had installed—bars near the toilet and in the shower, an extrawide entrance, an alarm system that chimed when the doors opened. He went the extra mile to be sure his grandfather was safe.

"It's good to see you, my boy. Come over here and set down." He pointed to the side of his double bed. Jude sat down gently and patted Mr. Matheson's hand.

"Glad to be out of the facility, I bet?"

"You know it," he said. "That food was about to kill me. And it was so drafty. My balls are probably permanently shriveled. I don't think they've loosened up since I got home. That's a good thing. No more whacking me in the knees."

Jude could tell by the smirk on his face that Mr. Matheson was trying to mess with him.

"Just keep those things to yourself, you hear me? How's it working out with Kyla?"

The old man raised his eyebrow and squinted at Jude. "She's okay. She lets me get away with more than you did. Isn't always after me to go to bed on time, get up from my naps and walk." His gaze drifted to the TV, and Jude thought he was done speaking until he said, "I was hoping she'd only be temporary. That you'd come back. It's just not the same without you here."

Mr. Matheson's eyes shot to the doorway, where Reese stood with his food and gave him a look that probably meant to knock it off.

"You can thank Jude's family for this delicious food you'll be eating for a couple of days." He set a standing tray over Mr. Matheson's lap, and Mr. Matheson's eyes bugged out.

"This looks tasty. You boys gonna eat?"

"We ate already," Bailey said from the doorway. "How are you feeling, Mr. Matheson?"

The old man's eyes sparkled, and he gestured for Bailey to come close. "Why, Jude, he looks like the spitting image of you. Come here, boy, and let me see ya."

Bailey couldn't stop smiling as he approached the bed with a hand out to shake. Mr. Matheson took his hand and looked him over.

"He looks like more trouble than you, though Jude, my boy. Son, you getting into trouble with the ladies? Or the boys, I should say in present company?"

Reese cursed, and Jude snorted. Bailey laughed nervously.

"Uh, no trouble. With either." He shrugged, and just like that, the awkward moment was over.

"You ever watch this movie, my boy?" He patted the side of the bed for Bailey to sit down, which he did, and he gasped.

"I haven't seen this, but that's a great TV, Mr. Matheson. You could do some serious gaming."

"Gaming? You mean them video games? Ain't never played nothing like that. Maybe you can bring yours over and set it up, teach me how to play. It's not like I got anything else to do, laid up here like I am."

Soon both of them were thoroughly engaged in the movie, and Reese gestured for Jude to join him in the other room.

THIRTY-ONE

"WOULD YOU take a walk with me?" Reese asked Jude, hoping to get a few moments alone. Jude looked over at his brother and Grandpa and nodded his head.

"Sure," he said. "Be right back, Bail."

Bailey waved at him, his eyes glued to the movie, and Reese gestured for Jude to head toward the kitchen. They walked silently through the house, into the backyard, and down the steps to the beach. It was sunset, and the air was chilly. Reese never minded the cold, but he noticed Jude rubbing the arms of his light jacket.

"Do you want my sweater?" he offered.

Jude shook his head. "I'll be fine," he said quietly, sneaking a glance at Reese.

"I know I've done just about everything wrong with you, and I'm so sorry for that. I wouldn't do you the disservice of asking for you to give me another chance, but I'd really appreciate it if you would consider moving back to stay with Grandpa. He really misses you. Kyla's great but—"

"I'll do it," Jude said. "I miss him too."

They walked along the shore, and Reese tried to channel the calming vibe of the waves as they had their conversation.

"I can't tell you how much we'd both appreciate that. I'll have my things moved over to Toby's tomorrow. You can come back whenever you are ready."

"What about you? I know how much you wanted to spend time with him. Why would you move out? You just had that room added on."

Reese felt his emotions climbing to the surface. "I don't want to make you uncomfortable. Or your family. They weren't okay with me living with you."

"It's not their decision," Jude said firmly.

Reese stopped walking. Jude turned to face the water and wouldn't look at him. It was frustrating as all hell to not reach out and touch Jude when Reese wanted to give his everything to him. In the waning light, Jude's serious features softened some as he looked out over the horizon.

"My father said only my God would judge me and that he didn't think he would judge me because I've lived a good life. I *have* lived a good life. I've fought with myself for years because I couldn't find resolution with my faith and who I am. It's not like I thought I'd go to hell for being gay or anything, but I finally had to stop listening to the Bible literalists who tried to tell me it was a sin. If things feel wrong, I don't do them. That's how I live my life." He turned slowly to look at Reese. "I never felt wrong about you, how I felt being with you."

Reese felt his own frown melt a little at Jude's confession. "I'm glad." But then he didn't want to interrupt. He wanted Jude to keep talking.

"What I *did* feel wrong about was being dishonest with my family and your grandfather. That's where I felt I'd sinned. I may not go to church much anymore, Reese, but my faith is still strong. We're not religious nuts. At least I'm not. We're Filipino and Catholic. We have strong traditions. I probably should have explained that a bit—"

"No, Jude. That was me being an ass. An ignorant ass. I'm so sorry."

Jude chuckled and looked away. Hope bloomed in Reese's chest.

"Hurricane Reese," Jude murmured. He turned back to Reese with a smile. That was it. Reese couldn't stand it. He held out a hand, and the millisecond it took Jude to take it nearly broke him. But he kept control. He merely gave Jude's hand a squeeze.

"Thank you for coming back to stay with Grandpa. It means a lot to us both."

"You'll be there. This arrangement can't keep you from seeing your grandfather."

Reese shrugged. Could he come to the house and exist in the same space with Jude and not give in to his desires?

"I don't want to crowd you. I'll see him, but I won't live there. I know I won't be in your life again as we were, so I don't want to invade your space." That was not at all what Reese wanted, but he'd do what he had to in order to make up for his huge disaster—to make it up to Grandpa *and* Jude.

"You don't know a damn thing, Reese Matheson."

Jude tugged Reese to him, and their lips met in a tentative kiss that just about buckled his legs. Reese wanted to fall to his knees and beg. He'd told himself he'd be content with the situation—he'd have to be if he had any hope of repairing what had gone so wrong. But Jude's kiss made him want everything they'd had and so much more.

When Jude pulled away, his eyes remained closed for a moment. When he opened them, Reese fought every physical urge and remained still.

"Don't stay away. Let's try to do it right this time."

"I want to do right by you, Jude. I promise, I'll—"

"Just *be*, Reese. I don't want you to *do* anything. No promises or declarations. I just need you to *be*."

Reese was willing to do just about anything, even if he had no clue how.

They held hands as they walked back up the beach and the lights embedded into the stairs illuminated their path. Reese wished he could stop time and hold on to his hope that he and Jude might climb the right path this time.

THIRTY-TWO

J UDE AND Bailey moved into the house on New Year's Day. Their parents wanted them all under the same roof until it was time to go back to school. They spent that time catching up on their lives since the last time they had seen their parents. Jude loved having his family back together. He'd been lonely without his parents and his siblings on a daily basis.

Bailey received a stern talking to about moving in with Jude.

"You will behave for your brother, and you will be respectful of Mr. Matheson and his needs."

"Of course I will, Papa. I'm not going to screw up. I swear. You can trust me."

"Jude is in charge. You do what he says."

"I got it. I got it."

"And both of you boys will come to dinner once a week, at least, at our new place and once on the weekends with the whole family. Now that we're back, family needs each other."

Jude cringed a little at that agreement. Things were fine, but he wasn't sure he wanted a weekly family gathering. That might be *too* much family.

Bailey was off-the-chain excited about having his own room. At seventeen years old, he'd always shared—first with Jude, then with Brianna and their little cousin. Jude got a kick out of watching Bailey organize his things and arrange them over and over until he was fully satisfied.

Mr. Matheson loved having fresh blood in the house to convert to his music, and he loved having someone who laughed at his jokes. Bailey hooked up his Xbox to the giant TV in Mr. Matheson's room, and Reese bought Bailey a gamer chair that could easily be pushed out of the way if necessary. Once Bailey taught Mr. Matheson how to play *Call of Duty*, Jude had to fight with them nightly to get them to go to bed.

The preproduction of *The Boy on the Corner* was in full swing, and Reese and Toby spent long hours every day at the venue they'd selected in Santa Monica. Reese came over in the evenings and spent time with his grandfather, and Toby came along most of the time. Bailey listened intently and asked a lot of questions as they talked about the planning and choreography.

Jude and Reese had no alone time, which was good, Jude supposed. But it sucked. Royally. He could hardly stand it. Reese would move close to him, brush against him as he passed. He smelled so good. They shared glances and private smiles. On a few mornings, Reese even came over early to surf, and Jude had to endure his wetsuit maneuvers. He got caught ogling more than once. Reese seemed to enjoy the torture, but Jude couldn't help but wonder if he was losing interest. He hadn't spoken any reassuring words. In his defense, it wasn't as if they'd had any private conversations, but Jude thought just maybe he'd been a passing fancy, and Reese had moved on. But then Reese would wink at him, touch his hand accidentally-on-purpose, and Jude's heart would flutter again.

One morning Jude let his curiosity get the better of him, and he decided to take Reese a surprise lunch. Kyla came over to stay with Mr. Matheson while the physical therapist was scheduled to visit. Jude hugged her, and she followed him to the door.

"So what's going on with you two? I asked Reese, and he just said he was trying to do things right this time. What the hell does that mean?"

Jude sighed. "I wish I knew. If doing things right means being a huge tease, I'm all for being wrong."

Kyla burst out laughing. "Jude, I've never heard you talk like this. If I didn't know any better, I'd think you were sexually frustrated, but—"

"But what? You try spending time in that man's wake. He must secrete, like, industrial-strength pheromones."

"He must if he's got you in such a state. You're the picture of self-control, Jude. What're you going to do?"

He had no clue. "I guess I'm headed into the eye of the storm."

REESE AND Toby finished meeting with Jesse and her assistants to go over the final choreography and plans for casting. Auditions for dancers were in two days, and there was excitement in the air. They'd hired phenomenal musicians, and Reese couldn't have been happier.

They'd decided to cast all unknowns because they didn't want it to be a vehicle for anyone. The story needed to be told for many reasons— for his grandfather's music, for a love story that ended abruptly, and for the many people who refused to accept what they were and who they loved because they feared reprisals. No more. No one should have to be afraid to be with the person they loved. People deserved to love and be loved by someone special—someone like Jude.

It was painful to leave the house every night. Thankfully Reese had the show to keep him occupied or he would have fallen apart and forgotten his resolution to do things right this time. He'd give it until the end of the show, and if Jude didn't make a move, he would assume they were finished.

Oh, he flirted. He couldn't help that. It was in his nature to flirt. And he could tell Jude was affected, but he never said a word. What did that mean? It wasn't like they had any privacy, but it was getting harder and harder to be around Jude without getting harder and harder. He brought Toby over to act as a buffer or he'd have Jude up against a wall.

He couldn't think like that. It was unproductive—like the boner he was sporting. *Great.* He had four more hours of rehearsal before he could head to the cottage.

He'd always had music to keep him focused, to be his outlet. He poured his heart out in song. So he would drill those guys through the entire show for the rest of the afternoon and see if that didn't get his head on straight.

"Mr. Matheson?" His production assistant Carly stood at the edge of the orchestra pit. "You have a visitor." She looked up into the seats, and Reese followed her gaze.

"A visitor, huh," Dwayne commented. Dwayne had been in bands with Reese since college, and was a mutual friend of his and Toby's. And he loved to give Reese shit whenever possible.

"Yeah." Reese ignored Dwayne's teasing when he saw Jude standing in the dim light with two white paper bags and a nervous expression.

"I brought you lunch," Jude said. He shifted on his feet, and his eyes darted around as though he might run if someone said *boo*. Reese would chase him down if he did. Reese licked his lips. It was the opening he'd been waiting for.

"I'll be right out," Reese said, and then he excused himself. He told the rest of the group to take a nice long lunch break. They'd been trying to hide their exhaustion for the past half hour, and a grateful moan followed Reese out of the pit. He hurried to the seating area and ignored shouts for his attention. Hurricane Reese was on course, and nothing was going to get in his way.

When he stood before Jude, he could barely contain himself.

"You came. You brought me lunch."

Jude nodded and cleared his throat. "I didn't know if you'd been eating very well. I just wanted—"

"Follow me." Reese was no longer able to maintain a modicum of cool. He grabbed Jude by the arm, spun him around, leading him up the ramp and out of the auditorium. He took a right up the steps to the balcony, which he knew would be deserted. The lighting crew wouldn't be back until auditions for the dancers began. He took the steps two at a time, forgetting that Jude was carrying lunch and that his legs were shorter than his.

"Hey." Jude laughed when he stumbled. "What's the hurry?"

They reached the darkened landing and Reese pulled Jude into an alcove. He shut the door behind them, and then they were in nearly complete darkness. The only light came from the crack between the doors.

"But lunch?" Jude asked on a breathless laugh.

Reese was all over him in an instant. The sound of the bags hitting the floor spurred him on, along with Jude's groan. Jude fisted his hair and pulled his head down for a heated kiss. Reese worried that he'd bruise Jude, but it had been too long. He was out of control. Hurricane Reese was reaching Category 5, and he prayed the only thing he would destroy was the wall that stood between their two hearts.

Reese had Jude's fly open and was on his knees before Jude could protest. He heard Jude curse as his grip tightened on Reese's hair, but Reese never let up. He held on tightly to Jude's perfect ass and assaulted him with his lips and tongue until Jude's whole body shuddered.

"Goddamn you, Reese," Jude growled as he came. Reese smiled as Jude completely lost composure and crumbled into his waiting embrace. They lay on the floor with Jude gasping for air and cursing at him.

"What the hell was that? I was just coming down here to bring you lunch."

"And you fed me." He kissed Jude deeply, and their tongues twisted together like the dance they'd been doing for the past two weeks—dancing, flirting, teasing. Reese pulled back and smiled.

"God, I love making you lose control like that. You taste so fucking good."

Jude cursed again. "Yeah, well, when you sneak up on me like that, I have no defense."

Shit. "I'm sorry, Jude. I've just been waiting for some sign that we were okay, that.... And you came here for me. I'm sorry. Did I misread your visit?"

Jude barked out a laugh and pulled Reese closer. "I think you read me loud and clear. I gave up hoping you might talk to me at home, so I thought I'd try coming to your territory."

Reese snuggled up closer. "And how'd that work out for you?"

"Pretty fucking good," Jude said, and he kissed Reese's hair. "I've missed you, babe."

Reese's heart melted into a pool of happy. "I missed you. I can't stand this. Please say you—"

"Yes," Jude said hurriedly as he resumed their heated kiss. Then he returned the favor. And it was Reese's turn to lose control. He loved every minute of it.

THIRTY-THREE

"**S**O TONIGHT when I come for dinner, I'm telling Grandpa you're mine, and that's it," Reese declared as he finished his sandwich.

Jude rolled his eyes sarcastically. "If you insist, although you know he's going to start up with the fairy comments."

Reese scoffed. "That old man has no room to talk. He's as big a fairy as they come."

Jude put down his water bottle so hard that water shot out the top. Reese laughed and handed him a napkin.

"What are you talking about?"

Reese wadded up his sandwich wrapper, tossed it overhand into a nearby garbage can, and shot up his arms in victory as it landed perfectly. "It seems the younger Thomas Matheson told a little fib. Well a big one, really. Remember I told you how he met my grandmother? How he loved her red hair? Turns out that little story—one I based my whole concept of their marriage on—was a sham."

"Again, what are you talking about?"

Reese smiled. "Jude, the musical is called *The Boy on the Corner*. That story? That was about him meeting a *guy* on the corner in Las Vegas."

"No. Fucking. Way. You are shitting me, Reese Matheson."

"I shit you not, Jude Joseph De La Torre. I think that's adorable, by the way. JJ. Why don't you go by JJ with anyone else?"

"Don't change the subject. Really? Your grandfather had a gay romance?"

"Indeed he did. Told me about it not too long ago. He thought he was telling my father. Said he wanted him to know because his grandson —that's me—is like him, 'always prancing around the stage.' Well, he's right. I'm in love with a man, and I couldn't be happier."

Jude leaned forward and gave Reese a chaste kiss on the lips.

"Nor could I."

THAT NIGHT they all sat down to dinner—Reese, Jude, Bailey, Toby, and Mr. Matheson. Reese, being the drama queen that he was, tapped his glass with his spoon as he stood from his place next to Jude at the table.

"Gentlemen and gentlemen, I have an announcement to make." He held his glass up to Jude and smiled. "From this moment on, I am publicly declaring my love for Jude De La Torre. I love him, and I plan on making him my husband someday very soon."

Jude closed his eyes and wished for that disappearing power, which never seemed to work when he needed it.

"Yeah, well, good for you. Pass the potato salad," Mr. Matheson said, and he went back to his meal.

The others looked at each other, and Reese frowned. "That's it? You're not going to bust my balls, old man?"

Mr. Matheson shoved a bite of food into his mouth and waved his hand at Reese. "You love who you love, son. Big deal. It's not like I ain't seen you two pouting enough around here. Get on with it." He took a drink of water and then scowled at Reese. "You ain't gonna wear a dress, though, are you?"

The five men burst out laughing at that.

"Maybe. I could rock a formal gown. What do you think, Toby? Want to throw something together for me?"

Toby rolled his eyes. "Please. Honey, no one in their right mind would even try to fit you for a gown. Remember when you tried drag in college? Hmmm? I rest my case."

Bailey's eyes flared. "*You* performed in drag?"

Reese shrugged. "A few times. They didn't make shoes big enough for me, though, so I had to go barefoot. And I got a rash from the lace. That shit is itchy as fuck. Besides, I make one ugly woman."

Jude doubted that was possible, but the thought of Reese in a dress did nothing for his spank bank.

The rest of the meal was full of talk about the show. Reese reached over and grabbed Jude's hand on the table, and Jude took it and smiled.

JUDE WAS still floating on a cloud three days later when his phone rang. He recognized the number as coming from the kids' school.

"Hi Jude. It's Mrs. Martinelli again. I was wondering if you knew why Bailey hasn't been at school the past two days? No one called him in ill."

Jude's grip tightened on the phone, and his mouth went dry. "He's not in class?"

"I'm afraid not. He's missed all of his classes today, and he was out yesterday as well."

"I dropped him off there. Both mornings. Oh my God. I'm sorry. Thank you for letting me know. I'll get to the bottom of this."

They disconnected, and Jude tried not to panic. Where could Bailey be? He couldn't be out looking for a job. That dilemma had been solved when they moved in with Reese. Then where? He started to call his parents and then thought better of it. He needed to find him first. He'd hate for his parents to think Bailey was messing around under Jude's watch. He didn't want to let anyone down.

As he held the phone in front of him, he remembered the app that let you know where your devices were. He and Brianna and Bailey were all on the same plan, so he turned on the app and chose Bailey's phone. The map moved around on the screen. When it stopped, Jude cursed. Then he called Kyla and asked her to come sit with Mr. Matheson.

The twenty minutes it took her to arrive were long and filled with terrible thoughts. Was it drugs? A girlfriend? *Prostitution?* Why the hell would he leave school? Kyla rushed him out the door, and he drove like a bat out of hell to the location on the app. He didn't ping it because he wanted his arrival to be a surprise. He planned to catch his brother in the act, beat the shit out of him, and march him before their parents.

He parked the truck and nearly broke the window when he slammed the door. Then he stalked up the steps to the front door and flung it open. He followed the same path he'd taken when he brought lunch to Reese.

Reese. There were two asses he'd be kicking that night.

As he entered the auditorium, he saw Toby sitting next to a blonde woman a few rows from the top. They had their heads together and were whispering. Jude spotted Reese's mop down in the orchestra pit at the piano. A group of dancers was performing a number, and they ended as Jude walked in.

"Thank you. Can we please see numbers thirty-two, seventy-six, fifty-four, and twenty-nine onstage?"

Toby turned the mic off as Jude approached them.

"Jude! Come here and have a seat. We're about to see the last audition group. I hope they're great, because so far I haven't seen anyone who really pops out, you know?"

Jude sat next to him on the edge of his seat. As the dancers took the stage, Jude cursed.

"Oh, I recognize number seventy-six," Toby said. "Jude, what—"

The music started and the dancers began the number. From the first eight count, Bailey danced circles around the rest. He was strong, confident, and so damn charismatic that Jude had no choice but to follow his moves. Tears welled up in Jude's eyes, and he covered his mouth.

Bailey was a star—a bona fide natural talent. What the hell were they going to do?

When the music stopped, Reese turned to speak with the bass player, and they laughed about something together. Being in the orchestra pit meant Reese couldn't see the stage. But Jude and Toby stared at each other—Jude in horror, Toby in sheer titillation.

"We've found our lead," Jesse was saying. "Who is this kid, and why are we seeing him last?"

"His name is Bailey Francisco De La Torre, and he's in big trouble."

"Uh," Toby laughed nervously into the mic. "Reese? Can we see you up here? Like now?"

Reese turned, squinted into the lights, and made his way out of the pit and up the aisle to where they sat. He smiled happily when he saw Jude was there, but his smile faded to concern quickly.

"Oh God, is he okay? Did something happen? Oh, God Jude."

"No. He's fine. Grandpa is fine. It's *him* who's in deep shit." Jude pointed to the stage where Bailey was holding court with a couple of young women.

"What's he doing here?" Reese asked with a frown.

"He's our lead?" Toby said nervously. "I'll let you two discuss this. Jesse? How about we, umm, *getthefuckoutofhere?*" He shooed her toward the aisle and Reese, who stood with his hands on his hips, looking perplexed. Once they'd gone, he made his way to Jude's side and sat down.

"I got a call from his counselor saying he'd cut school the last two days. I found him by using the locator app on my phone."

Reese was still frowning. "Sonofabitch." He paused for a moment with a curious expression on his face. "And how was he?" He turned to look at Jude, and his eyes grew wide. "I had no idea. You have to believe me. I'd never let him cut school."

Jude sighed. "He was fantastic. He was born to do this."

Reese nodded and looked back to the stage. Then he picked up the mic and turned it on. "I'd like to see that last group again. Band, take it from the top."

Reese sat back and reached for Jude's hand. Jude leaned forward and pressed his lips to Reese's knuckles as he watched his little brother soar.

EPILOGUE

F eedback Magazine
    January 2017
    Sammara Gunderson

A VERY *special production is being rehearsed in Santa Monica, California on this dreary winter day. Despite the gray skies and cold temperatures, the cast of* The Boy on the Corner, *an original musical by Reese Matheson and Toby Griffiths, are sweating and smiling. Leads Sean O' Reilly and Bailey De La Torre are currently running through the pivotal scene where Boy meets Boy. De La Torre is stunning as the clever musician caught by surprise at his irresistible attraction to the red-haired Boy. He sets a seductive tone to their encounter that seems to catch O'Reilly by surprise despite the fact that they've rehearsed their routine many times.*

The production is personal for Matheson and Griffiths. The creators are determined to show society, once and for all, that love is love, no matter what form it takes. I spoke with the two men at length just before the show's debut in Hollywood.

"I almost lost everything because of intolerance and ignorance. I've come to realize that I had just as much intolerance and ignorance within

myself, and together with my partner, Jude, I'm learning how to accept what I don't understand and to teach others that same acceptance. My grandfather's music laid the foundation for the story, and the rest came from, well, experience."

Reese's grandfather, Thomas Matheson, was a pianist for Frank Sinatra. He wrote the music decades ago, and Matheson and Griffiths pieced it together to create the score for their musical. The elder Mr. Matheson, 87, is recovering from a fall he took back in November. He also suffers from Alzheimer's and was unable to contribute to this article. The show is dedicated to him.

Griffiths had this to say about the show's purpose. *"As a teen growing up gay in conservative Orange County, I experienced a lot of hate and was the victim of violence more than once. Reese was one of my first friends in college, and he saw me as more than just the queer boy who liked to sing. We've been making music together ever since. I've been looking for a way to express my feelings about my past for a long time, and when Reese decided to take this direction with the show, I was totally on board. And he was in love. Someone had to have a level head!"*

Levelheadedness might be questionable with these two. They decided not to wait for producers to take on their labor of love, and did it themselves with the help of some very influential celebrity friends. But it almost fell apart over the casting of De La Torre, a seventeen-year-old high school student and the younger brother of Reese's partner, Jude De La Torre. When Jude discovered Bailey had been cutting school to audition, they discussed it with their families. The De La Torres forbid Bailey to miss school, and he was ready to refuse the role until choreographer Jesse Martin-Black, a former teacher in Hollywood, stepped in and agreed to homeschool him while the show has its run. His family agreed, and the show will go on.

"This show is important to me for so many reasons," said Bailey when we sat down after rehearsal. *"My brother has always encouraged me in dance and he's been a father figure to me for many years. Our culture has a difficult time accepting homosexuality because of our Catholic beliefs. But I love my brother, I love his partner Reese, and I don't think it's right that they, or anyone else, ever has to hide who they are from their loved ones. Love is love."*

Feedback Magazine *is a proud sponsor of* The Boy on the Corner *and the subsequent print project, the proceeds of which will go to benefit GLSEN, the Gay, Lesbian and Straight Education Network, which works to make schools safe for all children, regardless of sexual orientation or gender identification. This magazine has made it a priority to bring attention to issues that affect our music community. After the suicide of guitarist Gavin West from the metal band Hush and the beating of Maggie's Bones' guitar tech Knuckles Franklin outside of a gay bar in Dallas, Texas, it's time more of us enter this conversation. Be a part of the change. #loveislove*

ACKNOWLEDGMENTS

I OWE my eternal gratitude to my husband, my children, and my parents for supporting me in my writerly endeavors. Without you, all of this crazy would still be in my head. I love you. I promise I'll get the laundry done.

Infinite thanks to my writing partners Ellay Branton and Kimberlie L. Faye. You've been there for me through whatever zany chaos I dragged you into, and I know you'll always hold my hand. You're the angel and devil on my shoulders, and I'll cherish you forever.

To Cynthia St. Aubin, Kerrigan Byrne, Brandon Witt, and Kelli Collins, thank you for listening to my many freak-outs about pitching, querying, contracts, and the editing process. Your advice and friendship are invaluable.

To Mary Margaret and Danielle James, thank you for reading early drafts of the story and giving your input about caring for Alzheimer's patients. I admire you for your dedication and compassion, and I'm glad to have you in my corner. And thanks to Tricia for catching a boo boo after all these years! I appreciate you and your great brain.

Thank you to Elizabeth North and Ariel Tachna for not asking me to leave the table at RT 2017 when I pitched a romance featuring a gay odd couple and an octogenarian with wayward balls. I'm grateful you believed in my little story.

Thank you to Rebecca Hunter for your fabulous online course. Hurricane Reese got its start there and with your encouragement, I made it here relatively unscathed!

All of my love to the members of the San Francisco Area RWA chapter for your mentoring and collective wisdom. Special thanks to Karysa Faire and Stacy Finz for giving me that extra push I needed.

Thank you to the members of This Filipino American Life's podcast. I enjoyed hearing your stories about nurses in the family, dating life, and Christmas traditions.

To my friends John Diamonon and Reggie Deanching, thank you for your helpful tips on Filipino culture. John, we've danced together many times, but I'm still waiting to do karaoke.

Stay Tuned for more Rock 'n' Romance!

READERS LOVE THE FORCES OF NATURE SERIES BY R.L. MERRILL

Hurricane Reese

"I'm still in book hangover heaven."
   —Love Bytes

"Excellent book and there is so much to learn about both of these characters. Never assume you know a person just as they appear to be on the outside."
   —Diverse Reader

"How do I even begin to explain the love I have for this book? It was unexpected, surprising, and incredibly emotional...."
   —OptimuMM

Typhoon Toby

"With a strong plot, an expertly crafted cast of supporting characters, and deep empathy, Merrill's novel will keep readers hooked."
   —Publisher's Weekly

"This was definitely a book that I'm thrilled to have read and I'm excited to see the next story in this series"
   —Gay Book Reviews

And here's what readers have to say about the new series *Summer of Hush*:

"The Queen of rock 'n' roll romance rules again with another heartfelt tale of complex heroes whose epic love is destined to be. With Silas and Krish both recovering from the heartbreak of losing their best friends, they're looking toward the Warped Tour for fresh starts and the healing of their scabbed-over wounds.

"Summer of Hush" is secret identity meets secret crush meets mutual hero worship, all rolled up in one. The sweet, pulsing rhythm of the music enhances every scene and deep, emotional undercurrents-- Merrill's trademark--always strike the right chord. Five stars.
   -Author Kilby Blades

"Overall, this was a tender and compelling story that kept me invested from the first page to the last. This book juggles happiness and honesty and hopefully both can be part of their lives. I highly recommend the Summer of Hush and hope you give it a try."
   -Bayou Book Junkie

"I especially loved Silas' band Hush, what a fascinating group of guys. I enjoyed getting to know them. They are more like brothers rather than bandmates. From the tidbits of information given, I can tell some of them have sad pasts and their own story to tell. I NEED to learn more about all of them. Hopefully, R.L. Merrill will continue their stories in the next book....."
   -Dawn Nicole Costiera

About the Author

R.L. Merrill brings you stories of Hope, Love, and Rock 'n' Roll featuring quirky and relatable characters. Whether she's writing about contemporary issues that affect us all or diving deep into the paranormal and supernatural to give readers a shiver, she loves creating compelling stories that will stay with readers long after. Winner of the Kathryn Hayes "When Sparks Fly" Best Contemporary award for Hurricane Reese, Foreword INDIES finalist for Summer of Hush and RONE finalist for Typhoon Toby, Ro spends every spare moment improving her writing craft and striving to find that perfect balance between real-life and happily ever after. She writes diverse and inclusive romance, contributes paranormal hilarity to Robyn Peterman's Magic and Mayhem Universe, and works on various other writing and mentoring projects that tickle her fancy or benefit a worthy cause. You can find her connecting with readers on social media, educating America's youth, raising two brilliant teenagers, trying desperately to get that back piece finished in the tattoo chair, or headbanging at a rock show near her home in the San Francisco Bay Area! Stay Tuned for more Rock 'n' Romance.

Connect with Ro:
    Website: www.rlmerrillauthor.com
    Twitter: @rlmerrillauthor
    Facebook: www.facebook.com/rowritesrocknromance
    Stay Tuned for more Rock 'n' Romance.

Other Books By R.L. Merrill

Other Books By R.L. Merrill

Haunted Series: (Contemporary Romance)

Haunted

Fated

Bated

Jaded – (Coming Soon)

Minded Series: (Paranormal Spinoff of Haunted Series)

Minded

Blossomed

Father F'in' Christmas

A Peculiar Prom Night

Magic and Mayhem Universe: (Funny Paranormal Romance in the universe created by Robyn Peterman)

Shifted

Ghoul Me Once

Gator Me Twice

Magic and Mayhem/Shifted Collection

Fang Me Three Times

Fangtastic Four

Five Fanger Witch Punch

Hollywood Rock 'n' Romance Trilogy: (Contemporary Romance)

Teacher

Teacher: Act Two

Teacher: The Final Act

Contemporary Romance Series:

The Rock Season

Road Trip

You Fell First

The Heart Knows (Re-Releasing Soon)

A Match Made in Spain

LGBTQ Romance

Pinups and Puppies (Originally in Love Is All Vol. 2)

I Want, More – Bolder Breed Studios #1 (Love Is All Vol. 3)

Love and Pride – Bolder Breed Studios #2 (Love Is All Vol. 4, out solo November 2021)

Everything's Better With You: An MM Sports Romance

All I Wanna Do — Bolder Breed Studios #3 (Email Ro for a copy)

LGBTQ Romantic Suspense

Under His Sheets: Accidentally Undercover (April 2024)

The Banes of Lake's Crossing (Historical Horror Romance)

The Fourth Man (The Banes of Lake's Crossing) (Historical Horror Romance)

The Redemption of Nathaniel Bane

The Absolution of Jonah Bane

The Gifted Series: (Supernatural Suspense/Paranormal Romance)

Healer

Connection

Protector

Sundowners (M/M Paranormal Romance

Sundowners Book One

Sundowners Book Two (Coming 2024)

Forces of Nature Series: (Gay Contemporary Romance)

Hurricane Reese

Typhoon Toby

Earthquake Ethan (March 2024)

Summer of Hush Series: (Gay Contemporary Romance)

Summer of Hush

Brains and Brawn

You Can Do Magic: Carnival Of Mysteries (A Summer of Hush Tie-In)

Carnival Of Mysteries Book Two Coming Soon

Anthologies:

Thanksgiving Day Parade From Hell (Worst Holiday Ever) (Gay Contemporary Romance

Valentine's Day From Hell (Worst Valentine's Day Ever) (Gay Contemporary Romance)

Salty and Sweet (Summer Fair) (Lesbian Contemporary Romance)

The Fourth Man (The Banes of Lake's Crossing) (Historical Horror Romance)

A Piece of Him (Gone With The Dead) (Horror)

Breaking Bread—Dark Divinations from HorrorAddicts.net Press (Horror)

Exchange (Renewal) (Science Fiction)

Tap-Tap-Tap (Impact) (Horror)

Human Sacrifice (Innovation) (Horror)

The Sitter (Clarity) (Horror)

Joy Is A Phone Call Away – A More Perfect Union (Lesbian Contemporary Romance)

The House Must Fall – Haunts and Hellions from HorrorAddicts.net Press – May 2021 (Horror)

A Kept Woman – BAQWA Presents: Horror Show 2021(Lesbian Horror Romance)

Gods of Rock 'n' Roll (Free on Wattpad)

How Bittersweet is Karma? Free on Wattpad)

Let Me Stand Next To Your Fire (Queer Cheer)

Midnight in the Renaissance Elevator

Holiday Romance

A Peace Offering (Re-release) Crafty Tales Book One

Crafty Tales Book Two Coming Holidays 2024

Love and Pride – Bolder Breed Studios #2

Audiobooks

The Rock Season (Kiss App)

Brains and Brawn (Kiss App)

Teacher (Kiss App)

Hurricane Reese (Kiss App)

A Match Made in Spain

Healer: Gifted Book One

Non-Fiction

Horror Addicts Guide To Life Volume 2 - Edited by Emerian Rich

Death's Garden Revisited - Edited by Loren Rhoads (Out Fall 2022)